LONG TRAIL TO TEXAS

Clay Wade: Book One

A Fiction Novel Based On True Events

ART CLEPPER

ISBN: 978-1-4834-8379-5 (sc)
ISBN: 978-1-4834-8378-8 (e)

Lulu Publishing Services rev. date: 07/20/2018

CHAPTER 1

With night closing in the cannon and rifle fire had finally begun to slack off. The screaming and groaning of the injured continued. The darkness will not affect that.

When all the firing finally stopped, the medics came into the field to pick up the wounded and dead. Sometimes it's hard to tell one from the other. Bodies were strewn everywhere, blues and greys together, some lying on top of others, some of them still alive, for now.

Clay Wade was lying where he fell when his horse went down.

A cannonball hit the tree next to him and shattered it to splinters. Part of the tree went through his horse's stomach. Clay was thrown off to the side; the horse fell beside him kicking and screaming until Clay put a bullet in his head to put him out of his misery. That was the third horse shot from under him in four years of fighting.

A Confederate soldier saw where Clay fell, that's when the bullet went into his side. He landed next to his horse which shielded him and probably saved him from being shot again.

He knew he was in trouble. He didn't know where the rest of his unit was. They had been charging the confederate's line in mid-afternoon, with rifle and cannon fire all around them, men and horses were falling and screaming on both sides when he went down.

He must have passed out somewhere along there, because when he came too, it was almost dark, and he was lying beside his dead horse in a pool of blood. He didn't know if the blood was from him or his horse. He only knew he was in considerable pain. He tried to examine his wound and found the holes in his side.

He moved as close to the dead horse as he could, using him as a shield, and taking advantage of what little heat was still in the horse's body. His only hope of survival was the medics. If they found him before he bled to death, he may have a chance.

He tore off a piece of his shirttail and stuffed it in the holes, front and back, hoping to slow the bleeding.

That was the last thing he remembered. Everything went black again. When he regained consciousness again, he was shivering with cold. Middle of March in Virginia can feel like winter at times.

He saw someone coming toward him with a lantern. He called, but no sound came out. He tried to listen to the sounds to determine what was going on around him, but he passed out again.

The light kept fading in and out. Sometimes it was sunlight, other times it was moonlight, sometimes no light. He couldn't stay focused long enough to know what was happening. There were long periods of nothing, but silence accompanied by pain. Other times he was startled by screaming, cannons and rifles blasting away at his consciousness. Sometimes he was aware of people around him, and pain up and down his body, talking, then darkness until he was shocked into wakefulness again by more pain. At times he realized he was the one screaming.

As the awareness and painful periods gradually became longer, he was more aware of people around him, but couldn't stay focused on what they were saying or doing. However, he could associate the voices with the pain because he never got one without the other.

As he gradually became more aware of his surroundings, he began to remember other things, the canon and rifle fire, men charging through the trees and brush shouting, shooting, falling and dying.

The next voice he heard was a man telling someone, "I think he will make it if he doesn't get an infection. He's lost a lot of blood, and he'll be as weak as a kitten until he builds that back up."

Everything went black again.

Every time Clay woke up, he was in a new place, with new people. One time he felt like he was in a wagon with several other people, but was in so much pain, he couldn't be sure of anything. It was a blessed relief when he passed out again.

He woke up sometime later, still not knowing where he was but realized he was in a soft bed with covers up to his chin. He heard a man say, "About time you woke up. I was beginning to think you were going to sleep your life away."

Clay asked in a croaking voice, "Where am I?"

"You are in the hospital."

"How long have I been here?"

"Going on a week. You took a bullet through the side and lost a lot of blood."

Over the next several days, people came and went. They changed his bandages, put some awful smelling stuff on his wound and said he was healing fine. Couldn't prove it by him. He was still too weak to walk more than a few feet before having to lay back down. They told him he needed to eat lots of red meat to build up the blood he had lost.

The second week, he was eating everything he could get his hands on and felt much better. He was still sore and could hardly move his arm and leg on the left side.

A few more days and he could walk short distances without too much pain. He walked around the hospital grounds and sat in the shade outside every chance he got.

Then the best news of all came.

CHAPTER 2

The date of May 9th of 1865 is a date that will be remembered by every American for the rest of their lives. That's the date the civil war was finally over. Most people didn't care who won; they were just thankful that it had ended. After four long years of fighting and killing, maybe the world has come to its senses.

He was due to be released from the hospital in a few days to go back to his unit to continue fighting. However, with this great news, now he could go home. He had all this place he could stand for one lifetime. He was ready to leave all the smells, screaming of the injured and dying, no painkiller available, limbs being amputated and thrown on a pile to be hauled away and buried.

He didn't wait to be officially released. Gathering up all his belongings, which wasn't much, he headed for the door. A doctor tried to stop him but was told to "Get out of the way. I've just gotten the best dose of medicine anyone could give me; I'm going home!" Clay shouted.

The doctor said, "Good luck, soldier," as Clay went out the door.

Clay was twenty-three years old, stood at an even six feet and usually weighed about one ninety. But after his injury, and lying in the hospital for over a month, he guessed he wouldn't weigh much over one seventy. With broad shoulders and narrow hips, blond hair and blue eyes, he was considered by most women and girls to be a handsome man.

His side was still sore, but the doctor said it was healing nicely and wouldn't need any more doctoring.

All he had been thinking about for the last month while lying in the hospital, was Alice and his folks at home, and now that he was on his way the desire to see them was stronger than ever.

Alice is the girl who promised to marry him when he got out of the army.

Home is near Rogersville, Tennessee in Hawkins County, in the North-East corner on the Kentucky and North Carolina border.

He knew that was going to be a long walk, especially in his condition. He was weak from loss of blood and lying in bed for so long. But the doctor assured him there was no permanent damage.

Since his last horse was shot out from under him, and he had no funds to buy another one, he wasn't looking forward to this. If he had waited to be officially discharged, he would have gotten another horse and a rifle. But he didn't know that and would not have waited if he had known.

He asked a man on the street, "Which way out of here to Tennessee?" He directed Clay toward a road heading west and said, "Follow that road until it plays out. That will get you close. You can ask somebody for directions from there."

He started walking, slowly, because every step he took sent pain up and down his side. It wasn't comfortable, but he could tolerate it since he was going home.

Clay had not gone very far, just to the edge of town, when he realized he was going to need some supplies if he was going anywhere. All he had on him were the clothes on his back, a pistol taken off a Confederate officer and twenty-seven dollars. He had no idea how he got out of there with money in his pocket. They must have thought he didn't have anything, so didn't look.

He remembered passing a mercantile on the right, so he backtracked to the store and went in. They had just about everything a body could ever need, and a whole lot of stuff he could think of never needing. The smell of the store reminded him of Armstrong's back home. The fruits and vegetables, the leather goods, the smell of the new clothes, made him homesick.

Right then he decided he needed some different clothes. Where he was going this blue uniform was not going to set well with a lot of people. Of course, if he were wearing grey, it would not set well with a lot of people either. He figured the best thing to do was part with some of this fortune he was carrying and get a new outfit.

He found two pairs of pants, two shirts, a hat, long handles and some socks. He hasn't had socks in over a year. "Don't know if my boots are going to fit with socks," he mumbled. The boots were still good, so he kept them. They were more comfortable walking than high heel boots anyway. He got a bag of coffee and jerky; didn't know what kind but didn't care. "Maybe I can shoot some fresh meat along the way," he thought. He picked up a few other things that he thought would come in handy, like two blankets, a raincoat, skillet, coffee pot, canteen, a ground sheet, and tarp.

Before leaving the store, Clay went in the back room and changed into his new clothes and dumped his old uniform in the trash can.

He got the storekeeper to throw in a feed sack to carry it all in. He tied a knot in the top and threw it over his shoulder, after paying the guy fifteen dollars and thirty-eight cents and hit the road again.

According to the man in the store, the distance to Tennessee is about five hundred miles. As he walked out the door, he was mumbling to himself, "In my condition, I am not going to get very far in a day, so I will have to take it slow and easy."

As the day wore on, he got slower and slower. It was almost noon when he started out. By late afternoon he guessed he had gone about ten miles and he was dragging. He started looking for a likely place to camp for the night. He had to rest for a spell first, so he sat down beside the road, just two ruts with grass growing in between, and leaned back against a tree.

Must have fallen asleep right away because when he awoke it was almost dark, and he could hear what sounded like a wagon coming down the road. He waited until it was almost up to him and stood and held both hands in sight, so they could see he meant to do them no harm. When the wagon got closer, he saw it was one older man all by himself. Clay said hello and got a "hello" in return.

"I wonder if you would be willing to give a tired man a ride?"

The man said, "Well, sure, how far are you going?"

"To Rogersville, Tennessee."

Without hesitation he said, "I ain't going that far, but I'll take you as far as I'm going. Climb onboard."

Clay put his bag of supplies in the back of the wagon and climbed into the seat beside the driver asking, "How far would that be?"

"I got a little farm about another hour up the road. You are welcome to spend the night. My wife's a pretty good cook. Be glad to feed you and give you a place to sleep."

"I'm Clay Wade" and held out his hand. They shook, and the older gentleman said, "I'm Jeremiah Ellis, pleased to meet you."

Mr. Ellis looked to be fifty-five or so, with a short greying beard, which just covered the chin and a mustache that appeared to get trimmed regularly. He was wearing bib overalls and a faded blue shirt, high top, low heeled work shoes and a floppy hat that sagged down over his ears.

"Well, Mr. Wade, what are you doing walking out here?"

"I just got out of the hospital in Richmond and headed home."

"Which side of this war were you on, if I might ask?

"Does it make a difference to you which side I fought on?" Clay asked him.

"No, don't make a hill of beans difference to me. The whole damn mess was the stupidest thing I ever heard of, and a whole lot of good men got killed, and what did it prove?"

Clay responded, "I don't know if it proved anything. Some folks said it was about slavery. But I fought with a lot of boys that never owned a slave and don't know anyone who did."

They talked about this and that for the next hour, doing their best to avoid talking about the war.

An hour or so after dark they pulled up to a house with a light in the window, a barn out back, pole fences for the animals. A creek ran right through the fenced pasture behind the barn.

They drove around back and parked the wagon. Clay helped unhitch the horses and took them to the barn, fed and watered them.

"Grab that other bag of stuff and come on in, Ma will have supper on the table in a few minutes."

As they went through the door, he called, "Hey, Ma, we got company. Meet Clay Wade, picked him up on the road. He's headed to Tennessee. I told him he could spend the night and you would feed him."

"Hello, Clay, glad to make your acquaintance. Just park yourself down there at the table. The coffee is ready, and I'll have supper on the table in a jiffy. Why are you going to Tennessee? I'll bet you got a cute little girl down there you are just dying to see. Right?"

"Yes ma'am, I do have a girl if she is still waiting for me. I haven't heard from her in over two years. I've been laid up in a hospital for a while, and it's going to be another month or more before I can make it home."

Mrs. Ellis put a mighty fine meal on the table, and they ate pretty much in silence.

When they were finished eating, Clay told them, "If it's ok, I'll sleep in the barn, and I'm so tired I think I'll turn in. I will see you before I head out in the morning."

Mrs. Ellis said, "You certainly will. You will eat before you leave."

Clay was moving very slow by the time he reached the barn. He couldn't remember ever being this tired. He pulled some hay down from the stack in the corner, threw his bedroll on it and was asleep as soon as his head hit the bed.

By noon the next day he was seven or eight miles on down the road. He figured if he could make 20 miles a day he could be home in a month. If he got lucky and caught a ride, he could cut some time off that.

He walked what he estimated to be twelve to fifteen miles a day the first three days. He thought that was making good time what with having to rest every hour or so.

It was mid to late May and was getting warm during the afternoons. Clay was getting used to walking and was building up his strength. From here on, he figured he should be able to make the twenty miles a day if the weather would stop interfering. Every day thundershowers forced him to find a place to hang his tarp to try to keep dry. In his weakened condition he didn't think it was a good idea to get a chill, so he accepted the delay when necessary. He wasn't opposed to stopping early and sleeping late either.

He got lucky and a wagon loaded with freight picked him up on the 4th day out and took him all the way to Greensboro, North Carolina. That took almost two weeks. They stopped at several towns along the way to deliver or pick up shipments. In exchange for his help loading and unloading the freight, the driver paid for Clay's meals and hotel rooms, when there was one available.

When they arrived in Greensboro, and the driver announced this was the end of his route, Clay thanked him for the ride and the company, threw his sack over his shoulder and started walking.

His wound wasn't bothering him hardly at all now, so he was able to step out and put some miles behind him. He still had over half way to go, but the last two weeks had been a lot better than walking. It allowed his wound to heal, gave him time to rest and build up his strength.

Walking with no one to talk with can get tedious and lonesome. Alice and the folks at home were on his mind constantly. Every day he tried to find new ways to keep his mind busy, but it kept straying back to Alice, the girl who was waiting for him, he hoped.

He was walking through a heavily wooded area with the trees and brush coming right up to the road when he heard voices coming from around the bend ahead. Not wanting to meet any trouble he just stepped off the road and behind a large tree where he could see who was coming before they saw him.

He heard them talking long before he could see them. They were talking about what they had done with the farmer's daughter and wife. One of them was laughing and said "did you see the old man's face when I put my knife across his throat? I thought he was going to die right there and save me the trouble of slitting his skinny throat." They were still laughing as they went out of sight.

Clay remained hidden for another ten minutes or so thinking about what he had heard. "I am going to have to be better prepared in case I meet up with any more of their kind." He was thinking about what he could have done if they had come upon him unexpectedly and started trouble. With four like those, he wouldn't have had much of a chance.

The pistol he was wearing was a Confederate issue,1858 Remington cap and ball. It was considered the best handgun to have during the civil war. The Confederate officer he took the pistol, belt, and holster from, also had two extra cylinders that he carried loaded and, in the pouch, attached to the gun belt. That makes it a lot faster to reload if it came to that. Just pop out the empty cylinder and pop in a loaded one. Each held six rounds. That gave him eighteen shots before he had to take the time to reload.

That night, he was sitting by the fire back off the road, hidden in some thick trees and brush. He was still contemplating the situation he heard the men talking about, and wondering if there was anything he could, and should, do about it. Before falling asleep, he decided all he could do was inform the law in the next town.

In the meantime, he decided he better get more practice using his Remington. He had always been a fair shot as far as hitting what he aimed at, but he had never worked at perfecting a fast draw. There was no need for a fast draw growing up on a farm. But now Clay decided he would work on that since he had nothing else to do while he was walking, and it may come in handy farther down the road.

Mid-morning of the next day he was walking and practicing his fast draw, which wasn't very fast when he saw a farmhouse just off the road backed up against a hill with shade trees all around, and a barn out back.

He thought he might be able to get a free meal and maybe replenish his food supply if anyone was home.

He turned off the road walking toward the house. As he approached, he became aware that something was wrong. The smell of something dead hit his nostrils. Buzzards were feeding on something in the front yard, and a couple of horses were standing with their heads over the fence looking toward the house like they were waiting for someone to feed them. They should have been fed and out to pasture or put to work by this time of the day.

The closer he got to the house, the stronger the smell got. One reason was, the buzzards feeding on a dog by the front porch.

Suddenly, the conversation he overheard the day before between the four men on the trail, came back to him. He stopped in his tracks, not wanting to find what he knew was there.

After looking all around to make sure there was no danger lurking, he slowly approached the front porch. The buzzards went flapping and screeched away. He covered his nose with his bandana, but he couldn't tell if it did any good.

Pushing the door open and stepping inside, he immediately saw a man lying in a pool of blood on the floor with his throat cut.

The house looked like a tornado had hit it. Furniture was overturned, and broken dishes shattered on the floor, windows knocked out.

He forced himself to check in the first bedroom. That's where he found what he assumed was the wife. She was lying on the bed with her throat cut and no clothes. It was obvious she was badly treated before she was killed.

Across the hall, he found the daughter in the same condition.

The four men had apparently spent quite some time here before they finished their horrible deed and moved on.

Clay went back outside to get some fresh air and check out the rest of the place. The barn was torn apart like the house. It looked as if they were searching for something that wasn't here. It didn't appear these folks had much before this happened, now they have nothing, not even their lives.

He fed and watered the horses, let the milk cow in with her calf and opened the gate so they could get out to graze and get water. He found a shovel in the barn and proceeded to dig three graves. That took him the rest of the day. He had to take it slow and stop to rest often. Just before dark, he wrapped the three bodies in blankets off the beds and laid them to rest near a large oak tree on the hillside. He said a few words that he remembered the preacher saying at several funerals he had attended back home.

After covering the graves, Clay realized he didn't know any names to put on the markers that he intended to make, so he went back into the house looking for anything with a name on it. He finally found several envelopes addressed to Michael and Sally Winthrop and Mary. He got three boards out by the barn, and with his knife carved their names and stuck them into the ground at the head of each grave. He figured he had done all he could do.

That night he slept in the barn on a stack of hay. He didn't get much sleep though. The thought of what went on here just two days ago had him dreaming some crazy dreams and waking up every few minutes in a cold sweat.

He woke up for good when the roosters started crowing. He fed and watered the horses, opened the chicken coop so the chickens could search for food. If left in their pen, they would starve to death. By letting them out to run free they would probably be eaten by coyotes or wolfs, but at least they would have a chance.

He found some eggs in the hen house and smoked ham in the cellar, so he built a fire in the kitchen stove and made himself breakfast. He packed the rest of the eggs and meat into his pack. If left here it would just go to waste.

CHAPTER 3

He had no idea how far it was to the next town where he could report this to the authorities if there were any authorities. He wished he had the tools, such as guns and transportation, to go after those four. They needed killing in the worst way. But, he realized he couldn't do it. The best he could do was report it to someone who could.

He would write a letter to the return address on the envelopes and let them know what had happened to their loved ones.

Now he had a decision to make. There were two horses in the corral, a saddle in the barn, no one around to take care of them. Did he take them with him? Would he be accused of horse thievery? It sure would save him a lot of time and many miles of walking.

The temptation was too much to pass up. Clay decided he would ride to the first town where he hoped to find some law enforcement. There he would report what had happened, leave the horse there if necessary and see if the sheriff, or whatever law there was, could arrange to sell it and get the money to the nearest relative.

With that decision made, and after eating a good breakfast, he saddled the horse that looked like the best of the two, tied his bag of supplies on the back of the saddle, along with the saddlebags he found in the barn. As he rode away, he was feeling much better about his traveling arrangements, but he couldn't clear his mind of the tragedy that happened here to this little family.

Now he had a whole new game plan. He planned to travel thirty to forty miles a day if the horse could stand up to that.

Still practicing drawing his gun, he found that while riding, he could get it out much faster if he wore it on his left hip with the butt forward for a cross draw.

After the first day, he had a blister on his hand, but he was getting better at getting the gun out and in firing position. He had no ammunition to waste, so he was just concentrating on the draw. In fact, the only ammo he had was what was in the gun and the two extra cylinders. He had removed the cap and balls from the cylinder and practiced drawing and dry firing the weapon. When he got tired of practicing, he reloaded the gun with a loaded cylinder and put it back in the holster on his left hip, just in case he should need it.

The borrowed horse was holding up good, and he was averaging forty or so miles a day. At that rate, he should be home in less than a week.

Late that afternoon he came to the first settlement since leaving the scene of the murders. It wasn't big enough to call a town, just a small store that sold just about everything, one saloon with only four tables, and a blacksmith shop. Across the road, which did duty as the main street, was the office of the city Marshal, and a feed store. The saloon had a sign over the bar saying they served meals.

Clay went to the marshal's office, but no one was there, so he looked up and down the street for any sign of the lawman, and not finding one, he went in the saloon. There were only four other people in the place. Three of them sitting at one table carrying on a conversation, the fourth one sitting alone across the room. He looked like he had been there quite some time. There was a bottle of whiskey three-fourths empty sitting in front of him, and he looked like he had consumed all of it without any help.

Clay walked up to the bar and ordered a whiskey. When the bartender brought his drink, he asked about the marshal and was directed to the three sitting together. He was sure glad it wasn't the drunk sitting alone.

Taking his drink, he strolled over to the table and asked, "Which one of you gentlemen is the Marshal?"

The man sitting to the back side of the table, facing the door, looked up at Clay and said, "I'm the marshal, Allen Davis, what can I do for you, young fellow?"

Clay motioned to the vacant chair and said, "Mind if I have a seat? I need to report a murder." That got all their attention.

"Murder, where did this happen, and when?"

Clay told the story, beginning with leaving the hospital in Richmond and heading home to Tennessee, to explain why he was on the road in the first place. He told of overhearing the four men talking and then finding the bodies and burying them. He reached into his pocket and pulled out the envelopes with their names on them and handed them to the marshal.

All this time the marshal and the other two men sat in silence, listening. When Clay finished his story, the marshal looked at the names and read them off to the other men. All three of them knew the family, although not all that well. They came into town to do their shopping on a semi-regular schedule but didn't seem to have any other connection. Much like most of the families living around here.

Clay asks, "Is there anything else I need to do Marshall?"

Marshall Davis told him he would need to come to his office and make a report. "Then I will send it to all the neighboring towns. Did you happen to get a good look at these guys? Would you recognize them if you saw them again?

"I am pretty sure I would recognize the one who was laughing about cutting the man's throat. He was riding a scruffy looking gray horse. The others were riding a black and two sorrels. One of the sorrels had one white stocking on one of the back legs. Don't remember which leg." "Well, that will sure help in identifying them. If anyone has seen these guys, they will probably remember them," said the marshal thankfully.

One of the other men sitting at the table suddenly sat up straight and said, "I remember seeing them. They came through here about five or six days back. Left the horses at the livery and snuck out early the next morning without paying Sam for the boarding and feed. A sorry looking bunch. It seems all of them were wearing some parts of Confederate uniforms. Mostly caps and pants."

Clay and the marshal walked across the street to write out the report. It was getting late in the day when the marshal asked Clay what his plans were for the night.

"I don't have any, other than to find a place to throw my blankets and get some sleep after I get something to eat," Clay anxiously replied.

The marshal says, "Come on I'll treat you to supper, and if you don't mind, you can sleep in one of the cells back there. The bunks are not too bad. I have the blankets and such washed when they need it. They don't get too much use. Just a drunk now and again."

Clay thanked the marshal, took his horse to the livery stable and arranged for his keep and feed for one night.

The next morning as Clay was having breakfast at the café, the Marshall walked in with a young man who looked to be about nineteen or twenty years old. He had a strong resemblance to the marshal who introduced him as his son, Walt.

"Walt will be riding over to the county seat to report the murders to the sheriff. If these guys get caught, we will need you to come back to testify as to what you heard them say. Even then it will be your word against theirs."

"Marshall, I plan to be way on down the road toward home by late today. There won't be any coming back. I've seen all this country I care to see. But, I have another problem."

"What is that?"

"That horse I am riding. It belongs to the murdered people. I borrowed it, so I could get here and report what happened. I could sure use it to get the rest of the way home if you see a way to let me keep it. I'll be glad to sign a note for whatever you think he's worth. Then when we find the relatives, I can send them the money. Do you think we can do that?"

"You seem like an honest young man. You didn't even have to mention the horse. I would never have known."

Clay bowed his head and said, "Maybe you wouldn't, but I would."

The marshal thought about that for a minute or two. "That looks like about a thirty-dollar horse, wouldn't you say?"

"I'll be glad to send you thirty dollars as soon as I get it. I will even go higher if you think I should. It should take me five or six days to get home, depending on what I run into along the way. I should be able to get the money and send it to you when I get there". He didn't know if the relatives would ever see the thirty dollars, but at least his conscience would be clear.

Four more days and Clay rode into the main street of Rogersville, Tennessee. During those four days, Clay had been practicing with the handgun. He was getting much faster, and the gun was coming out smooth and lining up with the target naturally.

The place didn't look too different. Clay couldn't decide if the sign over the mercantile was new, or if the old one got painted. The street was still just as dry and dusty as always, except after a heavy rain, when it turned into a mud pit. A few people were strolling around the few businesses.

Clay didn't have any idea what day of the week or month it was. He figured it must be getting close to mid-July since he had been on the trail most of two months if he had been keeping track of the days.

The home place was about five miles out of town up in the hills at the edge of Clinch mountain. The farm isn't all that big, but they could grow some of the healthiest rocks and boulders you have ever seen. Unfortunately, there isn't any money to be made from that crop, but the scenery makes it all worth the effort.

His Pa had a few cows and a fair to middling stud horse, and four mares that gave them four new colts almost every year. Breaking and training the fresh horses had been Clay's job since he was about twelve years old.

He came walking his horse down the main street of Rogersville, Tennessee about mid-morning. There were a few new businesses, one more saloon, a livery stable and blacksmith shop that were not there when he left four years ago.

CHAPTER 4

He was anxious to get home and see the folks, then hurry over to see Alice. They had decided to wait until he got back from the war before they got married and built a place of their own. Everyone was saying the war would only last a few weeks.

He saw the owner of the mercantile store, Mr. Campbell, sweeping his front porch and waved to him. He looked at Clay like he saw a ghost. Well, it has been four years.

The sheriff was sitting on the bench in front of his office. Charles Campbell has been the sheriff of Hawkins County since Clay was a boy. His brother, Allen Campbell, had the mercantile next door. He waved. The sheriff got up and walked out into the street and shook Clay's hand and said, "Glad to see you back all in one piece, Clay. A lot of folks have missed you around here. How have you been?"

Clay replied, "Fair to middling, I guess. Still living and have all my limbs."

"That is a lot more than a lot of the boys can say. There's quite a few who won't be coming back, I'm afraid. Have you been out to the home place yet?"

"No, I'm just heading that way now. How is everyone?"

The sheriff dropped his head and scuffed the toe of his boot in the dirt, looked off down the street, then back up at Clay.

"Have you heard anything about your folks lately?"

"No, in fact, I haven't heard anything from anyone in over two years."
"Clay, why don't you get down and have a cup of coffee with me? We got a lot to talk about," the sheriff said reluctantly.

Clay didn't like the way that sounded but, he got down from his horse and gave the reins a turn around the hitch rail.

"Come on in, the coffee is probably pretty strong by now, made it first thing this morning, but it's hot," the sheriff said stalling.

When they had their coffee, and the sheriff was sitting behind his desk, with Clay across in a straight back chair, Clay asked, "What has been going on, Sheriff? Why are you looking so concerned?"

"There have been a lot of changes since you left. Not all of them to the good, I'm afraid. You won't recognize things around here. The war sure tore some things apart."

Clay was getting more worried by the minute, and the sheriff wasn't helping any by dragging it out.

"Come on, out with-it Sheriff; it can't be all that bad. What about my folks?"

The sheriff looked like he had swallowed a chaw of tobacco. He started stuttering and stammering and couldn't get anything out.

Clay said, "Come on Sheriff, tell me, what about my folks?"

"Clay, I sure hate to be the one to tell you this, but your folks passed away about two years ago."

"NO, what happened?"

"Sickness went around. Several families got it. Most of them pulled through, but your ma and pa were sick for a while, just kept getting weaker and weaker. They passed away about three days apart. Your mom went first, then your pa."

That set Clay back on his heels. He had to swallow the lump in his throat and turn his back, so Sheriff Campbell wouldn't see the tears rolling down his cheeks.

A couple of minutes went by before he could ask him, "So, no one is living on the place now?"

"The place was sold about six months ago for back taxes. A fellow from up north came in here just before the war was over and bought up all the property that was behind on taxes. He must own over half the county by now," the sheriff tried to explain.

"How can he do that? Don't the tax people know I will be coming back and pay the taxes?"

"That's the other thing, Clay. Your mom and dad got a notice from the war department that you had been killed. We all believed you were dead. That is really when your mom and dad started going downhill, I think. They were grieving over you. I couldn't believe my eyes when I saw you coming up the road."

"Everyone thinks I'm dead? How about Alice. Does she think I'm dead, too?"

"Well, yes. Alice's dad came down with the same sickness as your folks. He was another one that died. After he died, Alice and her mom had no way to make a living. That's when Johnny Smithfield came courtin' and convinced Alice to marry him, and he would take care of both of them. So, she did. I don't know if she loves him or if she was desperate. They are now living out at his dad's place and got a little one on the way. I'm sorry to be the one giving you all this bad news. I know it hurts. If there is anything I can do to help you out, you let me know, you hear?"

"Sheriff, I have just about enough money left on me to get good and drunk. I feel like that's what I want to do. Care to join me?"

"I'll join you for one drink. Well, maybe two. But I am buying." "Thanks, Sheriff, but it's going to take more than two to get me through this."

"Look, Clay, drinking is not going to make the problems go away. All you will do is wake up tomorrow with a headache, and the problems will still be there. Then you have to face them with a bad headache. Is that what you want?"

"No, right now I don't know what I want."

"Come on, let's get those drinks."

They walked across the street to the first saloon they came to, took a table up front by the window where they could see everyone who came along the road.

Clay sat there sipping his whiskey and thinking all kinds of thoughts. Some of them would have gotten him hung if he carried them out. One of the things he started thinking about was the sale of the farm for back taxes.

"Sheriff, just what did the buyer get when he bought the farm for the back taxes?"

The sheriff says, "He got the property, the house, and all the other buildings and fixtures."

"What about the personal property? The things inside the house and the horses and cattle, saddles and such?"

"As far as I know those things are not mentioned in the sale papers."

"Then they still belong to me? There is no tax on livestock and personal possessions, so they couldn't be sold for back taxes, since there is no tax owed on them, right?"

The Sheriff said, "You're talking lawyer stuff now. You're way over my head. But you may be right. Maybe you need to see a lawyer. There is one next door to the bank. I'll take you over there and introduce you. He seems like a nice fellow. He may be able to answer your questions."

"Do you know if the buyer has done anything with the livestock since he took over?"

"No," the sheriff said. "Nothing has been done. That feller is still too busy running around buying up more property. Although, I'm not sure he is buying all the properties he's taking over. I have heard some rumors, but can't prove anything, yet."

"Maybe there is still time for me to salvage something out of this. Let's talk to that lawyer," Clay said sounding more clear-headed.

"His name is White. Right nice fellow, what little dealings I've had with him."

"That sounds like a good place to start."

They got up, put money on the table for their drinks and left.

Leonard White was like the sheriff said. Looked to be about thirty years old, well-built but not heavy. Looked like he would be able to make a showing if he had to protect himself. About five feet ten or so weighed about one-eighty. Dark hair and dark eyes with a friendly smile.

When Sheriff Campbell introduced Clay, Mr. White recognized the Name. "Were Samuel and Irene Wade your parents?"

"Yes, they were."

"What can I do for you, Clay?"

"My folk's homestead was sold for back taxes. I want to know what was included in the sale. What does the buyer legally get?"

"My understanding is, if there is a lien on the personal property, such as borrowing money using the livestock as collateral for the loan, then the livestock would be part of the sale. The buyer would pay off the loan to the bank, or whoever held the note, and he would own the livestock."

"How do we find out if there was a lien on any of the personal items or livestock?"

Lawyer White asks, "Where did your dad do his banking?"

"Right here in town, at the local bank."

"That's where I would start. Go to the bank and ask to see your father's bank records for the last four or five years and ask if there was an outstanding loan when they passed away."

"Thanks, I'll do that."

"If you need any help with this let me know."

"I sure will, thanks,"

As they were leaving the lawyers office, Clay asks the sheriff, "Who bought my dad's farm anyway?"

"That would be a fellow by the name of Rafe Burdette. He came in here just before the war ended and started buying up everything that had back taxes owed. He apparently knew the South was going to lose the war eventually, and a lot of people would be hurting. He struts around like a proud peacock, knowing that everyone hates his guts and seems to thrive on it."

"Any idea where he got all his money?"

"Just a rumor, but I heard he was running guns to both sides during the war. Making deals out of both sides of his mouth, collecting from both the north and the south. Don't know how he was making it work, but that's the rumor going around."

"Burdette. What does he look like?"

The sheriff nodded his head down the street, "Just like that man coming down the street in the fancy carriage, with the high stepping horse, and the beautiful woman on his arm."

Clay looked where he was pointing and saw the fancy carriage and the beautiful woman followed by four rough-looking men riding better horses than a cowhand could afford. They didn't look like cowhands either. Looked more like hired shooters, and they had that attitude about them that dared anyone to give them any trouble.

As they went by, Burdette never looked in their direction. Clay asked, "Who is the woman, is that his daughter?"

"Oh no. That's his wife. She must be twenty years younger than he is. But, that's what money can get you."

"Who is in charge at the bank. Who do I talk to?"

Sheriff says, "I guess the man you should see is probably Edward LaGrange. He keeps the books."

Clay walked into the bank and saw one man behind a counter with an iron-barred window in front of him and another sitting at a desk off to the side. He went to the man behind the window and asked to see Mr. LaGrange. He pointed to the man across the room. Clay walked over and introduced himself.

"How can I help you, Mr. Wade?"

When Clay explained the situation, LaGrange turned around, pulled a book off a shelf, flipped through it until he got to Wade. He looked at it for a minute or so before asking, "What are you looking for, Mr. Wade?" "I want to see how much money was in the account when they died, how much is there now, and if he had any outstanding loans." Mr. LaGrange looked back through the account records and said, "Looks like he had $35.33 in the account. I don't find any record of any outstanding loans."

"Ok, I'll take the $35.33 and close the account."

He thanked the banker for his time and left the bank with the money in his pocket. The sheriff was still standing out front, so he asked him to have another drink with him because he had some questions for him.

When they were seated at the same table as before and had their drinks, Clay told him he was going to get his property from the farm.

"You did say there is no one living on the place now, right?"

"To my knowledge, no one is living there. Burdette spends most of his time here in town when he is not out looking at more property to buy," the sheriff said.

"Where does he stay when he is in town?"

"You're not thinkin' of startin' no trouble, are you?"

Clay said "Not really. I think the right thing to do would be to let him know I will be coming to get my personal property, cattle, and horses. Don't you?"

"It might be the right thing to do, but you will be askin for a peck of trouble. You saw them big fellows ridin' along behind him? That man don't go anywhere without them. Nobody can even get close to him."

Clay asked again, "Where does he stay when he's in town?"

"He has what they call a suite of rooms on the top floor of the hotel. Even when he is not there, he has a man stationed outside the door guarding the place."

"Well, when and where does he eat?"

"He usually eats about seven in the morning at the Rogersville Diner down the street in the next block. Sometimes he eats dinner there too, but most of the time he eats around six in the evening at the hotel dining room with his wife."

After thinking about that for a few minutes, Clay said, "Probably the best place to talk to him will be when he is having dinner with his wife, wouldn't you think? Less likely to cause trouble if she's there."

The sheriff was getting uncomfortable with this line of talk. He wanted no part of it. "I'm not asking you to get involved, Sheriff. I understand you live here, but I am determined to get what's mine. If Burdette wants to cause trouble, I will just have to deal with it when it comes."

After thinking about it a couple of minutes, Clay remarked, "Maybe I better ride out to the place and snoop around to see if the cows and horses are even still there. No point in making a fuss if everything is gone. If that is the case, I'll have to go after him for the money, if I can prove he is the one who took them. That will be a lot harder to prove."

All this time Clay's horse has been standing in front of the sheriff's office. He felt terrible about that when he realized what he had done.

He led the horse to the water trough and let him have his fill, tightened the girth and mounted. As he turned down the street, the sheriff said "Clay, you be careful. That's a mean bunch."

"Ok, I will."

CHAPTER 5

It was about a five-mile ride, should take no more than an hour and a half, he thought if he went slow and easy and watched his step, so as not to run into any of Burdett's men.

Having grown up here, he knew this country like the back of his hand. He planned to circle and come in from the south. There is a creek that runs down from behind the house, past the barns and on down through the valley. There is a lot of cover along the stream. He should be able to get close enough to see if there is any activity around the place. That will also give him an opportunity to scout the area where the cattle and horses should be if they are still here.

He knew all the best places to hide and still be able to see a lot of country without being seen. Riding along the creek bottom until he was directly behind the house and about one hundred yards out, he tied his horse to a bush and crawled up to where he could just see over the top of the ridge. He removed his hat and made himself comfortable.

One look at the place and he almost broke down crying. He had expected to come home to a welcoming family, a future bride, and a future raising cattle and horses. But, the place was run down, and overgrown with weeds and brush, right up to the front and back porch. The pens, where he had worked the horses, were in bad shape. The fences were broken and sagged in places; the gate was hanging loose, about to fall over. Nothing had been in there in months. Probably not since his Dad got sick over two years ago. He could tell by the looks of things no one was staying here permanently. He could see everything from here but didn't see any movement at all. He laid there for about ten minutes, just to be on the safe side and saw no action.

Deciding to have a closer look, he came up behind the barn and bunkhouse, hopefully without being seen, if someone should be here. They certainly were not doing any work around the place.

He came up to the back of the bunkhouse first, as quiet as he possibly could, which was not easy to do with all the weeds grown up right against the wall. Moving up to the window, which was open, he listened for a couple of minutes, not hearing anything, he peaked in, all he saw was a room torn apart like someone was searching for something.

With no one in the bunkhouse, he checked out the barn. Keeping the barn and bunkhouse between him and the house he made his way to the end of the barn and peeked in. Again, nothing, nor any sign that anyone has been here recently.

That made him feel pretty sure there is no one in the house, so he quietly walked up to the back door, listened but heard nothing, slowly push the door open and looked inside. It looked pretty much like the bunkhouse.

He walked through the house with tears rolling down his cheeks, remembering all the good times growing up here. He could still see Mom and Dad sitting at the dining table, drinking coffee and laughing about something. Usually something stupid that Clay did, like falling in the creek, or getting bucked off a horse.

It was a sad homecoming. Everywhere Clay looked brought back memories and broke his heart that much more. He thought he could even smell the food his mother prepared coming from the kitchen.

Not finding anything in the house that he would come back for, he checked the barn. There were a couple of saddles, bridles, ropes and the usual stuff that you find around a horse barn.

He went back to where he had left his horse and brought him up to the back door of the barn. He tied on both saddles, the bridles and all the other gear that he could get to stay there, then led him back into the brush along the creek.

There he stashed everything out of sight. It wouldn't take much of a tracker to tell where he had been. He wiped out any tracks as best he could and rode away. He knew if someone looked around the back of the barn, they would see where he had come and gone. He didn't think Burdette's men were going to be too anxious to go prowling around in the brush. They look more like the type to sit around doing nothing but cause trouble.

Now that he had established no one was staying here, he could ride around and check on the cattle and horses.

There is a beautiful little valley to the east and north of the home place where they always grazed. There are also a couple of canyons that open off the valley, with streams coming down off the hills, which feeds into the creek that runs behind the house. Those canyons have several hundred acres of good grass and timber. It is not part of the homestead, but you couldn't get to it without crossing the homestead.

He was still cautious and watchful as he rode. He mumbled to himself "I don't want to meet up with any of Burdette's men. I could easily enough explain what I'm doing here, visiting the place where I was born and raised before I move on. But I don't think they would take that explanation with a smile on their face."

Keeping to the high ground, without sky-lining himself, he scouted the north side of the central valley, riding in a north-easterly direction.

He was seeing some cattle here and there, but not close enough to see a brand yet. As he approached the mouth of the first branch canyon, he came upon several cows lazing around in the shade, chewing their cud, and they all had the bar W brand. That was his dad's brand, a simple bar over a W.

That was making him feel much better. He started trying to get a head count but, without driving them out of the brush so you can see all of them, that was hard to do. From what he could see, just riding across the country, there is several hundred head here, and he hadn't gotten into the canyons yet. Clay was feeling good about this. But, he was starting to worry about how to get them out of here without having to fight the whole Burdett crowd.

He hasn't seen any horses yet, but he knew where they would be if they are still here. They always favored the north end of this first branch canyon where the stream comes off the mountain and flows through the middle of the valley. As Clay rode into the canyon, he began to see signs of unshod horses and his hopes were soaring. If those horses are here, he would have the beginning of his horse ranch. All Clay needed to do was get them out of here and find a new place to settle down. But he didn't know if it would be around here. Tennessee has some beautiful country, and he had friends here, or he did before the war.

He and Alice had planned to build their house on that rise of ground right back there, overlooking this whole valley. That thought brought another lump to his throat. "Makes me not even want to carry on anymore. Just catch one of my horses and head west and see where I end up," Clay's mind wandered.

"But there is something about this Burdette that sticks in my craw. I am not about to ride out of here without getting what's mine. I can see already that there are enough cattle and horses here to give me a good start if I can get them sold without getting killed."

He continued circling the valley, staying in the trees. He had to be sure he was alone here before he did anything else.

Northern Tennessee, in Hawkins County, on the edge of the Clinch Mountains, is one of the most beautiful places in the entire area. The high peaks covered with trees, waterfalls cascading down in several places, makes a man want to stay right here forever.

Along the streams in the shade, perch were jumping where the deep holes have been washed out by heavy rains over the years. Clay pulled his horse to a halt and just sat taking in the quiet and the beauty of the place. Knowing if the horses are still here, they are probably back up this canyon. So, he carefully rode along the creek, staying in the trees and watching for any sign of humans in the area. There are open areas in the trees and a few small pools along the creek where water stands the year around being fed from springs on the side of the mountain.

About halfway up the canyon, he saw the horses. There was quite a herd of them. Apparently, no one had been taking care of them since his dad died. They were left to run and breed freely for four years. Even the ones who were babies when he left home now have babies.

Riding over to where they were dozing in the shade, he recognized a few, but there were some he had never seen before. He got off his horse, walked over to Splotch, the gray appaloosa broodmare with the white blanket across her hips, that was Clay's favorite. Clay petted and talked to her while the other broodmares, there were two sorrels and a black, came over to be petted. He stood there for a long time talking to them with tears rolling down his cheeks. They were old friends that he had missed.

Off to the side were the two old mules they had used to pull the plow and wagon and do the farm work around the place. They had to come up and get petted also. They all acted like they were starving for attention.

A couple of the younger ones that he remembered came close enough for him to get his hands on them. These are the ones he was working with before he left home. There were four that he had been riding.

He was able to get a rope on one of them while he was petting and talking to him. He apparently remembered Clay, because he didn't act up at all as he fashioned a halter, leaned on him and put his weight on his back.

After a while, he mounted the borrowed horse, which he had started calling Bud, and lead the young gelding. He called him Stormy because his coloring looked like dark clouds. He also had the white blanket across his hips like his mother.

He led him back to where he had stashed all the gear. He put one of the saddles on Stormy and cinched it down. He still didn't act up, so he put all the equipment he had taken from the barn on top of Bud and tied it down and secured it all with ropes and tied Bud to a bush. Stormy was led off a few paces so he could get accustomed to the saddle again. When Clay mounted him, he only put in a token effort to unseat him, but he wasn't serious about it.

Leading Bud with all the gear strapped to his saddle, they headed back to the horse herd. It was getting close to sundown by the time they got there.

He quickly got ropes on the other three that he had been working before he left. They would be about six years old now and had about six months of training; they had not been handled or worked for more than four years. He was wondering how much they remembered.

He put them on lead ropes, put the extra saddle on one, then decided to put the third saddle on another so that they could get used to it on the way back to town. It would be dark by the time he got there, but that was a good thing. No one would see him riding into town leading four horses.

On the way, he took turns riding the young horses. That brought back fond memories, and he enjoyed every minute of it. They obviously remembered the training they had because they didn't give him any trouble when he mounted them.

When he reached town, he came in by a back street and went to the sheriff's barn behind the jail. He unsaddled the horses, rubbed them down, gave them a scoop of oats, petted and talked to them while he was doing it.

He had been so excited about finding all the horses and cows that he forgot he hadn't eaten since early morning. He went to the diner and ordered a large steak with potatoes and gravy, beans and a pot of coffee.

While he was eating, who walks in but Mr. Burdette himself, being followed by two of his bodyguards. Burdette took a table in the back facing the door, his two men take another next to him, but also facing the door. If you came in after they did, you would not know they were together.

Clay was contemplating should he let him know that he was going to be removing his cattle and horses from his farm, or wait and let him find out, hopefully after they were all gone. After some thought, and looking at the two men with Burdett, he decided on the safest way. Don't tell him. All it will do is cause Burdette to put a watch on the place to prevent him from getting what is rightfully his.

The best plan he could come up with was to ease in there when no one was around, and quietly move all the cattle into the second canyon, farther away from the home place. When he had collected all he could find, he would try to sneak them out of the country quietly. That was not going to be easy. Four hundred or so animals make a lot of noise and dust when on the move, and the trail they leave is impossible to hide.

When he finished eating he walked over to the jail. No one was around, so he found the cell that looked the cleanest, threw his bedroll on it and was fast asleep in minutes.

The next morning as he was eating breakfast at the diner, Burdett and his bodyguards walked in. They took the same table they had occupied the night before. It looked like everyone knew that table belonged to Burdett.

It wasn't long until one of the men turned to Burdette and asked, "Boss, when do we start moving the livestock off that Bar W Place?"

Burdette thought about that a while before he said, "We need to go check out that new place up north first and see what we can do with it. Probably have to run that old man and his woman off. I'll give them one week to vacate. If they are still there, we will move them. Make it look like they left on their own. So, I would say by the latter part of next week we can start rounding up everything at the Bar W."

Clay was sitting close enough to hear their conversation. Today was Monday; so, he would have less than two weeks to get everything out of there. He would have to find some help darn quick.

He left the diner and got to the sheriff's office just as he was pouring himself a cup of coffee. When he saw Clay walk in, he reached for another cup and filled it. Motioned for him to sit. He walked around his desk and sat down, put his feet up and leaned back and took a big slug of coffee.

He was looking at Clay with a little grin on his face, and says, "I found a beautiful bunch of horses in my barn this morning. What do you think I should do with them? They ought to bring a darn good price."

"I thought you would like them. When I was out to the home place, I located about forty horses and probably four hundred or more head of cattle that have been running wild back there in the brush. I brought those four in because they are the ones I was working with before I left home. There are still some beautiful animals out there that I want to get out."

Clay continued, "I heard Burdette and his men talking this morning. They are planning to start rounding up all the livestock on the Bar W late next week. I am going to need probably four or five good men to help me get them out of there as soon as I can. Do you have any ideas where I might get them, like by tomorrow? Oh, by the way, Burdett said they were going up north to move someone off their place. He said he would give them one week to move; then they would move them and make it look like they left on their own. Thought you might want to check up on that. It sounds like they are going to cause someone some grief."

"Thanks for telling me. I will do some looking around and see what property he may be talking about."

"Now, let me think about this a minute. I know Willie Stanton just got back from the war and is looking for work. You remember Willie?"

"I sure do, we worked a few roundups together. Do you know where he's staying?"

"He has a widowed aunt that lives about a mile out of town to the west. Off to the right with a rundown fence. You might ride out there and see if he is still around."

"Ok, do you know anyone else I may be able to get? I would like to have at least five, plus myself. We ought to be able to handle four hundred, don't you think?"

"It's been a long time since I was on a trail drive. I probably have forgotten everything I ever knew about it. And another thing."

"What's that, Sheriff?

"I am not about to try to relearn it," the sheriff says shaking his head.

"Now, where is the closest market for a herd of cattle that we could drive to in a hurry?"

"There ain't none that you can drive to in a hurry. The closest is Sedalia, Missouri and that is over seven hundred miles. Take you over two months to make that drive. That's the closest railroad to here. From there they ship it to a packing company in Chicago. Wait a minute; I just saw something in the paper the other day. Let me find that."

After looking through a stack of papers for a few minutes, he came up with the article he was hunting. "Here it is, a guy by the name of Phillip Armour has opened a meat packing plant in Chicago where most that beef gets shipped. I think Chicago will be closer than Sedalia. Let's look at a map I have here."

He spread a map out on his desk and leaned over looking at it. Clay said, "According to this map, Chicago is considerably closer than Sedalia." They did some measurements and decided it was about two hundred miles closer. "That will cut about two to three weeks off the drive and probably get more money by cutting out the cattle buyer in Sedalia."

CHAPTER 6

That decided, he saddled Stormy and went looking for Willie Stanton. He wasn't that hard to find. There was only one house about one mile out of town with a run-down fence around it.

Willie saw him coming up the lane and met him on the front porch. They shook hands like old friends. Aunt Maddie invited him in and served them both a cup of coffee and cookies.

Aunt Maddie was an attractive woman in her early forties, with black hair, brown eyes, beautiful smile, and a good figure. Too young to be a widow. Clay had the fleeting thought that she would be a good catch for some man. They shared small talk for a few minutes about what they have been doing. Of course, they both had been in the war and came back alive with all their parts. They could be thankful for that.

When the idle talk died down, Clay asked Willie, "What do you have planned for the next two or three months?"

Willie gave Clay a funny look and asked, "Why you ask? You got something you need help with?"

"I sure do. And it has to be done quickly. I need about four or five more just like us."

Willie's curiosity got the better of him. He said, "This sounds like something big. What's up? We goin' to rob a bank?"

They both laughed, "No, nothing like that. Do you know about this fellow Burdett, and what he is up to?"

"Yeah, I've heard some talk about him buying up property for back taxes, and possibly running people off their place, and taking over. How does that affect us?"

"My folk's place is one that he bought, for practically nothing. He got the land and buildings, but all the livestock is still mine, and I mean to get it off the place before Burdett decides to take it. I heard him and his bodyguards talking this morning at breakfast. They plan to start moving everything off the latter part of next week. We have about eight or ten days to get everything off the place without him knowing we are doing it."

Willie asks, "Do you think we can get it done that quick?"

"All depends if we can get the men and get started, like tomorrow."

"Well, let me think a minute. The two Carter boys are around, Ed and Jim. If we can get them, that'll make four of us. Then there is Slim Campbell, the sheriff's nephew, and his cousin Able Thornton. That will make six. Is that going to be enough?"

"Let's hit them up and see if they are interested. But, I got to tell you, this may turn out to be dangerous. All depends on how rough Burdett wants to play."

"Well, it can't be any rougher than what we just went through, and we seem to have handled that ok."

"Do you know where we can find these guys?" Clay asked as he headed for the door.

"Let's go into town and start asking around. Someone will know where they hang out."

Thirty minutes later they were sitting in the sheriff's office. The sheriff was telling them where he thought the men might be. They split up, each going a different direction to cover more area.

Clay rode to the Carter farm and asked if Ed and Jim were around. Their mother, Mrs. Carter, was shocked to see Clay standing on her porch. "Clay, oh my gosh, we heard you were dead. What happened?"

"I don't know, Mrs. Carter, must have been a mix up in paperwork. You know how the government operates. But it sure has torn my life apart. I'm looking for Ed and Jim, are they around?"

She pointed him to the north, saying they are working in the field over that way.

After another short ride, Clay saw two men shocking hay. When he rode up to them, they were as shocked as their mother to see him. They had been friends since boys, and to hear he was dead and see him riding up was quite a shock.

They were more than glad to see him. It gave them a chance to take a break. They had not seen each other in over four years, then to think he was dead, it was like a homecoming, with handshakes, back-slapping, and such. Finally, things settled down, and Clay could tell them why he was there. They were both eager to help him out. Anything to get out of the hay field.

After some discussion and explaining to them the danger that they could expect from Burdett and his men, they agreed to meet that night at Willie Stanton's aunt's place. It seemed the safest place since it was out of town and not near any other houses. They didn't want any of Burdett's people to see them or, take a chance on someone else seeing them together, and word somehow getting back to Burdett.

They were instructed to bring their rifles and handguns, if they had any, bedrolls and horse and saddle, of course.

From there, Clay headed on over to the Thornton farm. Willie had gone to see Slim Campbell.

Just before dark, all six of them gathered outside Aunt Maddie's barn. Clay began by outlining what he had planned. "Ok, guys here's the plan. If any of you want out after you hear what we are going to be doing, I'll understand, no hard feelings. There may be some trouble from Burdett and his men, and you may not want to get involved, but I don't have a choice. I have got to do this."

Clay stood up and continued, "I plan to round up every head of livestock I can get off the home place before Burdett knows what we are doing. We'll drive them to a box canyon at the far end of the valley, where we can hold them for a few days, while we continue the roundup. When we have as many as we figure we are going to get, or until we run out of time, we will push them out by the home place and head toward Chicago. The drive will probably take about two months, give or take a week or so. When we get the herd sold, I can pay all of you the going rate of thirty dollars a month, plus a bonus, if everything turns out like I hope it does. Aunt Maddie said she had coffee and cookies ready for us, so I'm going to go up to the house and get mine while you all talk it over. Any questions?"

They all looked from one to the other, shook their heads "no." Clay walked into the house and got his cup of coffee and a couple of cookies and sat down on the porch to wait for the men to make their decision.

Wasn't but a few minutes until Ed and Jim Carter came walking up with their heads down, and Clay figured he had lost them.

Ed began, "Look, Clay, we don't know if we can get away on such short notice, what with the hay in the field that needs to be shocked. If it's left on the ground, it will ruin, and all that work will have been for nothing, plus the cows and horses won't have anything to eat this winter if we don't get it done."

"I understand that, Ed. How long do you think it will take you to finish it?"

"We were figuring by the end of this week we should have it all done." Clay thought about that a minute or so. "Ok, how about this. You all finish your hay and join us as soon as you can. I figure we won't be leaving before the first of next week anyway. While you all are doing that, the rest of us will be rounding up everything we can and try to be ready to pull out by the time you join us. How does that sound?" "That sounds good to us, right, Jim?"

"Yeah, we will hurry it up as much as we can. Where do you want us to meet you?"

"You know our old home place, right? Ride right on past it, don't let anyone see you, and head north-east down the valley, following the creek. Everything dead ends back there so you can't miss us. We will be in one of the box canyons on the north side of that valley. We'll be keeping a lookout for you, and anyone else who may be around. I would like to get this done and be gone before Burdett gets wind of it. By the way, do you know of anyone else we can get to help us? We could use a couple more if we can get them. The more of us, the safer and easier it's going to be."

Ed and Jim looked at each other, shrugged their shoulders, shook their head, and said, "Can't think of anyone right now, but if we do we will see if they are available."

Clay said, "Thanks, guys, that will be a big help." With all the plans made they all headed home.

Before they left town the next morning, Clay went to the mercantile and picked up another skillet, a Dutch oven, a week's supply of flour, sugar, salt, some cans of peaches and tomatoes, and everyone's favorite, beans. At the last minute, he thought they would need a pack saddle. They could use one of the mules to carry all their cooking and camping gear.

He knew they would run out of almost everything, and someone would have to make a trip back to town to get more supplies before they started the drive to Chicago.

He saddled Stormy and Bud, tied all the new supplies on Bud, mounted Stormy and leading the other three young horses, met Slim, Willie and Able on the outskirt of town.

When they arrived at the Wade farm a couple of hours later after taking a long way around, Clay told the others to wait for him down by the creek in the trees. He needed to make sure there was no one at the house.

Again, he left his horse tied back in the trees and snuck up on the back side of the barn where he could look over the place. He saw no one nor any sign that anyone had been there since his last visit.

When he returned to the three men, he suggested, "Since we will be riding through this valley anyway, we may as well drive as many as we can." He told the men, "Spread out across the valley and start moving everything ahead of you. Keep it as quiet as you can. I don't think there's anyone around but no sense in advertising what we are doing."

Slim asked, "Are you sure what we are doing is legal?"

"I spoke with the lawyer; he assured me that all the livestock belongs to me. I'm just playing it safe because I don't think Burdett is looking at it the same way I am, so I'm expecting trouble, sooner or later."

Riding slowly, they moved everything they saw ahead of them without getting them excited. Before the men realized it, there was a small herd of forty or so cows and calves with a few bulls thrown in. It took just about an hour to reach the entrance to the first canyon. With a little gentle prodding, they moved through the opening into the canyon. The men pushed them all the way to the far end, then came back almost to the entrance and set up camp in a grove of cottonwood trees beside the stream.

At this point, the canyon was narrow enough that if any of the cows tried to get past them to leave the canyon, they were sure to hear them.

They constructed two windbreaks with the tarps. If they didn't get a hard-blowing rain, they would be dry enough, but it got chilly at this altitude after the sun went down.

With a fire going behind the trees and bushes, they made coffee and roasted a couple of rabbits, ate the peaches and laid around talking.

There was still enough light to see the horses when they came up to check out the fire. Some of the young ones probably had never seen a man before Clay showed up.

There were several each of the three, four and five-year old's that could be broken to the saddle and used on the drive. That would take some time, but they had a week to ten days left to get it done. That would give them enough horses in the remuda for the drive. They decided they would start on that tomorrow.

Clay was not one to tie a horse to a post or tree, throw a saddle on it, climb on, and turn it loose to see how long he could ride. To him, that did nothing but break a horse's spirit and took a lot longer to get the horse to a point where he was usable. Working slowly to gentle them and gain their trust, then work up to the saddle, then the rider had always worked well for him.

First thing next morning they rounded up all the horses and drove them to the second canyon. Then they cut brush and limbs and built a fence across the entrance to both canyons, to keep the cows and horses from straying when the men were not around.

For the next three days, they were busy from daylight to midafternoon rounding up cattle and pushing them into the first canyon.

By stopping the roundup at mid-afternoon, that gave them the rest of the day to work the young horses. That became their favorite part of the day. Each man would catch up the same horse each day and work with them for an hour. Then they would catch up another young one and work it for an hour. So, each man was working two horses each day. That was eight new horses that would be rideable in a few days. They still would not know anything about handling cattle, such as reigning, roping, driving and all the other things necessary to be a good "cow horse."

By Friday night Clay estimated they had close to four hundred head hidden away in the canyon and four more horses available. Four more of the young horses were coming along nicely and would be ready in a couple more days.

CHAPTER 7

Late Friday evening Willie was on lookout up on the side of the hill overlooking the big valley when he saw three riders coming their way. They were expecting Ed and Jim to arrive tonight or tomorrow morning, but three threw them into a rush to get into position in case this meant trouble.

All the men except Clay were hidden back in the trees with their rifles, where they could see the camp and the riders, but not be seen. Clay was lounging by the fire drinking coffee like no one else was around. The thong was off the hammer of his pistol, and his rifle was leaning on the log beside him.

As the three approached the camp, Willie came out of hiding and announced, "It's Ed and Jim, but they have a girl with them!"

Clay couldn't believe it. "This is no place for a girl. What could they be thinking?"

As they rode into the camp and dismounted, everyone had their eyes on the girl. She was about five feet six inches tall, slim but not skinny, and she filled out the shirt and jeans in all the right places as a girl should.

Clay came walking up, staring at the girl. "Ed, Jim, what is the meaning of this? This is no place for a girl. Where did you find her?"

Ed and Jim had a sneaky look on their face like they were hiding something. The girl was looking Clay square in the face when she said, "Hello, Dirt Ball."

Clay's mouth dropped open, but he was speechless. The only person who ever called him that was Ed and Jim's little sister, Ellen. "Dirt Ball" was a play on his name, "Clay."

"No way. You can't be that little skinny, freckled faced brat that followed us around all the time."

"Yep, It's me."

She was not little or freckled faced anymore. Here is a woman, in every sense of the word.

"Ellen, what are you doing here? This situation could get very dangerous if things don't go just right."

"I don't need anyone's permission to go where I want to go. I decided you men all need someone to cook and take care of you, or you will get yourself killed."

"There is likely to be shooting and no telling what all. You can't stay here," Clay tried to argue.

Ellen gave him a disgusted look and asked, "Why not? I can shoot, ride, and rope as good as you, and you said you need more help, so here I am."

Clay was still stammering, "Yes, but this is going to be a long drive to Chicago. Could be two months or more. We can't take you with us."

"You just try and stop me, Dirt Ball."

"Ed, Jim, do something."

"Hey, don't look at us. We have never been able to tell Ellen anything. She pretty much does as she likes."

"Does your maw and pa know you are here?" Clay demanded.

"I just told them I was going with Ed and Jim, that I would be back when they came back, that we were going to help you drive some cows to Chicago. No big deal."

"No big deal? You are out of your mind if you think you are going with us. It's going to get dangerous, don't you understand that?"

Ellen was standing her ground, looking Clay directly in the eye. "No more dangerous for me than for you. What's the difference?"

Clay threw up his hands and stomped away.

Ellen turned around and looked at the rest of the men and asked, "What's for supper?"

Ed, Jim, and Ellen had their bedrolls and camping equipment and enough food for several days. They threw everything down by the fire.

After eating they were sitting around talking about what was coming tomorrow and on down the road ahead.

Clay told Ellen, "If you are dead set on coming along you will need to carry your weight around here."

"Don't worry about me; I'll work you into the ground every day. Just tell me what you want me to do."

"Do you think you can handle the remuda without losing them or getting yourself trampled?"

"I can do better than that. I'll have all of those horses broke and trained to handle cattle before we leave."

Clay laughed, "That'll be the day."

CHAPTER 8

Saturday morning was the day Clay had decided to start moving the herd to canyon number two because all the grass in canyon number one had been eaten down to the roots already.

First thing Saturday morning, Clay rode back to the home place to check it out. He knew there would be lots of noise and dust when they started moving the herd. He wanted to make sure there was no one around to cause them trouble.

Not expecting anyone to be there, he rode up to the back of the barn, instead of leaving his horse hidden and walking up. That was a big mistake.

As he came around the corner of the barn, he was met face to face by two men. They didn't look like they were any happier to see him than he was to see them. They all were surprised.

Clay recognized two of Burdett's men.

Clay took the offensive first, asking "what are you all doing here? "Who are you?"

Both men looked like they got caught with their hand in the cookie jar. Both were riding horses much better than a cowhand could afford. Their clothes looked like they were almost new. Guns tied down. One of them was tall and slim the other shorter but heavy build. Neither seemed like he had been doing any work that would break a sweat.

The tall one finally said, "We work for the owner, Mr. Burdett. Who are you and what are you doing here?"

"I am Clay Wade. My folks owned this place until it sold while I was away. I'm just back visiting the old place before I ride on."

The tall one was doing all the talking. "I think you have seen all you need to see. How about you just turn around and ride on down the road. There is nothing for you here. If you keep snooping around it might get you hurt."

Clay's temper was rising at a rapid pace. Fortunately, he had removed the thong from his Remington before he rode in here, but he quickly decided now was not the time to start shooting. If he got killed, these guys might start looking around and discover the men and Ellen. That's what he was trying to avoid. So, he chose to agree with them, for now, and headed out toward the road.

When he reached the road, he turned to the left, away from town, and continued riding in a relaxed trot like he was in no hurry to get anywhere. After a mile or so he came to the top of a hill. After crossing over and started down the other side, he stopped and rode back to where he could just see over the top.

He dismounted to let his horse take a breather while he looked over his backtrail. After about ten minutes he saw no one following him, so he cut back through the woods toward where the men and Ellen were waiting. He was sure they must be wondering what had happened to him. He should have been gone only thirty minutes or so, but here it was probably over an hour. He was hoping they had stayed where he left them and not gone to the house looking for him.

He hurried as much as he could, which wasn't very fast due to the thick brush, up and down the cliffs, crossing streams and such. Some of the terrains were almost straight up and down, so it took a while to find his way through and around it. Knowing this country as he did, it was a lot easier for him then it would have been for someone else.

As he topped the last hill separating him from the big valley, Clay saw he was about halfway between the home place, where he had run into Burdett's men and the first canyon where the cattle were.

He stopped to give Stormy another breather and to look over the canyon. It was a good thing he did because he saw two riders coming along down the middle of the valley, following the creek. At this distance, he couldn't identify them, and he didn't recognize the horses. They could be Burdett's men; he didn't pay much attention to their horses, other than to see they were above average in quality, and they were both sorrels, as were both of these. But, there were a lot of sorrel horses around.

From where he was sitting, he would have to cross the valley to get to the other side where his people are. If he cut across here, they would see him before he got a hundred feet. He had to figure another way to get there, and he had to get there before the two riders did.

He knew he had to get to the far east end of the valley, cross over to the other side, staying out of sight in the trees while doing this.

He remembered there used to be a trail, probably made by deer, or wild hogs, back down the side of the hill away from the valley. If he could get to that path, he could make better time around to the end of the valley. He could cross over there in the trees and come back up to the second canyon, where he hoped his crew was still waiting. Having no time to waste, he took off as fast as Stormy could make it through the thick trees and underbrush. A few minutes later he found the trail and turned onto it, as he put his heels to Stormy and let him have his head. That's when he found out that horse loved to run.

They were up and down hills, across creeks, dodging trees and around twists and turns in the trail. Stormy never let up.

By the time they reached the end of the valley and turned around the end, Stormy was wet with sweat, foam around his shoulders and flanks, but he showed no signs of slowing down.

They turned back to the west toward the canyons. He had to cross the stream coming off the side of the mountain. He let Stormy have a drink, not too much, just enough to help his thirst and give him a breather.

Clay guessed he still had about half a mile to go, but he didn't see the two riders anywhere. He hoped he had beaten them.

Just before reaching the second canyon, he slowed Stormy to a slow trot. He didn't want to go rushing into something without knowing what it was. Keeping a sharp eye out for trouble, he pulled his rifle from the boot and eased into the canyon. Everything was quiet. That was not a good sign.

He reached the campsite to find it empty. All the camping gear was still there just as it was when he left this morning. No sign of trouble here. Turning back to the canyon entrance, he headed for the first canyon.

He was getting worried now. If those two men came upon his people, would they know what to do? Probably not. Then there was Ellen. He couldn't let anything happen to her.

He stayed in the trees, as close to the canyon wall as he could, and still ride as fast as Stormy could manipulate the brush and trees. They were moving much slower now because of all the twisting and turning they had to do to get through this tangled mess.

About fifteen minutes later, he was approaching the canyon entrance. Again, he had slowed to a fast walk, not wanting to make any unnecessary noise. He moved out toward the valley to get a better look back up to where he had last seen the two approaching men. He didn't see them anywhere, but that didn't mean they weren't there. They might have turned back. But then again, they may already be in the canyon. Maybe they already had the men and Ellen under their guns.

When that thought hit his brain, he quickly pulled Stormy back into the trees, tied him, pulled his rifle from the boot again, and headed into the canyon on foot.

Easing through the trees and brush like an Indian, he made very little noise. All the time he was listening for any sound that may give him a clue as to where they were, and what was going on.

He was carrying his rifle across his chest, in what the army called the port arms position. Every few yards he stopped to listen. He had gone a hundred yards into the canyon when he started hearing voices. He speeded up some because now he knew where they were. He didn't know who, but he knew where. When he could hear the voices clear enough to know what they were saying, he could tell some were not his people.

This area was covered with huge trees, some of them two and three times as big around as a man, He lined up behind one of them and continued to close in on the voices. Eventually, he could see where everyone was. All his people were sitting in a half circle with the two Burdett men standing in front of them holding handguns. Clay had to circle to get behind Burdett's men. Both were facing the same direction, so when he reached that point when their backs were toward him, he started easing closer.

When he was only about twenty yards from them, he heard one of them telling his men and Ellen that they probably should just kill the men, and let the girl entertain them for a while, before they returned to town to report to Burdett.

Clay continued to move toward them as silently as he could. Finally, there was no more cover for him. That's when Ellen first saw him. She gave a little gasp, then settled back down. After that, she never looked in Clay's direction again.

Clay slowly eased his rifle to the ground and pulled his Remington. He was only ten yards behind them when he pulled the hammer back on the 44, they heard it and started to turn around.

Clay gave them fair warning, "If you move, you are dead. Pitch those guns on the ground out in front of you, now. One wrong move and I start shooting. At this range, I can't miss."

When they had done as ordered, Clay told Willie to get the guns, "Don't get between them and me."

When Willie had retrieved their guns, he then frisked them to make sure they had no more weapons. Clay reminded him to check their boots. He found each had a hideout gun and a knife.

Ellen got up from where she was sitting, walked over to Willie and told him, "Give me one of those guns. I am going to love shooting that tall skinny one for threating to kill all of you, and for what he planned to do to me."

Clay interrupted her and told her "Not now, Ellen. You can have the gun, but we have to figure out what's best to do with them."

"I know what's best. Just give me that gun. I will take care of it. He's nothing but a scumbag anyway; no one's going to miss him. Probably all his friends will be glad to see him dead if he has any friends, which I doubt."

"Ok, Jim and Ed, tie 'em up until we decide what to do with them. Willie, you, Abe, and Slim keep them covered, if they make a move, shoot them. Just make sure you kill them if you have to shoot. We don't have time to be fooling around with a wounded thief and murder."

Willie suggested, "Why don't we load them on their horses and go back to camp. It's almost sundown now, by the time we get there it's going to be dark."

Clay agreed. "Ok, let's get them loaded up. I'll meet you on the way. I left Stormy tied up back here. Give me a few minutes to make sure there is no one else around."

They arrived back at the camp without further incident.

The two prisoners were placed in sitting position, with their hands wrapped around a tree and tied. They were facing away from each other on opposite sides of the campfire about twenty feet apart.

Ellen started preparing their supper. Ed & Jim took the horses to the stream to drink their fill. Slim got water to make coffee and got it going; Able was keeping an eye on the prisoners.

Supper all came together about the same time, so they were eating and drinking coffee not long after dark. The tall, slim prisoner asked if they were going to get anything to eat.

Ellen informed him quickly, "I am not wasting good food on the likes of you. You can starve to death for all I care, after what you had planned." They gave each a plate of food and a cup of coffee and untied their hands, but there was a man with a gun sitting in front of each of them while they ate. When they finished eating, they both said they needed to take a walk behind the bushes. So, one at a time, they were walked away from camp by two men with guns, then brought back and tied to their tree again.

Ellen said, "You guys are going to fall in love with that tree before you leave here. Maybe we can get a preacher out here to marry you. How would you like that, Scumbag?"

Scumbag yelled back at her, "You are going to regret you ever saw me, smart mouth."

"Ellen shouted back at him, "I already regret ever seeing you, and if I get half a chance I'll put a bullet right between your eyes."

"When Burdett finds out about this, you will all be dead and buried where no one will ever find your bodies," threatened Scumbag.

Clay wanted to know, "Is that what he has been doing with the other people who sold him their property dirt cheap and then supposedly left the country overnight?"

Scumbag asked, "Where did you hear that?"

"Oh, there is talk around. You guys aren't nearly as smart as you think."

The other prisoner chimed in, "Ike, shut up. You are going to get both of us killed running your mouth off."

Clay asked, "So, your name is Ike. What's the rest of your name?"

"That is none of your business."

"Well, I just thought you might want your mother to know what happened to you. And, we'll need a name to put on your grave marker in case she wants to see your final resting place."

"I don't want my mother to know anything."

"Why, doesn't she know that you are a thief and a murderer, as well as a rapist. After what you had planned for Ellen? I am sure she would want to know what you were doing and how you died. Don't you think so, Ike?"

"Shut up; I don't want to hear any more of this!"

The second prisoner said, "Come on, Ike, they are just trying to get you all riled up, so you will start talking. If you do, Burdett will kill you himself, and you know it. You've seen him do it."

"You shut up, Luke, and mind your own business." Clay asked Luke, "So, Luke, what is your name." "Luke Wilson and I don't have a mother."

Ellen chimed in, "I can understand that. No woman in her right mind would claim either of you as her son."

Clay asked them," How did you all get hooked up with Burdett?"

Luke answered, "He was looking for men and offering to pay top wages."

"What were you hired to do?"

Ike yelled at Luke, "Luke, shut up. Don't tell them anything!"

Luke kept talking,

"Burdett told us we would be helping him take over new properties he was buying and driving cattle to market."

"Have you driven any cattle to market yet?"

"Yeah, last week we took a small herd to Knoxville."

"Burdett has a buyer in Knoxville?" Clay asked.

"Yeah, some guy he knows. I only saw him once for a few seconds."
"Do you know his name?

"No, I never heard it mentioned. Burdett tried to keep us away from him, and him away from us."

"Do you know where he does his business?"

"Yeah, he has a ranch out of town a few miles. We drove the cattle there." Luke said.

Clay asked him, "Do you think you could find it again?"

"Oh sure, that wouldn't be a problem."

Ike butted in again, "Luke, you sorry, lily-livered coward. I knew you were no good the first time I met you. All the times we were kicking people out of their places you always stood back and did nothing. Like you were afraid of getting your hands dirty. You are a worthless piece of...." "Look, Mr. Wade," Luke said, "I've never liked working for this

Burdett fellow. I never met Ike until I started working there. I've never done anything against the law. If you trust me, I can show you where the buyer lives and even help you on the drive. I'll work for you for the same pay as these folks are getting."

Clay thought about that for a minute. He turned to the other members of his crew, "What do you all think about that. You all were there when they showed up. What part did Luke play in it?"

Ellen spoke up first, "Now that you mention, he never said a word. He had his gun drawn, but he never really threatened us with it. Ed, Jim, what do you think."

"I agree with you. I never saw him make any threatening move." "Willie, what is your opinion?" Clay asked.

"Well, I have to agree with them. I didn't see anything to indicate he might shoot us."

"Abe, how about you?"

"Same goes for me."

Clay said, "Ok, let me propose this. Tomorrow morning, we'll leave Ike here tied to his tree. He seems to be falling in love with it as Ellen said. The rest of us will start moving the cattle and horses out of here. We need to get them far enough from here that Burdett will have to look hard to find them. It's going to be impossible to hide the trail of over four hundred animals, so we are goin' to have to be on the lookout for anyone following us. We need to find us a safe place somewhere long enough to get brands on all these animals. That's goin' to take a lot of work and probably a week or so to get it done."

Ellen asked, "Why do we need to brand them?"

Clay answered, "If we are driving them to Chicago, we will be crossing several state lines and a bunch of counties. I don't want to run into trouble with any lawman about ownership. The bar W is my Pa's brand. I can have that transferred over to my name; then we only need to brand the unbranded younger stuff. That will save us a lot of work and time.

"Do any of you know of a place where we can hide for a week or two to get all this done?"

Luke said, "There are plenty places up along the Cumberland before you get to the Gap."

"That will probably work. We'll be going that way."

"Luke, do you have any idea how much Burdett got paid for the cattle he sold?"

"No, as I said, he kept us apart, so that we couldn't hear anything."

Clay said, "We will ride down there and have a talk with this gentleman. It will probably be a wasted trip. I'll bet he didn't pay half what they are worth, and Burdett would be glad to get it because the cattle he's selling are not his anyway."

Willie agreed with Clay and said, "When you take into consideration the cost and the risk involved with a long drive, you can afford to take less and sell here and still probably come out ahead."

Clay shook his head and agreed with Willie. "Ok, is everyone in agreement?"

They all shook their heads yes." "Luke are you in, or out."

"Oh, I am definitely in if you all will have me. From what I've seen while you've had me tied up here, I think I will like working with you all a lot better than Burdett."

Ike chimed in again, "Luke if I ever lay eyes on you again I'll shoot you on sight."

"Then I guess I'll have to make sure I see you first."

Clay reminded them, "The first thing we have to do is get all the cattle and horses out of this canyon and the valley. But, I guess the first thing we better do is untie our new hand."

Ellen wanted to know, "Are we just going to turn him loose and trust him not to cut our throats in our sleep?"

Clay answered, "Oh, no, we are going to have a guard awake all night, and Luke won't be allowed to have a gun until he proves he can be trusted. You agreeable with that, Luke?"

"I sure am. You won't have any trouble with me; I promise you that." Ellen told him, "We better not. I'm goin' to have my eyes on you the whole time. If you look cross-eyed one time, I'll put a bullet between them before you know what's happening."

CHAPTER 9

Willie untied Luke and set the guards for the night. Clay agreed to take the first watch for two hours, then Jim, Ed and Able.

Luke got his bedroll from the back of his saddle, threw it on the ground across the fire from the others and was soon asleep.

First thing the next morning when everyone was up, had eaten breakfast and saddled their horses for the day, Clay called everyone together to lay out the day's work.

Clay asked them if they knew of any place they could leave the four broodmares, the stallion, and the eight younger horses. "We can't take them on the drive to Chicago, so I have to find a place to leave them while we are gone."

Able volunteered, "Back behind our barn there is a fenced pasture, should be big enough for that many horses."

Clay wanted to know, "What is in there now?"

"Just a couple of old workhorses."

Do you think Blackie will be a problem with them?" "Shouldn't be."

"Ok, the first thing will be to get those over to your place. How about we get lead ropes on one of the mares and the stud. The others should follow along. Three of us should be able to handle that. After we get them delivered, I will go into town to get more supplies. While I am there, I will talk to the livery guy and the sheriff to see if they may be able to find a buyer for several of them."

It didn't take long to have the horses ready to go.

Ellen volunteered to go along. Said she needed to get some things in town before they hit the trail.

Since Able knew where there they were going, he took the lead with the mare and stallion. Clay and Ellen followed and kept the others moving. That turned out to be a bigger job than expected. None of the animals wanted to leave the home ground. By the time they reached the west end of the valley near the home place, the younger ones had decided it would be much easier if they played along.

At that point, Clay called a halt while he checked the place out. After making sure no one was around, they passed the house and hit the road toward Rogersville. They saw no one along the way. A few miles before they reached the town, they turned off and cut across country to Able's place. After leaving the horses, they all went into town.

They went first to get the supplies they would need. With everything packed and tied onto their saddles, they went to see the sheriff. He said he would ask around to see if he could find a buyer.

Then they went to the livery, introduced themselves, told the livery guy their problem of needing to sell some of the young horses. He said he would ride out to Able's place to look at them. Clay explained the four broodmares and the stallion were not for sale, and the others were all less than two years old and have never had a rope or saddle on them.

"I would like to get at least fifty dollars each for them." Clay said. "See that gray over there? They are all full or half brothers and sisters to him. You won't find a better bunch of horses anywhere for that price."

The livery owner, Mr. Bates, looked at Stormy and remarked, "That is a good-looking horse all right. Do you want to sell him?"

"Well, I hadn't thought about it. That one is my favorite. I would sure hate to part with him. What would you be willing to pay for him?"

"Let me walk over there and look at him."

After walking around Stormy, lifting his feet, looked in his mouth, he said, "I can give you sixty dollars for him. That's high as I can go."

Clay shook his head and said, "No, to part with him I have to have at least a hundred. So, I guess I'll keep him."

Mr. Bates walked around the horse a couple more times and asked, "Mind if I ride him?"

"No, go ahead."

Clay was already thinking which horse he would use to replace Stormy. He would only sell him if he got his price, but, he needed the money for supplies for the two to three months while on the trail.

Ellen and Able were standing by watching the haggling and couldn't believe Clay was considering selling Stormy.

Finally, Mr. Bates came back to Clay, scratching his head. "Ok, I can go seventy-five, but that's all I can do."

Now Clay was scratching his head and said, "How about ninety?"

Mr. Bates came back with eighty.

They shook hands on the deal. Mr. Bates paid Clay in cash.

Clay told him, "I'll need to ride Stormy back to the ranch to get another horse, I'll be back later today."

Mr. Bates said that would not be a problem.

With the money he had now, they went back to the store and bought more supplies. He asked Mr. Campbell to pack them up and hold them until he came back later today.

As they walked out the door of the mercantile and headed for their horses, they met Burdett and three of his hired bodyguards, one of them being Ike.

It took Clay and his party by surprise, but Clay recovers quickly and spoke to Ike, "Well, hello Ike, I'm surprised to see you here. What's the matter, didn't you like our company?"

Burdett spoke up, "Wade?"

"Yes, I'm Clay Wade, I'm afraid I haven't had the pleasure of meeting you. What's your name?"

"Don't get smart with me; you know who I am. I hear you have been trespassing on my property."

Clay replied, "If you mean gathering my property to remove it from your property, then I guess you could call it trespassing."

"You don't have any property on my property, and if I catch you there again, I'll have my men remove you and anyone with you, by force if necessary. Do you get my message?"

"Oh, I heard you talking, but your message doesn't mean anything to me. You see, I'm not like a lot of other folks around here, Burketts, I'm not afraid of you or your goons. If you want to try to keep me from taking what's mine, then you just come on. But, I'll tell you this, we will be there until we finish our business, which should take about two more weeks, then we will be gone, and you can have the place to yourself. How does that sound?"

"First, the name is Burdett; you will do well to remember it. Second, you don't have two weeks."

"Third, I'll have guards on the place, and anyone who shows up there will be shot on sight. How does that sound?"

"Well, Burkett, even though you have a big mouth, it sounds like you may have bitten off more than you can chew, and If Ike here is an example, you are going to need a lot more men."

"Wade, I told you once, I won't tell you again, the name is Burdett."
"That's good because I don't want to hear it again. Now if you and your goons will step aside, we'll be on our way."

With those parting words, Clay pushed his way right through the middle of them, bumping shoulders with Burdett and the man next to him. Ellen and Able follow him as they walked to their horses, mounted up and slowly rode out of town.

None of them ever looked back. That must have infuriated Burdett more than anything Clay had said.

Once they were out of sight of Burdett and his men, they put the spurs to their horses and lit a shuck back to the ranch. When they arrived there, they didn't sneak in a back way but continued right through the yard. Just as they passed the house, two men came running out with guns blazing.

Clay went one way around the barn; the other two went the other. As soon as they were behind the barn, all three pulled their horses to a sliding halt.

Clay told Ellen to hold the horses. He and Able each ran to a different corner of the barn. Just as the two shooters were reaching the front of the barn, Clay and Able stepped out and opened fire, hitting both men before they could get off another shot.

They approached the downed men carefully. One was dead; the other was hit in the shoulder and again in the upper thigh. Clay kicked his gun out of reach. The man looked to be no more than nineteen or twenty years old. Too young to be in this business. Clay bent down to examine the wounds and told him, "You will live if you get out of this business and clean up your life. Otherwise, you are going to die young. It could have been right here. Do you get my message?"

The kid was in considerable pain. He just shook his head yes and gritted his teeth, trying not to cry. Ellen came walking up leading their horses. She ripped a piece off the dead man's shirt and wrapped it around the injured leg and made a pad to place over the shoulder wound. She tied it tight to help stop the bleeding.

They caught up the horses belonging to Burdett's men and tied the body across his saddle. The kid said he could ride back to town, but Clay tied his hands to the horn of the saddle, so he wouldn't fall off before getting there if he should happen to pass out.

Clay told him to tell Burdett if he sent any more men after him the same thing would happen to them.

After they rode out of the yard, Clay, Ellen, and Able continued on their way back to camp.

CHAPTER 10

The other men, Willie, Luke, and Slim, met them about halfway, saying they had heard shots.

Ed and Jim had stayed with the cattle.

When they all reached camp, Clay explained what had happened in town and at the home place.

"By the way, how did Ike get loose?"

Jim explained, "When we came back to camp after you left this morning, he was still tied over there. We went to check on the cattle and came back a couple of hours later and found him gone. It looks like he rubbed the rope through on the tree. I guess we should have been checking it a lot closer than we did?"

"No harm done. We would have had to let him loose sooner or later anyway."

"So, we can expect trouble from now on. We have to be on our guard at all times, day and night. I told Burdett we would be out of here in two weeks. Hopefully, he will think he has that long to do something about us. That should give us time to get on up the trail. What do you all think about pulling out of here tomorrow morning at daybreak?"

They all shook their heads in agreement.

Ellen said, "I'll start packing up everything and be ready to go. But, you have to take Stormy back to town and pick up the rest of the supplies you bought."

"Yeah, you are right."

Able asked, "Are you going to want someone to ride back with you to watch your back?"

Clay thought about that a few seconds, then said, "No, it will be dark by the time I get there. I'll come in a back way and leave the same way."

Ed asked, "What if someone is waiting at the house when you come back?"

"I'll come in on that hidden trail we've been using."

With that settled, Clay caught up another of the horses. This one could have been a twin to Stormy. Same mom and pop, same coloring. This one was called Smokey. He was one year younger and had not been handled at all until they arrived here about a week ago. But, it's time he started learning the ropes and earning his keep. He had been ridden almost every day and was coming around nicely.

Clay caught up one of the mules to carry the packs and told Ellen she could use the other one to bring all her cooking and camping gear.

When Clay left camp, he was riding Smokey, leading the mule and Stormy.

He went out the hidden back trail, so he wouldn't pass the house if other Burdett men had shown up there.

When he arrived in town by back streets, he left the mule behind the mercantile and took Stormy to the livery for Mr. Bates. Then he went to see sheriff Campbell. The deputy on duty told him the sheriff had gone home for the night. Knowing where he lived, Clay walked around the corner to the sheriff's house.

When he knocked on the door, Mrs. Campbell opened it. She was a motherly type, in her mid-fifties or so, with salt and pepper hair and a pleasant smile.

"Hello, Mrs. Campbell."

"Well, Clay Wade, What a surprise! Come in; I heard you were back. I am so happy to see you. But, I'm sorry about your family. That must have come as a big shock."

"Yes, it did, Mrs. Campbell. How have you been?"

"I'm fine, Clay. Come on in; the sheriff is in the kitchen eating. Have you eaten? Let me get you a plate."

"Thanks, Mrs. Campbell."

Clay took a seat across from the sheriff. Mrs. Campbell served him a cup of coffee, then a plate loaded with fried chicken, potatoes and green beans.

"Ma, you know what they say about feeding stray animals. You can't get rid of them." the sheriff said.

"Well, if that's all it takes to get a young, handsome man around here, I'm ready."

Clay laughed and said, "That's very tempting, Ma'am, but I'm afraid the law in this town would frown on that."

"You're probably right; he's a real stick in the mud."

"So, what can I do for you, Clay?" the sheriff asks.

"I need to give you some money to send to a family's relatives. I came across them a day or so after someone killed them. That horse I rode in here on belongs to them. I made a deal with the local town marshal to buy the horse and send the money to the relatives when I got home. But, when I got here, I found there was no money. I just sold one of my horses to Mr. Bates, so now I have the money. Can you handle that for me?"

"Sure. I'll deposit it in the bank and have the bank mail them a draft.

Only cost a dime I think to send it."

"Great, here is the thirty dollars that the sheriff valued the horse at, and here is the address to send it to."

Clay gave him the money and headed back to pick up the mule with the supplies. When he rounded the corner of the mercantile where he had left the mule, he saw Ike and another of Burdett's men standing there waiting for him. Clay kept walking toward them and asked, "What can I do for you fellows?"

He stopped when he was about twenty feet from them.

Ike said," There you are. I thought I saw you come into town leading this mule."

"OK, so you did. Did you want to buy a mule?"

"Oh, you are a real funny one. We are going to teach you who's in charge around here; then we are going to ride you out of town on a rail."
"I know you two don't have brains enough to come up with that plan on your own. Did Burdett tell you to do that?"

"No, we came up with it ourselves."

Clay said, "Then you have no one to blame but yourselves for what happens to you."

They started walking toward Clay.

He held up his left hand and said, "Hold it right there. If you think I'm going to stand here and let you walk over here and start beating on me, you are dumber than you look, and that's pretty dumb."

They stopped, glanced at each other and went for their guns.

He felt the recoil and smelled the gunpowder before he realized he had dropped to his right, drawn and fired off four shots. Both men were hit twice in the chest. Both collapsed to the ground.

Clay laid there for a moment getting his wits about him. It was a few seconds before he realized he had no severe wounds. He discovered a bullet hole in his left sleeve and one in his shirt collar that just grazed his neck leaving a bloody mark, but nothing else.

Clay heard people running his way. He quickly exchanged cylinders in his Remington, giving him six new rounds ready in case he needed them.

By then a crowd had started to gather, everyone asking what happened.

Mr. Campbell came from the store with a double barrel shotgun. The sheriff showed up a couple of minutes later. "What happened here, Clay?" He wanted to know.

Clay told him exactly what happened, that they were waiting for him, and drew first. He had no choice but to defend himself.

Mr. Campbell stepped forward and said he had seen the whole thing from the back window of his store. The sheriff examined the bodies and saw both had a gun in their hands and both shot in the front. Mr. Campbell said he saw them draw first, so the Sheriff ruled it self-defense.

Sheriff Campbell said, "Looks cut and dried to me. Somebody go wake up the undertaker and help him get these bodies out of here. Clay, come by the office and fill out a report, just for the record, then you can go."

"Ok, Sheriff. Mr. Campbell, can you get my supplies loaded while I do that? I would like to leave town as soon as I can. I don't want any more trouble."

"Sure, Clay, I'll have it loaded when you get back."

The Sheriff and Clay walked to the sheriff 's office. It didn't take but a few minutes to write out the report explaining what happened.

When he returned to the store, the sheriff walked with him and waited until he was riding out of town by a back street. He couldn't make fast time leading a loaded mule, but he still arrived back at camp before midnight.

When he reached the entrance to the canyon where the camp is, Slim challenged him, and Clay answered and rode on in. Luke came out to help him unload the mule and hobble him, so he would be easy to find in the morning and offered to take care of Smokey for him.

Clay walked away toward camp but kept an eye on Luke to see how he took care of the horse and mule. He was pleased when he heard Luke talking to them while he rubbed them both down with a handful of dry grass.

Clay was dead tired and was asleep about as soon as his head hit the bedroll.

Early next morning, Ellen brought a cup of coffee to Clay. He was still sleeping. When Ellen touched him on the arm, which was lying across his chest, Clay came awake with a start, grabbed his pistol and tried to sit up, but Ellen put her hand on his gun hand and shook him again, saying "Clay, wake up, it's me, Ellen." She was still holding his hand when he opened his eyes and looked around, trying to place where he was. Finally, his eyes fell on Ellen's face a few inches from his. He stared at her as if he had never seen her before.

"Wow," he said, "for a minute there I thought I had died and gone to heaven." He released the gun onto his chest, turned his hand over and squeezed Ellen's hand, brought it up to his lips and kissed it.

"You know, for a skinny little freckled faced kid, you have sure turned into one hell of a beautiful woman."

"Well Clay, you shock me. If I didn't know better, I would think you were making love to me."

"I can't think of anything I would rather do."

"Here, you better drink your coffee before you make a fool of yourself."

She walked away, but stopped and looked back, saw he was watching her, smiled and went back to the fire.

A few minutes later, although Clay was groggy from lack of sleep, they were all sitting around the fire eating breakfast and drinking strong, black coffee. Clay filled them in on what happened in town. They were shocked to hear that he had outdrawn and killed two of Burdett's men.

"Because of all this trouble, Burdett is probably going to be on the warpath looking for scalps. We need to hurry up and get out of here. The biggest problem is, the only way out of here is right by the home place. There's going to be a fight if Burdett has men there. So, what I think we better do is get the cattle and horses moving that way. Before we get close enough for them to hear us at the house, a couple of us will ride up to check it out. We will have to decide how to handle it after we see how it stacks up. Everyone in agreement?"

Everyone said, "Yes."

"Ok, let's get ready to do it."

The sky was just beginning to lighten in the east when they moved out from camp. Ellen was leading the pack mule loaded with all the camping and cooking gear. Everyone helped drive the horses out of the canyon into the valley and turn them west toward the exit. On the way, they went into the first canyon and moved all the cattle out into the big valley.

It took a while for the cattle and horses to get lined out and headed in the right direction. All the men and Ellen were riding young animals that had no experience handling cattle. That only made the job that much harder, but they would learn.

They were trying to keep the noise down as much as possible to keep from alerting anyone at the house.

CHAPTER 11

The herd was about halfway up the valley when Clay called a halt. He, Willie and Ed moved forward to the brush and trees overlooking the home place. The first thing they noticed was three horses in the corral. They moved forward on foot until they reached the back of the barn. They still had not seen or heard anyone. Moving forward to the bunkhouse put them within about fifty feet of the back door of the house. From there they could hear talking coming from inside.

Clay motioned for Willie to move up to the south side of the house, Ed to move to the north side, Clay would cover the back door.

The temperature was hovering around ninety degrees, so all the doors and windows were wide open. They could hear talking but could not distinguish what was said.

Clay moved up beside Willie, removed his hat and eased his eye around the window facing. One quick glance showed him three men sitting around the table drinking coffee. Two were facing the back door, one facing the front. Clay whispered to Willie, telling him to go to the front door, "When you hear this window shatter, barge through the door and cover them. I will have them covered from here. I'll go tell Ed to cover them from the back window by the table."

"Ok," Willie said.

Clay quietly moved to the back corner of the house where he could see Ed at the opposite corner. He motioned for Ed to cover them from the window. Ed motioned that he understood and moved to the edge of the window. Clay returned to his window, listened a moment, then smashed through the screen covering the window with his gun leveled.

"Hold it right there; you're covered from three sides. One wrong move and you're dead meat. Ed, go inside and keep them cover while the rest of us come in. We are going to have us a party."

Ed came in the back door; Willie came in the front, then Clay came in through the back door. Ed had already taken their guns. They had them stand one at a time while they searched them for other weapons. When they were sure the men were clean, Clay said, "Let's take our guests out to the barn, there is a good strong cross beam that should hold all of them without any problem."

One of the men said, "Wait just a minute, you can't hang us. We haven't done anything to you. We were told to come out here and don't let anyone take anything from this place. Nobody said anything about getting hung."

Clay answered, "Well, you see, that's the price you pay when you work for a thief and murderer."

"What are you talking about?"

"You work for Burdett, don't you?" "Yes, but…."

"Get some rope, Ed. Tie their hands behind them, and march them out to the barn."

Three ropes were thrown over the cross beam and looped around each man's chest under his arms. They pulled the three men up until their toes were just barely touching the floor.

Wiping his forehead Clay says, "That should keep them until someone comes along to turn them loose. You tell Burdett, that if he causes us any more trouble, I am going to make it very uncomfortable for him in this county, and if any of my people get hurt in the process, I'll be coming for him. You be sure he gets that message, and that he understands it. Then my advice for you three is to get out of the county. Because if I see your faces around me again, I'm going to assume you are after me, and I will react accordingly. Got that?"

The one doing all the talking nodded that he understood.

With that taken care of, Clay, Willie, and Ed returned to the herd and motioned for the rest of the crew to get them moving.

The first several miles were a fight to keep the herd together and moving in the right direction. None of them wanted to leave their home. They were born here and had never left it.

Ellen was having her troubles with the horses as well. Luke saw it and dropped back to give her a hand.

That first day they only made maybe seven or eight miles. Toward late evening, they came to a small valley with a stream running through it and decided this would be the place to stop for the night.

While the men circled the herd to get them bedded down, Clay rode back along their back trail to see if anyone was following them. He watched from the top of the last hill they had crossed until it got too dark to see, then returned to camp.

Ellen had set up camp back on the edge of the woods that backed up to the side of a hill. From there they could see the entire valley where the cattle were bedded down. She had a friendly fire going, coffee boiling, a Dutch oven full of biscuits, a skillet with bacon and beans. Made it smell worth all the trouble they had getting this far.

When Clay rode up, Ellen handed him a steaming cup of coffee and told him supper would be ready in a few minutes.

All the men were out circling the cattle, making sure they didn't stray. Clay asked Ellen, "How are you making out?"

"Oh, great, didn't have to shoot anyone, didn't lose any horses, didn't fall off and get trampled."

"I call that a successful day then," Clay said. "Why don't you get a cup and come sit by me until the men come in?"

She poured herself a cup and came over to sit on the log beside him.

After a few minutes of silence, she asked him, "What are you planning to do when this drive is over, and you have money in your pocket?"

"My original plan, after I recovered from the loss of my folks, my girlfriend, my home, was to take what I could salvage from this, and go someplace and start over, get married, have a dozen or so kids..."

Ellen interrupted saying, "Hold it, I thought I might want to tag along until you threw in a dozen kids, but, you lost me there."

Clay burst out laughing, sloshing coffee all over his legs. When he could finally talk again, he said, "How about if we could agree to half a dozen? Would you still be interested in tagging along?"

"Cut it down to two or three, and we can talk about it." "It's a deal."

With that he leaned toward her, she met him halfway with their first kiss. Ellen pulled back and stared into his eyes, then she wrapped an arm around his neck and kissed him again. This time it lasted a lot longer. Neither of them wanted it to end.

Clay said, "This is either going to make this trip a lot more pleasant or a lot more miserable. But, I'll sure be glad when it's over."

About that time Ed and Jim walked into camp with sheepish grins on their faces. They apparently saw what their sister and Clay were doing.

Ellen dished up their supper, which they hurriedly ate, then the three men went out to relieve Slim, Luke, Willie and Able so they could come in. They decided it would be best to have three men night herding these first couple nights until the cattle got accustomed to the routine.

Clay, Luke, and Able took the first watch. Then they would wake up Slim, Ed, and Willie for the last shift. That would be rough on everyone for a couple of days, going with very little sleep, but he figured they would live through it.

That night everything came off as planned.

Early the next morning, Clay was awakened by a hand on his arm again, but this time he didn't panic like last time. Ellen was sitting by his side with a cup of coffee. When he was fully awake, she leaned over and kissed him on the lips.

"Now I know I'm dreaming," he said in a raspy voice.

"No, you aren't. That was a real kiss, and you better get used to it."
"That will not be a problem. Give me another sample of what I have to look forward to."

She did. Only this time it took much longer.

"Here, your coffee is getting cold. The men will be coming in soon.

I need to get breakfast ready."

As she was preparing the food, he sat, drinking his coffee and watching her. The men came in one at a time to get coffee and breakfast. As soon as Clay had eaten, he went out to relieve whoever was still riding herd. When they had all eaten, Luke and Able came out to relieve him.

Before he returned to camp, he rode to the top of the hill to scan their back trail while it was still dark. But, like yesterday, he saw no sign of a campfire anywhere. He just hoped that meant there was no one back there.

The sun had just shown over the peaks to the east when they prodded the herd into motion. They rebelled, trying to return the way they had come. But, after some quick horse work, with yelling, swinging ropes and such, the gang finally got everyone pointed in the same direction.

Clay asks Willie to take the point while he went back to help Ellen get the horses lined out. While riding along with her, he noticed one of the young stallions was causing a lot of trouble with the other studs. He was trying to act like the king of the herd and would probably be the one to challenge Blackie for his position when they got back home.

Clay watched him for a while and saw what was going on. He remarked to Ellen about it. She said, "Yeah, he acted like that all day yesterday. I thought about shooting him several times when he ran the other horses away from the herd."

Clay said, "We will fix that when we come to a place where we can camp for a week or so while we brand the cattle."

Ellen wanted to know, "How do you fix it?"

Clay glanced at her, then thought, well why not, she will probably watch it happen anyway, so he told her, "We will make a gelding out of him. That will take all the meanness out of him. He should turn into a first glass working horse then. He would surely make a good herd stallion if he weren't so mean. But the way he is starting out, he will only get worse."

After the cattle and horses had settled down and fell into the daily routine, Clay rode back to look at their backtrail again.

He spotted a dust cloud back about two miles or so. He watched it a couple of minutes, saw that it was moving fast in his direction. He turned around and raced back to the herd, which was by now a mile or so ahead of him. It took only a couple minutes to get there. He stopped when he reached Ellen and told her to push the horses as hard as she could up to the cattle. Then he raced to the first drag rider and told him to drop back and get ready for a fight. Then he went to the next rider and told him what was happening and told him to gather the rest of the men at the rear of the herd.

When they were all together, he told Ellen to keep pushing hard on the horses and cattle, try to keep them moving. We will set up back here somewhere and stop them before they get to you. "If they should get past us, you make a run for it. Don't worry about anything else, just save yourself. Got that?"

"Yes sir, Mr. Wade."

Willie had been riding point and pointed out that he had seen where the trail narrowed down just ahead. "If we can get the herd through there and set up our ambush at that spot, they will never know what hit them."

"Good thinking, Willie. Let's get them moving."

With a lot of yelling and crowding, they got the herd at a trot and covered the distance in a few minutes. As the last horse passed through, Clay told Ellen to keep them moving. "Willie and Slim will wait here, the rest of us will push the herd on through this gap and set up at the other end. We'll have them caught between us. But don't anyone fire a shot until I do. We need to find out their intentions before we do anything rash. They may not even be Burdett's men. Luke, you stay with me and let me know if you recognize any of them."

"Sounds good. I'll know anyone that was there when I was there."

"Willie, Slim, give me your horses. Get behind those boulders up there and don't let them see you until they have passed you. Ellen, wait for our horses at the other end and take them with you. I'll fire three quick shots when it's time to bring our horses back."

With the plan all worked out, everyone moved into their chosen positions.

They didn't have to wait but a few minutes until the group of six men came riding into the trap. Clay asked Luke if he recognized any of them. Luke said, "Yeah, that big fellow in the lead is one of Burdett's right-hand men. Calls him his enforcer."

Clay responded, "Fancy name for a murderer."

Clay waited until they were almost up to him, then he put a bullet into the ground right in front of the enforcer's horse.

Rock fragments and dust flew up in the horse's face, the horse went straight up in the air, whirled in a half circle and crashed into the riders behind him.

When things had settled down somewhat, Clay shouted, "Hold it right there, men. Want to tell me why you all are following us?"

The enforcer yelled back, "Who the hell are you?"

"I'm Clay Wade, who are you and what do you want?"

"None of your business. Get out of our way before we ride over you like a bug."

"Ok, Mr. Enforcer, I will lay it on the line for you. You are not going another foot. Now get off your horses. Drop all your weapons on the ground. Do it now, or we open fire and not one of you will leave this canyon alive. You have about three seconds to get moving."

The enforcer snapped back, "I think you are bluffing. You don't have the guts to take on all of us." One of the men beside the enforcer spoke to him; Clay heard him say, "Sam, this is the guy who gunned down Ike and Bob behind the store in Rogersville."

"What's it going to be men? Like I said, you aren't going any further. You can leave here alive, or we can plant all of you here. In case you haven't noticed, you are boxed in, front and back, and on top of that, we have you outnumbered, and you're sitting out there in plain sight. Now, get off those horses or start shooting."

Slowly, the men dropped their weapons, then dismounted.

Clay instructed them to step forward ten paces and stop. When they had done that, Clay fired four shots into the ground in front of their horses. They panicked and headed for home as fast as they could move.

Burdett's men all wanted to know, "Why did you do that? How are we goin' to get out of here without our horses?"

Clay told Ed and Jim to get all their weapons, "But don't get between them and us, and don't get close enough for them to get their hands on you."

When their weapons were all collected, and Clay told them to remove their boots, they went into a cursing fit.

"The choice is still yours, you can do what I tell you, or we can bury you right here. It makes no difference to me."

Slowly, they sat down and started pulling off their boots. Some were wearing socks; some were not.

Clay began to feel sorry for the ones who were just following the boss's orders. Clay told all of them, "You all had a choice when you took this job. You all know right from wrong, but you took it anyway. So now you suffer the consequences of your bad choice. You all remember this. We could have killed all of you right here, and no one would ever know what happened to you. If I see any of you on my trail again, we will shoot you on sight. You all get that?"

Some of them nodded their heads; some just stared at him. Clay figured those were the ones he would probably see again.

"Ok, start walking. We'll be watching so don't get any ideas for coming back."

They all started limping back down the trail. It had rocks of every size, and where there weren't so many rocks, the soil got unbearably hot during the heat of the day. When they had walked perhaps one- hundred yards, Clay lifted his Remington and fired three quick shots into the air, the prearranged signal for Ellen to bring the horses back.

When everyone had mounted again, they could still see the men hobbling along. It was going to take them a long time to reach Rogersville unless they caught some of the horses.

At the end of that narrow gorge, it opened into a pretty little flat with a creek running through it. Water was never a problem in these hills. The Cumberland Mountains have springs and waterfalls every few miles.

When they reached that little green flat, it was time for the noon break. The men circled the herd while Ellen got a fire going and put on the coffee. The cattle and horses found some shade and rested while the crew ate cold sandwiches and drank coffee.

Luke pointed out the dark clouds moving in from the west. "Looks like we may be in for some bad weather."

"Yeah, looks like it is moving fast, too. We better call it a day and get the tarps up," Clay said as he put down his cup.

Everyone pitched in. Tarps were tied to trees to create lean-tos. Ellen got a fire going under one. All the men huddled around, enjoying the feel of the brisk wind, the fire, and the hot black coffee. While they were eating, Clay filled them in on the rest of his plan. "We'll continue on this route until we get almost to the Cumberland Gap. There are lots of canyons and small valleys where we can hold up while we brand those that need branding. There are also a few young stallions that need castrating. They are just causing too much trouble, especially with all these young mares around. We will hold up there long enough for them to heal, and to get the branding done. While that is taking place, Luke and I will ride down to Knoxville to look up Burdett's buyer. If he pays a reasonable price, we can save ourselves a lot of hard work. But, I have my doubts about getting that fair price."

Just as they finished eating, the rain hit. It was a cold and blowing wind, to the point it almost tore the tarps from the trees.

Three men were kept on duty, circling the herd, because conditions were ideal for a stampede. The night herding duty was rotated every two hours. The men came in, got warm, got coffee, and got a little sleep.

At every opportunity, Ellen would be with Clay, keeping both warm. The storm moved on through before morning. Everyone slept late, except the three men riding herd. When they were relieved, they got a couple of hours sleep before they started the herd moving.

Several times every day, someone would ride back to where they could see their backtrail. Expecting at any time to see more Burdett men following them. But that never happened.

It took them all of seven days to reach the area of the Cumberland Gap and find a canyon that suited their needs. It was on the north side of the valley leading to the gap and was ideal. Perhaps a thousand acres with a stream coming down the mountain and flowing right through the middle. The grass was belly high, and the water was cold and clear.

They set up their camp next to the creek in a grove of tulip poplar trees and prepared to make it their home for at least two weeks.

They all were dead tired, bone-weary, saddle sore and aching all over from being in the saddle so long. They lounged around the rest of the day, one man at a time keeping an eye on the herd as they grazed and laid in the shade.

First thing next morning, they tackled the job of castrating all the young stallions. That was a backbreaking job. All of them were strong as bulls and most had never had a rope on them. They were thrown and tied down, so they couldn't hurt anyone, or get hurt, they were castrated and branded with the Bar W brand on the left shoulder. The wounds got smeared with black gooey fly repellent. When they were released, they walked back to the herd, but none of them caused any more trouble.

That took most of the day, so the men lounged around in the shade the rest of the day. In this box canyon, it only took one man on night duty, so everyone got plenty of rest.

The men had noticed the sudden close affection Ellen and Clay were showing each other. Behind their backs, the men were making bets about whether the wedding would take place before the drive was completed or after. The odds were the highest on "after the drive."

That evening, sitting around the fire, eating and drinking coffee, Clay told them, "First thing tomorrow, Luke and I will ride down to Knoxville to see that cattle buyer. Probably have to spend the night there or on the trail somewhere. The rest of you can carry on with the branding while we are gone. You will need to keep a close watch for trouble. I don't think we have seen the last of Burdett."

Ellen asked, "Would you mind if I ride along?"

Clay answered, "Of course not. If the men think they can get by doing their own cooking."

"Well, they can, or they can starve."

Ed and Jim both joined in saying, "That's no way to be treating your brothers."

"Get used to it." She said. "Clay, since we are going to be just riding, not working cattle or anything, I want to try riding that black filly with the white blanket, that looks just like that back gelding. I've had a saddle on her several times, and I think she is ready for me to ride."

Next morning, bright and early, after breakfast, Ellen had a saddle on the filly and was leading her around the camp area. After a few circles, she asks Clay to hold the filly while she mounted.

With Clay holding to the bridle, Ellen eased into the saddle. The filly twisted around a little, looked back at Ellen and relaxed. Clay led her around for a few minutes. Ellen dismounted and remounted a couple of times with no reaction from the horse like she had been doing this all her life.

While Clay and Luke were getting their horses ready, Ellen stood talking and petting her horse. "What do you think I should call her?"

Luke and Clay made several suggestions; she finally settled on "Black Night."

As they rode away from camp, Clay had a lead rope on Black Night, just in case she should decide to act up, but she didn't.

The trip to Knoxville was going to take over a day and a half, so just before sundown, they found a secluded place off the trail and made camp for the night.

Later that day before they reached Knoxville, the lead rope was removed, and Ellen was on her own.

The cattle buyer's place was north of town, so they came to it before Knoxville. A ranch hand said the cattle buyer was in Knoxville and wouldn't be back until late.

"Any idea where we might find him in town?" Clay asked.

"I would try the saloon first. That's the most popular meeting place."
"By the way, what's his name."

"Winwrite, Albert Winwrite."

Clay thanked him, and they headed for Knoxville.

It was almost dark when they got there. Clay asks Ellen to get them two hotel rooms while he and Luke took the horses to the livery stable and looked up Mr. Winwrite.

"We'll meet you in the dining room in about an hour," he says. They got lucky and found Winwrite in the first saloon. He was sitting at a table with three other men. Clay asked at the bar, and Winwrite was pointed out to him.

Clay walked to the table, excused himself, and asked which one was Winwrite. The tall, slim fellow with white hair and his back to Clay, turned around and looked up, said, "I'm Winwrite, what can I do for you?"

"I have a small herd of cattle I would like to talk to you about, see if you would be interested in buying them."

Winwrite stood up, pointed to another table and said, "Let's sit over here where we can talk without being disturbed."

"I'm Clay Wade."

"Glad to meet you, Mr. Wade. Now how big is this small herd you have to sell?"

"Total of four-hundred and twenty-five. That includes grown cows, calves, bulls. Most of it is young stuff, under six years old, obviously some or older, but most are under six."

Mr. Winwrite asked, "Why are you selling?"

"When I came back from the war, my folks were dead, and my girlfriend had married someone else. So, I decided I would sell everything and make a new start somewhere else."

"Sounds reasonable. How much are you expecting to get for them?"

Clay answered, "We were on our way to Chicago with them when we heard about you, so thought we would check with you. Maybe save us a long drive. In Chicago, I expect to get about thirty-five for the grown stuff."

Tapping the table with his knuckles Mr. Winwrite says, "Of course, this is not Chicago, and I can't pay their prices because I still have to get them there myself. I know the cattle buyers in Sedalia and Abilene are paying about twenty-five. I can probably match that price if that is satisfactory to you. I'll want to see the herd first before I make a final commitment. Where are you holding them?"

"They are up by Cumberland Gap." "Why there?"

"That's on the way to Chicago."

"So it is. Ok, I can't get away until the day after tomorrow. Can you wait until then to ride up there with me?"

Clay said, "I'm sure we can find a way to amuse ourselves until then."

"Where are you staying?"

"At the hotel."

"How about I meet you there for breakfast at seven, day after tomorrow?"

"Sounds good."

They shook hands, Clay returned to the bar and ordered a whiskey. He and Luke agreed not to be seen together in case Winwrite remembered Luke from dealing with Burdett.

Clay finished his drink and went to the hotel to find Ellen waiting in the dining room. He almost didn't recognize her. She had gotten a bath, changed into clean clothes, did her hair up in a bun in back, and was sitting at the table all prim and proper. That red-gold hair was just sparkling in the lamplight. All Clay could do was stare. He had never seen her look so pretty.

Clay was smiling from ear to ear. Ellen said, "Well, things must have gone pretty good to put a smile like that on your face."

"I'll say they did, so far."

"What do you mean, "So far?"

"He wants to see the herd before he makes a final commitment. But, right now he is offering twenty-five. That's Abilene prices. So, if he holds to that we can't go wrong. But, we have to wait around until day after tomorrow, so he can ride out with us to see what he is buying."

Ellen said, "So, we are stuck here with nothing to do until then?"

"Not necessarily, I can think of something to do."

"Oh, good. What would that be?"

"We can get married."

CHAPTER 12

Ellen gasped, covered her mouth, and her face turned red. She stared at Clay as if she had never seen him before.

Luke had just come in and taken a seat. He was sitting there with a big grin on his face, not saying a word, just watching.

Ellen started stammering, "But, but, but I don't have anything to wear, especially to my wedding."

Clay had an answer for that, "I bet we can find a store that has just the dress you need. We will go looking first thing tomorrow and get married as soon as we can find a preacher or judge or something. Ok?"

"Oh, Clay, you caught me totally by surprise."

Luke stood up, "Look, I'm going to leave you two alone. You sure don't need me for this."

Ellen called him back, "Here is the key to your room, number six, on the second floor. Mine is number four.

Clay and Ellen sat, talking, holding hands, looking into each other's eyes. After a long time, they got up and walked around town, looking in store windows. They found the dress shop where Ellen could get her dress.

When they returned to the hotel, they met Luke coming in the door heading to his room. Clay told him, "Luke, you don't have to hang around here all day tomorrow unless you just want to. You could go back to camp and tell the rest of the guys to hold off on branding any more of the cattle, since we may have them sold. You could also tell them that Ellen and I will be married tomorrow and bring the buyer out the next day."

Luke agreed to do that, said he would leave at sun up.

Clay escorted Ellen to her room. Sometime after midnight, he reluctantly tore himself away and went to his room but didn't get much sleep. He couldn't stop thinking about his wedding day tomorrow.

Long after sunrise the next morning, Clay knocked on Ellen's door. She was up and dressed and invited him in. After a proper good morning greeting, they went downstairs to breakfast. Afterward, they went to the dress shop.

Clay left her there to pick out her dress while he went to the livery stable to check on their horses. He went into each stall and talked to them while they were brushed and groomed. Smokey was the only stallion there not gelded.

Clay saddled Smokey and Black Night, rode out and down the street to the dress shop. Ellen was still in the store getting fitted, so he rode out into the country just to give the horses some exercise. After thirty minutes or so, he returned to town and saw Ellen walking toward the hotel. He caught up with her before she entered the door and asked her how it went. She informed him the dress would not be ready for an hour. They arranged to meet for lunch, then find a preacher.

At three that afternoon, they said their vows and became Mr. & Mrs.

Wade. The reverend's wife witnessed the affair, and it was all legal.

They returned to the hotel, and no one saw them again until seven the next morning when they came downstairs to meet Mr. Winwrite. He was already at the table with a pot of coffee and three cups.

Clay introduced Ellen, "Mr. Winwrite, I would like you to meet my wife, Ellen. This is Mr. Winwrite, he's the gentleman who is going to buy the herd." Mr. Winwrite stood and shook the hand that Ellen offered.

After breakfast, as they sat drinking coffee and engaged in idle chit-chat, Ellen offered to go to the livery and get their horses ready. Mr. Winwrite said, "We may as well all go, that's where I keep my horse."

When Clay and Ellen led their horses from the livery, Mr. Winwrite stopped and stared. Finally, he remarked, "That is a couple of the finest horses I have seen in many a moon. Where did you get them?"

Clay told him, "I raised them. We have more just like them if you are interested. I might be talked into parting with them if the price is right. These two are not for sale, and there is at least one other out with the herd that is not for sale."

Winwrite asked, "How many do you have out there?"

"How many, Ellen?"

"I believe there are twenty-one more."

"Are they all as good as these?"

Clay said, "They are all either full or half-brothers or sisters of these two."

"How much are you expecting to get for them?"

Clay hesitated a moment, then said, "I hadn't given any thought to selling them. I was planning to use them as my breeding stock to get started over, all except the geldings."

"How many of those do you have?"

"I believe we just gelded eight a couple of days ago. See, they have just been running loose, no one to look after them while I was in the war. When I came back there was this herd of horses. Only four of them were broke to ride. I did that before I left. Since I got back we have broken about eight more of the young ones. We have been using them to make this drive, so they have had a lot of work the last few weeks."

"I'm anxious to see the rest of them. I like what I see so far."

The rest of the day was spent in idle conversation until they stopped to camp for the night along beside a slow-moving stream in a grove of trees. They had brought along just enough food and coffee for a couple of meals. They turned in early so they could get an early start tomorrow.

Before the sun was up, they had eaten a little breakfast with the last of their coffee and was in the saddle. They arrived at the camp in the canyon in the early afternoon. Winwrite was anxious to see the horses more so than the cattle. But, while they were riding around looking at horses, he also took note of the cows, bulls, and calves.

When they were back at camp, Ellen served Clay and Winwrite coffee. She then joined Ed and Jim where they were sitting beside the stream, killing time by holding a pole with a hook on it.

They wanted to know how it went in Knoxville. Ellen informed them, "It couldn't have gone better."

Back at the fire, Clay and Winwrite were haggling over the price of the horses. They had already agreed on the twenty-five for the cattle, delivered to Winwrite's ranch outside of Knoxville.

Winwrite wanted those horses. He was pushing for fifty dollars a head; Clay was holding out for sixty. They both knew Winwrite was going to get them for fifty-five, but they had to go through the act.

When they finally settled on a price, the horses went for fifty-five, the cattle for twenty-five for all the grown stock, five each for the calves.

The money would be waiting for them in Knoxville. Clay asked for his money in cash, saying he had a crew to pay and other expenses he had to cover.

Six days later the herd of cattle and horses were delivered. Winwrite was waiting with the cash.

Clay, his crew, and wife went into town to celebrate. After they had eaten Clay paid the men what they were promised for the drive to Chicago, although it had only taken one month instead of the three they expected. Clay paid each ninety dollars. Ellen didn't get anything. She looked around at the others with their money, held out her hand and asked, "Where is my money?"

Clay just laughed and said, "That's why I married you, so I wouldn't have to pay you."

That got a laugh from everyone except Ellen.

Then Clay handed the thick envelope to Ellen with all the rest of the money in it, "Here, this is yours. Can I borrow enough to buy the guys a drink?"

"Only if you promise me no one will get drunk."

"That is a promise. But first, you and I are going over to the bank and open an account in both our names," Clay tells her as he turns to leave. "I'll meet you guys at the saloon, and the drinks are on me!" With a whoop and holler, the men took off in a run for the bar.

Ellen and Clay opened the account in both names. Either of them could draw from it. Ellen looked at Clay and said, "I don't know what to do with all this money, I never had any before."

Clay laughed and said, "You never had a husband before either, but you knew what to do with him."

Ellen slapped him on the arm, turning red in the face. She went to the hotel and got a room for her and Clay while he went to the bar to have a drink with the men.

When Clay arrived at the hotel to meet Ellen for dinner, he was shocked when he saw her standing in front of the mirror. She had had a bath, done up her hair, put a tiny bit of color on her cheeks, and had on the dress she was wearing at her wedding.

Clay stood, staring in awe at his new wife. He backed toward the door, saying, "Excuse me, Ma'am, I believe I have the wrong room."

Ellen put her hands on her hips and told him, "You better get yourself in here."

He did, but it was a couple of hours later before they made it to dinner.

Late the next morning, they all met for breakfast and then head home to Rogersville. That would be a full two-day ride. All the other animals were sold and delivered except for the two pack mules. Clay had the young black gelding with the white blanket on a lead rope.

Clay roped him and took him to the livery stable, where the rest of their horses were being boarded until they were ready to leave town.

When he saw Clay coming at him with a rope, he tried to make a run for it, but there was nowhere to go. He put up a good fight, but in the end, Clay led him out of the pen with the rope wrapped around his saddle horn. By the time they reached the livery stable, he had quieted down enough to be led into a stall. That was another new thing for him. He had never been in a barn or stall before. The other horses that he grew up with were in stalls next to him, so he settled down quickly, especially when Clay put hay and oats in the feed bin for him.

At noon on the third day after leaving Knoxville, they all rode into Rogersville. Six big, strong young men and one beautiful woman drew some attention. One of those who saw them ride in was a Burdett man standing in front of the saloon. He turned and went inside. Immediately, the one known as the "Enforcer" came out. He stared at the group as they rode by, then went back inside.

Clay and Ellen stopped at the sheriff's office to see how things stood around here since they had not heard any news since they left town over a month back. The rest of the men went to the restaurant.

The sheriff saw them riding in and was standing outside his office when they rode up.

Clay and Ellen dismounted, shook hands with Sheriff Campbell, Clay said, "Sheriff, I would like to introduce my new wife."

"Wife? Well, aren't you the lucky devil. Congratulations to both of you. When did this happen? Come on in and tell me all about it."

While Ellen was telling about the wedding, Clay was watching out the window. He saw the enforcer and three other men come out of the saloon and head toward the restaurant where Clay's men had gone.

He told the sheriff and Ellen, "I have to go. I think there is going to be trouble. Burdett's men are following our guys to the restaurant."

He rushed out the door with the sheriff and Ellen right behind him. When they reached the restaurant door, Clay heard loud voices inside. He pulled out his Remington and stepped through the door. All of Burdett's men had their backs to him. Clay's men were standing across the room facing them. The room was as quiet as a tomb. Clay stood there a moment, then pulled back the hammer, making that clicking noise that could be heard by everyone and said, "Don't anyone move." Ellen stepped up beside him with her gun in her hand. Clay calmly reached out and removed all the guns from Burdett's men's holsters".

"Looks like you guys never learn, do you? Did Burdett send you over here to cause trouble, or was this your brilliant idea?"

The enforcer said to Clay, "Wade, you have stuck your nose in our business for the last time."

"I have told you all before. Stay away from me and mine. Next time you cause trouble for me, I am going to shoot to kill. Sheriff, you hear that? They have been warned to leave us alone. I have done nothing to them, but every time I turn around Burdett's men are there causing trouble. I am through being patient with you. No more Mr. Nice Guy. From this minute forward, your life is in your own hands. Do all of you understand that? You keep hanging around Burdett and his gang; they are going to get you killed. My advice for you is, if you want to live, cut your ties with this bunch of crooks and leave the state. Now, get out of my sight and don't let me see you again."

"What about our guns?"

"You can pick them up at the sheriff's office when he decides to let you have them."

Mr. Enforcer turned to Clay and said, "You sure talk big hiding behind the sheriff. Why don't you meet me out in the street, man to man, without the law protecting you? Let's see just how big and brave you are."

Clay smiled and said, "Right now? Guns or fists?"

"Why, you little punk, I'll break you in half. Come on."

"Here, Ellen, hold my gun. If anyone butts in, shoot him."

Ellen said, "Clay, he's a lot bigger than you are."

Clay kissed her and said, "Just watch my back."

They walked into the street. Mr. Enforcer was making a big show of removing his vest, rolling up his sleeves, spitting in his hands, rubbing them together, prancing around.

Clay just stood there smiling, letting him show off. Being laughed at infuriated the enforcer even more.

Suddenly he rushed, with his head down, intending to tackle Clay and get him on the ground where his added weight would be to his advantage. Clay brought his knee up and caught his opponent on the point of his nose. The enforcer was stunned and staggered back a step, spit a mouth full of blood, and a tooth. He took a good look at Clay and growled, "I'll kill you for that."

Clay taunted him with, "You've been trying to do that for weeks, but you aren't having any luck, are you? Come on, stop wasting my time. I have other things to do."

This time he came with his fist up, starting a roundhouse swing. Before it could reach him, Clay delivered a straight left to the already smashed nose, another one to the belly, another one to the nose. They came so fast the enforcer didn't have time to counter with his punches. Clay kept coming, never letting the man get set. Every time the enforcer opened his eyes, there was a fist in it.

Clay had his man back peddling and never let him stop. He backed into the hitching post. As he leaned back to avoid another punch, Clay bent down, grabbed his legs and flipped him over the rail. He landed on his face in the dirt. Clay stepped back to give him time to get up. He wanted this to be a lesson this man, and Burdett, would not forget.

The enforcer struggled to his feet. He walked around the hitching rail and back into the street. Clay was waiting for him.

He cautiously came toward Clay. He was looking around for some of his men to help him, but no one was volunteering. They all heard what Clay had told Ellen. She was standing on the walk, holding Clay's gun as well as her own. The way she was handling them, they knew she could use them, and would if she had to.

Clay was standing in the middle of the street, his hands down by his side. "Come on, Mr. Enforcer, that is what they call you, isn't it? What's your problem, I thought you wanted to fight? What happened, did you change your mind? So far, I haven't seen you do any fighting. All you have done is back up and lay down. You aren't even making this interesting."

The enforcer was furious, but he was afraid to get within Clay's reach.

The crowd that had gathered was cheering for Clay to beat his brain out, stomp him and such taunts. All this was making the enforcer even more frantic, but he had lost his confidence and was looking for help.

Clay started walking forward; the enforcer was backpaddling again. Suddenly he lunged, Clay side-stepped, caught him in the kidney with a fist as he went by, when Enforcer straightened up and grabbed his back, Clay gave him a left in the ear as hard as he could swing. That ended the fight. The enforcer was face down in the street, blood running from his mouth, nose, and ears.

Clay became conscious of the crowd and the noise. He looked up and saw Burdett turn back into the saloon, motioning one of his men to follow him.

Clay knew the fight with Burdett was not over.

CHAPTER 13

He got his gun from Ellen, strapped it on and headed for the saloon. He motioned for Willie to cover him. Willie nodded and followed him in taking up a position beside the door with his back to the wall.

Clay saw Burdett talking to his man at a table near the far end of the bar.

Clay walked up to him, got right in his face.

Burdett looked furious, to think that anyone would just walk up to him without being invited.

Before Burdett could say a word, Clay told him, loud and clear, "Burdett, I am tired of you and your whole stinking, murdering, stealing gang. I want you out of this county for good. If I see you or any of your men around me or mine again, I will be coming after you. What you saw happen to your so-called Enforcer, is just a sample of what will happen to you. I'm talking about you, not your hired thugs. You have until sundown to get out of town or meet me in the street, and you can choose the weapons. Sundown, Burdett."

Burdett was so furious he was shaking. He came out of his chair saying, "Why, you sorry..." That's when Clay backhanded him across the mouth, knocked him back in his chair, then slapped him open-handed, three more times before he could say anything or stand up.

"How do you like it, Burdett? If you are still here after sundown today, you are going to get more of that every time I see you, or any of your men, anywhere near me, or anything that belongs to me. Have I made myself clear, Burdett?"

Burdett just sat there in shock; Clay backhanded him again, as hard as he could swing. Burdett's chair flipped over backward and spilled him on the floor. Clay sat the chair upright, picked Burdett up bodily and slammed him into the chair.

"You have until sundown. Don't make me come back here and kill you."

Clay turned and walked out the door. Willie was standing beside the door with his back to the wall, covering Clay's exit. Clay never looked back.

Willie followed him outside. Ellen was waiting across the street. When she saw him come out, she ran to him, threw her arms around his neck and hugged him so tight it hurt. "Oh, Clay, I was so scared, I thought they would kill you when you went in there."

"I think you will find I don't kill so easily." "I sure hope you're right."

"Ok, fellows, and lady let's get out of here before there's more trouble." Ellen asked, "Where are we going?"

"I thought it would be a good idea to go see your mom and dad. See if they have room to put us up until we are ready to head to Texas if you still want to go with me."

"I want to go where ever you go. If it's Texas, so be it," Ellen said with a quick nod.

"I understand there is land just waiting to be settled, and we're going to need a big place to raise a dozen kids."

"Oh, I just remembered. I can't go with you; I have to stay here." "Over my dead body, you will."

"Don't say that. It gave me goosebumps."

Able stepped up and said, "I think I'll just hang back and see if anyone has any ideas of shooting someone in the back."

"Thanks, but don't get yourself in a bind," warned Clay.

As a group, they mounted up and slowly walked their horses out of town. But they all had eyes in the back of their heads until they were out of sight of anyone watching.

Able caught up with them a mile out of town. Clay asked, "Any trouble?"

"Mr. Enforcer tried to get a rifle from somebody's saddle. I just told him if he touched it I would shoot him. He changed his mind."

When they arrived at the Carter home, there were seven men and Ellen. Slim, Able and Willie continued to their homes. Luke asked if he could hang with Clay and Ellen. "In fact, if you will have me along I would like to go to Texas with you. I've spent some time there and know the country. I can show you some beautiful places that would be ideal for raising cattle and horses.

Clay and Ellen both agreed, "That sounds like a plan. Probably save us a lot of time looking for the right place."

Ed, Jim, and Ellen went into the house. Clay was hanging back.

Mr. and Mrs. Carter greeted all their kids, asking how the drive went. "You all are back early; we didn't expect you for another month. What happened?"

Ellen explained about finding a buyer for the cattle and horses in Knoxville, so didn't have to go to Chicago. "Oh, by the way, I need to introduce someone. Come on in here."

When Clay walked in, Mr. and Mrs. Carter were surprised to see him, but said, "We know Clay."

Ellen said, with a mischievous smile on her face, "But, you don't know him as your son-in-law."

Mrs. Carter gasped, "Oh my God. You got married?"

"Yep, sure did."

Mr. and Mrs. Carter both came around to Clay. Mrs. Carter gave him a big hug, Mr. Carter shook his hand and welcomed him into the family.

Luke was invited in and introduced. Mrs. Carter wanted to know how they had met Luke. They all started laughing. Ellen explained that it was either hang him or take him along. Then she had to explain what she meant by that. Luke told them he got to cast the tie-breaking vote not to hang him.

An hour before sundown, Clay, Ed, and Luke rode back into Rogersville. They tied up the horses in front of the sheriff 's office and spread out up and down the main street.

Clay checked with the sheriff to see if Burdett was still around and was informed that Burdett and his whole crew had left town a couple hours back. But, if he returned and there was going to be a gunfight, Clay wanted the sun at his back. So, he walked to the west end of town and waited for Burdett to show.

Long after sundown, when it was almost dark, Clay went to the saloon.

The bartender told him Burdett had checked out of the hotel, took his wife and all his men, and rode out of town an hour after Clay had given him notice.

When Clay and the men got back to the Carter place, Ellen came running and gave him another one of those bear hugs, and a long, sweet kiss.

"What happened?"

Clay just said, "Nothing, they all left town." "I am so thankful to hear that."

After eating and visiting until dark, Mrs. Carter told Luke, "You can bunk in with Ed and Jim. Clay, if you didn't mind, since you are married, I guess you can share Ellen's room."

"Oh, no, Ma'am, that will be just fine."

"Mom," Ellen said, "you have always said I can't have boys in my room."

"Ok with me if you don't want him in there. But I don't consider Clay a boy."

"Ok, ok, he can come in my room," Ellen laughed.

Ellen and Clay thought the family would never declare bedtime so that they could go to their room. Tonight, would be the third night since their wedding night, almost a month ago, that they have been alone. They were both looking forward to it.

Everyone was at the breakfast table before sunup. Ellen and her mom put a big spread of food on the table. While they were eating Clay announced he was riding over to Able's place to check on his other horses that were left there.

Ellen said, "Wait for me, I want to go too."

When they were ready to go, Clay decided to put a saddle on the black colt with the white blanket and lead him along, letting him get accustomed to the saddle before he tried to ride him.

"We have to come up with a name for him. Any ideas?" asked Clay.

"Let me think about it. How about "Trouble?" Ellen suggested. "Trouble, you like that?"

"Yeah, that describes him perfectly."

"Ok, Trouble it is. I Hope Trouble doesn't live up to his name."

During the three-day ride from Knoxville, Trouble had grown accustomed to the rope, being led, tied, petted, brushed. He didn't mind having his feet lifted to inspect the hooves. He didn't have shoes yet, but that would happen next time they were in town. He had been kept in a stall in the barn and was accustomed to the halter, but when it came to the saddle, that was another matter. He didn't take to that so much. But with help from Luke, the saddle was gently placed on his back; the girth was brought up under his stomach and slowly tightened. He was watching everything that was happening to him, rolling his eyes and fidgeting. When the saddle was in place and secure, Clay stepped back. Luke led Trouble around the pen a few times. He gave a half-hearted effort at bucking the saddle off but gave up after a few lunges.

All the time Luke was talking to him and stroking his face and neck. It was a half hour ride to Able's family farm. When Ellen and Clay arrived, leading Trouble, Able met them at the door and went with them to look at the horses. They all looked perfectly content.

Clay informed Able that they would be leaving for Texas soon and they would be taking all the horses with them except maybe one.

"What is the deal with that one?" Able wanted to know.

"For letting them stay here while we were gone, you can have your pick of any of the young ones. The Stallion and the four broodmares will go with us, and any of the others that we haven't sold by then. Which one do you want? Or, do you want any?"

"Sure, I would love to have any of them. That is a beautiful bunch of horses," said Able.

"We won't be leaving for a few days, so take your time, just let me know when we come to get them, ok?"

Ellen and Clay headed back to the Carter farm. They came to a creek with fresh running water, lined with cottonwoods, blackjacks and ash trees. Ellen said, "I believe there is a nice little pool right up here. Make a good place to stop for lunch."

"It's a little early, isn't it?"

"Maybe, but you don't think I'm going to let an opportunity like this slip by do you?"

"You are a conniving woman; you know that?" With a big smile, she said, "Yes."

Ellen led the way up the stream a couple of hundred yards. Sure enough, there was the prettiest little pool, surrounded by big shade trees and a carpet of grass beside the pool.

They tied off the horses downstream and spread their bedrolls on the grass in the shade. Ellen reached into her saddlebags and brought out a coffee pot and coffee and a sandwich for each.

Clay got a fire going. While they waited for the water to get hot, they laid on the bedrolls, hugging and kissing. By the time they became aware of what time it was, the coffee had boiled dry and the fire was down to ashes.

They were laughing as they got dressed and put on more water. The young couple was finally able to eat lunch and have their coffee.

On the way home, they discussed the things they would need for the trip to Texas. The first thing was a covered wagon to haul all the stuff that would be necessary to set up housekeeping once they located their new home. There was a wagon builder in Rogersville. They would visit him tomorrow and hope he had one available. After that, they could start collecting all the other supplies, food, utensils, and appliances.

Ellen solicited the help of her mom and dad to make a list. Not knowing where they would settle, they had no way of knowing what would be available there, so they had to plan on taking all the necessities with them.

Over the next week, they were busy from daylight to dark collecting everything on the list. They had Luke running here and there picking up things to add to the wagon. Ed and Jim were also anxious to help. They even wanted to go to Texas with them to help them get settled. But, Mr. Carter put a stop to that. He needed them here to help run the farm. It was too big for one man to handle.

When Clay was in town the first time, after giving Burdett notice, he checked with the sheriff to see if Burdett was still around. "No, he and all his men pulled out that same day, and no one has seen them since."

That was a relief, but it worried Clay more than if he was still here.

Not knowing where he was or what he was doing had Clay watching over his shoulder all the time. He warned Luke and Ellen to be on the alert always. "Carry your guns loaded, and don't hesitate to use it if you have too."

Clay was still finding time almost every day to practice his draw. Only now he had money to buy ammunition, so he was getting practice shooting also. Then Ellen started going with him when he went to practice, so she started practicing. Wasn't long before she was almost as good as Clay. She could hit the target, but it took her longer to get the gun out and in position to shoot.

Clay decided next time he was in town; he would get her a smaller gun. The Colt Navy she was using was too heavy for her. It was the gun they had taken off Ike back at their camp.

CHAPTER 14

He went into town the next day to shop for a gun for Ellen and another pair of mules. The first person he saw was Willie Stanton. They went to the saloon to have a drink. Clay asked Willie, "What are you doing these days, Willie?"

"Not much, I have been looking for a riding job, but there aren't any around here. I'm thinking of going somewhere and get a new start."

"Have you thought about Texas?" Clay asked. "I hear it is wide open. Land for the taking."

"I would sure like to do that, but it takes money to homestead, what with all the equipment you need to buy to prove up on it."

"I have a proposition for you. How about you come with Ellen and me. Luke is coming along; he says he knows the country down there and can show us some property that we can homestead. If we can find the right place, you could work with us and homestead a place nearby. How does that sound?"

"Sounds good, let me talk it over with Aunt Maddie. I don't want to leave her here alone. I'm the only kin she has left."

"Once we get settled you can send for her," Clay suggested.

"Ok, I will let you know in a day or two."

"By the way, Willie, I need to pick up another pair of mules. Know anyone who has some they would be willing to part with?"

"I do know someone. Aunt Maddie has a couple that is just standing around eating. Since Uncle Ed died, she hasn't used them for anything. And, I bet she could use the money."

Clay asked, "Are you going home now? I'll ride out with you and talk to her."

It turns out Aunt Maddie was more than willing to sell the mules. They agreed on a price and Clay said he would be back in an hour or so with the money.

When he got to town, he went to the bank and got the cash. Then he went to the gun shop to buy a gun for Ellen.

The gunsmith had a small selection, but he had just what Clay needed. A Smith & Wesson, 32 caliber, rimfire, six shots. It was much lighter than the Remington or the Colt, so would be more comfortable for her to handle. The gunsmith also had several Spencer 7 shots, repeating rifle. Clay bought four of them for himself, Ellen, Luke, and Willie. If they should run into problems on the way to Texas, these guns could make all the difference.

Clay returned to get his mules from Aunt Maddie. She had all the harness to go with them and threw that in at no additional charge.

Clay put the harness on the mules and led them back through town to the Carter Farm.

They all agreed to leave the day after tomorrow.

CHAPTER 15

Later that afternoon, Clay headed out back to practice with his new weapons. Ellen tagged along just as she had since they were kids. There he gave her the new Spencer rifle and the Smith and Wesson pistol. She was excited, to say the least. She strapped on the belt and holster and dropped the Smith and Wesson in it. She drew it a couple of times to get the feel, then she turned and fired at the row of cans sitting on the fence. She missed the first two shots, but she knocked a can off with the next four shots.

Clay showed her how to reload. That was all it took. She was thrilled with it. She then tried the Spencer and was just as good with it.

The night before they were planning to leave, Willie came by, all packed and ready to go. They all sat around the dining table to plan out their route and try to decide the best place to start looking. They all had been asking questions of everyone who may know something of Texas. The big thing they learned was about the Comanche Indians who were causing problems in the northern part of the state; so, they decided to go to the southern part. Somewhere in the area north of Victoria, but south of San Antonio. They were told the Comanche usually don't come that far south.

They also learned of all the longhorn cattle that were running wild in that part of the state. Even before they set out from home, they were already talking about rounding up a herd to drive to market.

Earlier that day, they had driven all the horses over from Able's place and held them in the horse pasture close to the house for an early start the next day.

Everyone was up early and excited about beginning the trip. All except Ellen's mom and dad, who couldn't accept the fact that their little girl was leaving home. The distance to Texas was so far away; they were afraid they would never see any of them again.

The women were crying and hugging. Mrs. Carter kept saying, "You will write, won't you? Let us know where you land and that you made the trip ok?"

"Yes Mom, I'll write every chance I get along the way and let you know where we are and give you our mailing address when we finally get settled."

When they finally were able to get on the road, it was after nine o'clock. Their first major town on the way was Knoxville. They had just come from there a couple of weeks ago, so they knew the trail and where to camp for the two nights it would take to get there.

Late the third day, they parked the wagon in a grove of trees on the outskirts of Knoxville beside a quite running stream. They hobbled the broodmares and the two stallions, Blackie and Smokie, who were staked out on a patch of grass out of reach of each other. The young ones would not stray far, so they were left to run free.

At night, someone was always on guard. Ellen usually took the first watch for two hours; the men would share the rest of the night.

That night, Clay suggested they go into town and have a meal that someone else cooked for a change. Ellen jumped at that. But, then remembered someone had to stay with the horses. They were going to draw straws to see who stayed, but Willie volunteered. "Just bring me something."

Ellen, Luke, and Clay went to the diner and had an excellent meal, which included, a huge steak, potatoes, and gravy, followed up with a big slice of apple pie and coffee. They sat around talking and enjoying the break from the trail. Finally returning to camp, they found everything in a mess, all the horses gone, and Willie lying in a pool of blood.

Ellen screamed and ran to Willie. Clay felt for a pulse, found it stable, but rapid. Luke was looking around trying to determine what had happened. Willie was unconscious and couldn't tell them.

"We need to get him to a doctor," Ellen said.

They had a thin mattress that Ellen and Clay used in their tent. They lowered the tailgate on the wagon, made a bed across it for Willie.

While Ellen and Clay were doing that, Luke was hitching up the mules. Apparently, the thieves didn't think the mules were worth taking.

The doctor was already in bed, but he opened the door in his nightshirt. He looked at them and asked, "What the devil do you want this time of the night?"

When they explained they had a wounded man who needed care, he opened the door, and said, "Bring him in here. Put him on that table while I get dressed."

After the doctor had looked him over, checking his head, pulse, reflexes, he determined that Willie had a bad concussion, but he thought he would be ok after a few days' rest. "Leave him here, I'll keep watch over him in case he starts having convulsions. That's pretty common with an injury of this kind."

Clay and Luke took the wagon and mules to the livery stable while Ellen got rooms for the night at the hotel.

Early next morning, they were having breakfast in the diner when the sheriff came in. Clay invited him to join them at their table. When the sheriff was seated and had his coffee, Clay introduced everyone, then told him about the robbery and the injury to Willie.

The sheriff introduced himself, "I'm George Steel, sheriff of Knox County. He sat and listened to what they had to say. "I'll get a posse together and go after them."

Clay told him that would not be necessary. "You have your posse right here," indicating Luke and himself.

Ellen jumped in saying, "Don't leave me out of this. I want to get my hands on that scum."

The sheriff held up his hands, "No way will I have a woman in my posse."

"Then we will go without you, Sheriff. I suppose we can handle it without any help," Ellen informed him.

"I can't allow that either. Taking the law into your own hands makes you no better than those guys."

"Well then, get used to me being along." Ellen's mind was made up, and there was no changing it.

Clay asked, "When will you be ready to leave, Sheriff?" "As soon as I finish my breakfast and saddle my horse."

Thirty minutes later, they were all together in front of the sheriff's office. Clay, Ellen, Luke, and the sheriff 's deputy, Samuel Winwrite. Turns out he was a nephew of the cattle buyer.

When he saw the horses Ellen and Clay were riding, he remarked, "My uncle has a couple of horse that could be twins to those two."

Clay informed him, "They are brothers and sisters to these two. Mr.

Winwrite bought them from us, along with a bunch of others."

"Yeah, I saw that bunch of horses. The best-looking herd I've ever seen. I tried to talk Uncle out of one, but he wouldn't budge without me paying full price."

They arrived back at the campsite a few minutes later. They scouted around looking for tracks. When they determined which way the thieves had gone, it was easy to follow. The trail of that many horses is almost impossible to hide.

The Sheriff remarked, "Looks like they are heading for the Cumberland Mountains. That's some rugged country up there."

Clay said, "Ok, we know where they are going, let's go. We are wasting time."

Clay led off at a slow gallop that Smokey could keep up all day.

The sheriff was riding beside Clay, with Ellen and Luke following them, while the deputy was bringing up the rear.

After two hours at that pace, Clay called for a halt to give the horses a breather.

They started out at least twelve hours behind the thieves. They didn't know if the thieves had ridden through the night, or if they stopped to camp.

Along about noon, they saw where the thieves had stopped, had a fire, and apparently had coffee and food. From the tracks, they could tell the thieves are pushing the herd hard.

It became evident after a while that the young colts and fillies were having a hard time keeping up the pace. Some of them were only a few months but, most were one to almost two years. Those older ones were holding up good, so far.

After a thirty-minute rest, the posse took to the trail again with the pace at the slow gallop. After thirty minutes, the horses got a five-minute breather.

Just before sundown, they saw where the thieves had stopped again.

Apparently, cooked a meal and had coffee. Looking at the tracks, Clay and Luke agreed, the thieves have slowed down. They are now moving at a walk. Apparently, they thought they had a big enough lead that they could take their time.

The posse took another breather, stripped the saddles off their horses, rubbed them down, let them roll, and get a drink from the creek.

While the horses were taking their break, Ellen prepared a quick meal from the supplies they brought along in their saddlebags. They were all tired and stiff from so many hours in the saddle. But after another thirty-minute rest, the horses were saddled, watered again, and back on the trail. They galloped for thirty minutes, walked for thirty minutes, then galloped another thirty minutes.

Even at night with a bright moon, they could follow the tracks with no problem. They rode all night at that pace. By morning, they could tell they were only a short time behind the thieves.

At daybreak, they gave the horses another break, unsaddled, rubbed them down, and let them drink and graze beside the creek for an hour, while Ellen fixed a meal for the posse.

They all stretched out on the ground and got a few minutes sleep. They were all dead tired. They had been on the trail for twenty-four hours. The horses were showing the strain, especially the two belonging to the sheriff and his deputy. They were not of the same quality as the Wade horses.

While they were resting, the sheriff remarked, "I need to get me a horse like yours. Maybe I can get the county to buy two for my deputy and me. After this chase, I have a good argument in favor of it."

Back on the trail, they came to the campsite of the thieves. The ashes in the campfire were warm; the tracks were fresh, showing they had just left the camp a few minutes before the posse arrived. They were again traveling at a walk. Apparently, the babies were slowing them down, but they could see the value of not losing them.

The sheriff told them, "We are going to have to be careful from here on. We don't want to ride into them unexpectedly."

The posse moved out again, galloping for thirty minutes, walk for thirty minutes, then gallop again. They were eating up the miles and gaining on the thieves. Every time they stopped, they studied the tracks. They were fresher at every stop.

Around noon, they saw a dust cloud ahead of them. Clay said, "If we can see their dust, they can see ours if they look. Let's slow down and follow along until they stop again. Then we can move in and maybe take them by surprise without anyone getting hurt.

A few minutes later, as they topped a hill, they could see the horse herd ahead of them at a slow walk, the babies lagging, with a rider behind keeping them moving.

The posse took another breather. There are no worries about the thieves getting away now. The only problem now was to try to take them without anyone getting hurt or killed. Although Clay, Ellen, and Luke, were not too worried about the thieves getting hurt. In fact, they would like to see them hung from the nearest tree. If the sheriff and deputy were not along, that's what would happen.

At mid-afternoon, the thieves took another break.

Clay had moved out ahead about a half mile. When he topped the hill, he was only a quarter mile back. He saw them stopped, building a fire, and unsaddling their horses.

Knowing they would be there for a while, he returned to the posse and informed them what he had seen. He suggested they leave their horses here and approach on foot. There was plenty of cover, so they should be able to get right up to the edge of their camp without being seen.

Clay suggested Ellen stay with the horses, but she was having none of that. Just like the rest of them, she checked her pistol and her new Spencer rifle, to make sure they were both fully loaded and in working order, with no sand or grit in the working mechanism.

Clay finally consented. "Ok, stay right with me. Sheriff, how do you want to do this.?"

"How about you two," indicating Ellen and Clay, "move off to the left and come in from that side of their camp. Luke and Samuel, move off to the right and come in from that side. I will stay in the brush along beside the trail and come in from this side. Try to move as quiet as you can. We want to catch them by surprise. But don't anyone take any chances, if you must shoot, shoot to kill. No one does anything until I offer them the chance to surrender. After that, all bets are off. Ok?"

Clay cautioned them about not shooting toward the horses or at any of us.

With that, they all moved out, moving like shadows through the trees and underbrush. When Clay and Ellen arrived where they had a good view of the camp, and the horses were out of the line of fire, they each settled down behind a large tree and waited for the sheriff to make the first move.

They could see four men lounging around the fire, talking and drinking. Some were drinking from a cup, some from a bottle.

They didn't have to wait long. The sheriff called out in a loud, clear, voice, "Don't anyone move, we have you surrounded. I am Knox County Sheriff Steel; you are all under arrest. Keep your hands where we can see them. Don't make a move for your guns, if you do, we'll shoot."

For a couple of seconds no one moved, then mumbling was heard coming from one of the men, whom they assumed was the leader of the bunch of thieves.

They all slowly got to their feet, but suddenly, as if by signal, they all went for their guns. Clay had drawn a bead on the leader. As soon as they made a move, Clay pulled the trigger. His target grabbed his chest, folded over and hit the ground. He never moved again.

Ellen had sighted in on the one next to the leader. She didn't hesitate when they drew. Her shot caught him right between the eyes. He was dead before he hit the ground.

The sheriff, Luke, and Samuel also opened fire hitting all four of the thieves.

The posse closed in on the camp, cautiously watching each of the downed men to see if any of them were still alive. They weren't.

The sheriff just shook his head, "They brought it on themselves. They had their chance but chose the hard way out."

"Maybe not, Sheriff. I guess they knew they would hang and chose to go out this way. Not sure I blame them," Clay said.

Ellen added, "Their first mistake was stealing our horses and injuring Willie. I sure hope he's ok."

Deputy Samuel wanted to know, "What do we do with the bodies? If we try to take them back to Knoxville, they are going to be getting pretty ripe before we get there."

The Sheriff said, "Let's look through their gear, maybe they have something to dig with."

They found a small shovel and each of them took turns digging. They dug one hole large enough to hold the four bodies. They were laid in the hole, covered with a blanket, then covered with dirt, then rocks. Not knowing any of their names, and not finding any identification on any of them, they could only put a cross at the head of the grave.

Considering the horses were all worn out, they decided to make camp a little upstream and rest up through the next day before returning to Knoxville.

Clay, Ellen, and Luke looked all the horses over carefully. They didn't find anything except exhausted horses. Especially the babies. They were just laying around in the shade, taking it easy. The mothers were very attentive, letting them suckle when they wanted to. Ellen watched that with a smile and said, "Oh, how sweet."

Three days of slow riding, with numerous stops for rest and feeding, and they were back in Knoxville.

They turned the horses into the pen at the livery, arranged with the owner for their keep, which included oats and hay.

They thanked the sheriff and his deputy for helping get their horses back and checked back in at the hotel. Then they all went to the doctor's office to check on Willie. The doctor met them at the door, "Go on in; he's sitting up, feeling good and anxious to get out of here."

"That's good news," Ellen said with a big exhale.

After confirming with the doctor that Willie was able to leave with them, they all went to the diner for another excellent meal, then went to the hotel for a much-needed night's sleep.

Next morning, after a breakfast of ham, eggs, coffee and lots of hot biscuits, they retrieved the horses from the livery, hooked the mules to the wagon, and hit the trail for Texas once again.

Willie discovers that he couldn't take the jarring he got from riding a horse, so he asked to drive the wagon. That was the routine for the next week. With Ellen riding Black Night, Clay and Luke took turns riding all the other two-year old's. They figured by the time they got to Texas and established their homestead; these young horses would be a big benefit to them.

Ellen got a big kick out of watching Clay and Luke saddle and ride the young ones first thing in the morning. They saddled a new one every morning. One of them mounted the young one while the other one kept him tied up short to the horn of his saddle so that he couldn't buck. All he could do was twist around and kick up in the rear end. After an hour or so, he settled down and acted like a regular horse.

There were eight of the two-year old's, four from the four older broodmares, and four more from the five and six-year-old mares. By the end of the second week, all of them were broke to the saddle.

Six days out of Knoxville, they reached Chattanooga, Tennessee. During that six days, they only ran into one day of bad weather. It was mid-July, and the temperature was hovering around one-hundred degrees most of the day.

One morning it was chilly and windy when they awoke and prepared breakfast. The sky was cloudy, and the sun never showed itself through the clouds all day. Around mid-morning, it started raining. A hard blowing, cold rain. The men put on the rain slickers; Ellen was driving the wagon, so she slid into the back under the cover, and closed the front as much as she could. It was a miserable day, but they still made the estimated twenty miles. The lunch break turned out to be cold sandwiches and water. They all hovered in and under the wagon to keep as dry as possible. The rain slacked off toward late afternoon. They found a level area beside a fast running stream and set up camp for the night on the outskirts of Chattanooga. They placed the wagon so that it blocked the wind and tied down a tarp to form a lean-to where Luke built a fire for cooking. Clay had thought ahead and bought two tents, each large enough to sleep two men, or one man and one woman comfortably. Those were set up and a ground sheet placed inside, so their bedrolls and blankets wouldn't get wet.

All in all, it wasn't a bad night. It was much cooler than previous nights, and everyone slept well.

Seven days later, they reached the small town of Elyton, Alabama, (later renamed Birmingham).

That night, they parked the wagon at the livery stable, and put all the horses in the pen out back, except the two stallions who went into stalls inside.

There was no hotel, but there was a widow who rented rooms. She had two vacancies, so Clay took both for one night. They stashed their gear in their rooms and went to the only restaurant in town for a good meal.

Afterward, the men went to the barbershop for haircuts, shave and baths. While they were doing that, Ellen had a tub of warm water delivered to her room for her bath. Being able to sleep in a real bed was a treat that they all enjoyed. But early next morning, after breakfast, it was back on the road again.

Most days they passed through at least one small town, sometimes more. They were able to replenish their supplies whenever needed, so they didn't suffer from running short of food.

Part of the daily routine was practicing with their guns. Since there were only four of them, they had to be on the alert for anything that looked like trouble. So far, they had not had any problem, but they knew it was possible at any time.

They heard talk in every town they passed through, about gangs robbing travelers who looked vulnerable. So, they didn't want to look vulnerable. But they knew they presented a good haul for someone who could steal their horses, again, and the wagon load of supplies.

Eight days later, still averaging an estimated twenty miles per day, they reached Meridian, Mississippi.

Clay's group and the horses and mules were tired all the time, so they decided to rest up a couple of days. It would do all of them a world of good. They found a good camping spot upstream from the town, pitched their tents, hobbled the grown stock on a good patch of grass close to the creek, and all but one crashed. They took turns watching the horses, and the camp. They were not taking any chances of having everything stolen while they all slept.

After Clay and Ellen had rested until almost noon, they rode into town, found a café and had a meal, followed up with lots of coffee and chocolate cake. They strolled around town, looking in windows and just looking in general. Ellen picked up a few things she needed, and Clay got more ammunition for all their guns. Not knowing where they were going or what they may run into, he wanted to be ready for anything. They could always use it for target practice.

It was another two hundred miles from Meridian to New Orleans. That would take ten days, with no trouble. So far, they had been fortunate. They had no breakdowns with the wagon, no crippled horses, no problem with people on the road. An occasional rain shower here and there, but nothing to complain about. It kept the dust down.

CHAPTER 16

At New Orleans, Clay went to the dock to see if it was possible to get a ride on a steamship across the gulf to Victoria. If they could, it would save them weeks of travel by road.

He found an office that handled cattle coming from Victoria, and Indianola, and other towns along the Texas coast. When he told the man what he needed, he was more than glad to help. He said, "I have a boat leaving in two days for Indianola. It was going to have to return empty, but you can ride along for almost nothing. Just cover the cost."

Clay was overjoyed. He asked, "How long will the trip take?"

"Most of five days. We can drive your wagon right on the boat from the dock, and the horses will be driven on and put in stalls along the side. Should be no problem. I suggest you pick up some feed to give them on the trip."

The next day, they went to a feed store and bought several sacks of oats and hay and had it delivered to the dock.

When they arrived at the appointed time on the second day, the feed and hay were already loaded.

The mules were hesitant about walking up the ramp from the dock to the boat, so Luke and Willie took hold of their bridles and led them while Clay drove from the wagon seat. The wagon was parked in the middle of the boat to help with the balance. Willie and Luke led the adult horses on, and the younger ones with a little prodding from behind, but they saw their mommas going on, so they followed. Once everything was tied down and secure, the captain showed Clay and Ellen to their cabin, Luke and Willie to theirs.

The captain informed them they would be traveling at about eight knots per hour which would put them in Indianola in about five days. Going by road, at twenty miles per day, would take them about twenty-four to twenty-five days.

The trip was an experience they would not have missed for anything. None of them had ever been on a boat of this size, and certainly not out on the open water, out of sight of land. The captain enjoyed having them on board, especially Ellen. They were invited to dine with him in his quarters, which was nothing fancy, but beat eating on the open deck. He showed Ellen how to steer the ship, how to read the compass and stay on course. She enjoyed it as much as he did.

The weather held for the first three days, then a storm moved in, the water got rough, and waves were coming in over the deck. The men and Ellen were kept busy trying to keep the animals from getting too excited. The storm moved inland during the night, and the next day the water was calm, the sun bright and hot as blazes. If there had not been a good ocean breeze it would have been intolerable.

As enjoyable as the cruise was, they were all relieved when they set foot on dry land. The animals and wagon were unloaded and driven through Indianola to a vacant plot on the north side of town.

Clay and Ellen rode back into town to check with the land office about available land for settling. The agent informed them, "West and northwest, toward San Antonio and Austin there is very little settlement. A few farms, but most of those are small. Just find a place with no one close by and put down your roots. Stake out the area you want to homestead and go to the county seat and file with the land office. If it's filed on they can tell you before you put in any work."

Clay wanted to know, "Is that good grazing country out there. We're new to Texas, so we're not familiar with any of it."

"Oh, yes, some of the best grassland you will find anywhere. Belly deep to a tall horse."

"Sounds too good to be true. Why hasn't it already been settled?"

"Some of it was, at one time. But with the war and all, the men were off fightin'; the women couldn't make a go of it. Many of the men never came back, so the land was just left there. Most of it the taxes haven't been paid on it in years."

"Do you know of any place like that - was occupied but is now vacant?" "That's in DeWitt County. Clinton is the county seat. You will have to check with them."

"How far is it to Clinton?"

"About ninety miles or so, almost due northwest."

"Thanks for all the information," Clay said as he gave him a firm handshake.

"Good luck to you."

They spent the night at their camp and left the next morning for Clinton. It was late the fifth day when they got there, so they set up camp outside of town and went to the land office the next morning.

When they stated their business, the man reached for a big book on a shelf behind him, flipped through some pages, turned the book around so Clay and Ellen could see it. There were several vacant places. Some of them with houses and barns and other outbuildings.

Clay pointed at one of them, "How much would it cost to get that place?"

The book was turned back around; the man looked at some figures, did a little figuring of his own, and said, the taxes past due comes to two hundred and twenty dollars. That's what you can have it for."

"How far from here is that?"

"If you head almost due north, that will take you to Cuero, from there, there is a road of sorts, which will take you right to it. Be there in about a half day."

Ellen asked, "How will we know when we get there."

"When you leave Cuero, on the outskirts of town there is a wagon road to the north-west. Follow that road out about ten miles or so. You will come to the Guadalupe River. Anywhere along that river, you will find good grazing and lots of water. The old Locke place is along beside the river. That wagon road goes by the place."

"OK, Ellen, want to ride out and look it over? If it fits the bill, we will come back in to close the deal. Ok?"

"Sure, suits me."

"See you in a few days." Clay said.

When they walked out the door, they were so excited they couldn't talk. Hurrying back to the wagon, Willie and Luke were told what they had found.

They were so anxious to get there, they hooked the team to the wagon and headed out. According to the agent, they would be there about noon. The agent also told them it was three places joining. The typical homestead of six hundred forty acres, plus Mr. Locke had bought out two other properties adjoining his. So, the total was nineteen-hundred and twenty acres, all of it fronting on the Guadalupe River. With a house and barn already in place on two of the sites.

They talked about it all the next day as they traveled. It sounded ideal for Clay and Ellen to live on one, Willie and Luke could live on the other, and they would all work the three places as one.

CHAPTER 17

Mid-afternoon, they topped out on the hill overlooking the old Locke place. Clay was driving the wagon with Ellen sitting beside him. He stopped so they could look the place over from a distance before going down to the house.

The place looked like they expected. Overgrown with weeds and brush. Reminded Clay of his home place back in Tennessee when he saw it for the first time after coming back home.

Clay looked at Ellen; they were both smiling, liking what they saw.

From the top of the hill, they could see a long distance. The terrain was rolling hills with groves of trees scattered here and there. There were large open areas where the grass was knee high to a tall man with cattle grazing everywhere you looked. They could see a couple of ponds in the distance, surrounded by trees. They didn't know what kind of trees they were, but at this point it didn't matter.

The house was built with sturdy logs, long across the front with a porch from one end to the other. The house and barn looked like they might need some repairs, but nothing they couldn't do themselves.

When they arrived at the house, Ellen jumped off the wagon and ran to the door. It was not locked, she pushed it open and went in. It looked like someone had just stepped out and expected to come back soon. A sofa and matching chair was sitting in the living room in front of the fireplace. A dining table, with six chairs in one end of the kitchen. A large wood stove was at the other end.

Ellen was amazed at all the furniture left by the previous owners.

All the bedrooms had beds, chests, mirrors, and built-in closets. It was ready to move into with just a little cleaning.

Clay came in and was as amazed as Ellen. He said, "You know, we got a bargain. We can move right in and don't have to do anything. I feel sorry for the Locke's, to have to move away and leave all this behind. I guess it makes up for what I lost back home."

Willie and Luke came in from inspecting the other buildings. There was the barn, a bunkhouse, a horse barn with stalls for up to eight horses, with a covered shed attached that would protect much more from rain and wind.

The mules were unhooked from the wagon, unharnessed and turned into the pen connected to the barn. The horses were already grazing on the knee-deep grass that had been growing there for some time. There was a water trough, but no water in it.

The well was halfway between the house and the barn. Clay started pumping the handle, but no water was coming out. He took his canteen from his saddle and poured water into the pump to prime it. After a few more pumps, fresh, clean water came flowing. He tasted it. Smiled, said, "Cool and sweet. Can't get any better than that."

With a bucket from the wagon, he filled the water trough in the horse corral.

Clay and Ellen started cleaning the house while Willie and Luke were cleaning the bunkhouse. Ellen saw what they were doing and yelled, "Hey, why don't you let that go for now? There are three bedrooms in here. We can all sleep in here."

Ellen removed the bedding from the beds and put her own on them. She found plenty of wood in the box beside the stove and got a fire going. Coffee was boiling in a few minutes and supper was not long in coming. It was still camp rations, but eating at a dining table made it all taste better than sitting on the ground.

When they were eating, Clay asked, "Well, guys, what do you think?" Both started talking at once. They all laughed. Finally, Luke began again, "If the rest of the place is as good as this, I don't think you can go wrong."

Willie agreed, "We need to ride over the ground to see what kind of grass there is and check on the water availability. The river is just right there, but we don't know how easy it is for the animals to get to it. Like, how high are the banks? Is there quicksand? Those kinds of things."

Clay agreed, "We will ride over the whole place tomorrow, and check out the other two homesteads. See if the houses are as good as this one, and the barns, corrals and such. I tell you I'm so excited to have found this place; I have goosebumps all over me."

"You and me both," Ellen said.

After eating, they took their coffee and moved to the front porch to watch the sunset.

Long after it was good and dark, they were all still sitting there, saying nothing, just enjoying the quiet and the rest after such a long, tiring trip. Finally, Ellen broke the silence, saying, "I'm getting a bath and going to bed. Good night boys. Oh, one of you can share my room if you want to."

While she was still within hearing range, Clay said, "Want to draw straws?"

Ellen shouted back, "I heard that!"

When Ellen had had time to finish her bath and get in bed, Clay came into the room, said, "I drew the short straw."

"Well, aren't you the lucky one."

"I sure plan to be."

Long after the lights were out, Clay and Ellen lay holding each other, and making plans for what they were taking for granted was going to be their new home.

Next morning, while Ellen was cleaning up from breakfast, the men saddled their favorite horses and were waiting by the barn when she came out ready to ride.

They took their time riding all over the place, checking out the watering holes, the grass, what kind grew where and estimating how many cows they could run on it. Then they moved to the second homestead. That house was smaller, but in good repair, just needed some cleaning. The barn had four stalls, and a storage area that would hold several tons of hay, and other food for the animals.

The house was a two bedroom, with another room that made up the kitchen, dining and living room. Luke and Willie both agreed it would be perfect for them.

The third homestead just had a small cabin and a lean-to for the animals to get out of the rain and wind.

There were no fences between the three properties, but each of them had corrals for small groups of horses or cattle.

In their riding, they saw lots of longhorn cattle. They were as wild as the deer they saw, and there were plenty of those.

As they were riding up to one of the waterholes, Ellen held up her hand and whispered, "Hold it."

She quickly pulled her rifle from its scabbard under her leg. Slowly stepped down from Black Night, handed the reins to Clay, dropped to one knee. None of the men had seen anything so had no idea what she was going to shoot. When the shot exploded, the horses jumped and were hard to control for a few seconds. An eight-point buck burst from the brush and ran about thirty yards then dropped dead.

"There's your supper guys. I've done my part, you all take it from here."

Luke said, "You had the easy part."

The deer was field dressed and tied across the back of Ellen's horse since she was the lightest. She and the deer combined wouldn't weigh as much as Luke. Getting the deer on Black Night, and tied down, was a fight. She didn't like the smell of blood and had never had anything like that on her back.

They continued to ride around the nineteen-hundred acres, admiring it more and more all the time.

When they returned to the house, Clay asked all of them, "What do you think? Is this the place we want?"

Ellen suggested, "How about a show of hands. Who wants to stay here?"

All four hands went up. "Well, I guess there is no question about it."

"Tomorrow, Ellen and I will ride to Clinton, pay the money, and get the title transferred. Unless you all just want to make the ride, you can stay here, or go over and start getting your house straightened up. We'll be leaving right after breakfast. Probably need to spend the night in town. We don't know how long it will take to get the paperwork done and signed.

Willie said, "We've already talked it over. We'll stay here and work on our place. While you are at the land office, ask about any other places that are available. We don't have any money to pay back taxes, but we could homestead a place. In fact, both of us could homestead a place. That would add another twelve hundred and eighty acres. We could still work it all as one place if that is agreeable to you."

Clay said, "That sounds great. We'll check it out."

CHAPTER 18

As the sun was peaking over the horizon, Clay and Ellen were already on the trail to Clinton.

They arrived there right at lunch time, checked into the hotel, then went to the land office. The man behind the counter was glad to see them. "How did it go? You all like the place?"

"Ellen said, "We sure do. We're ready to sign the papers."

I'm glad you got here when you did. There was a fellow in here yesterday. Said he had seen the place and liked what he saw. He was trying to get it for a lot less than what is owed. I didn't like his looks, so I stalled him, hoping you all would come back before he did. If you see him prowling around out there, you better be careful. He looks like he could be a troublemaker. He talks and acts like he's used to getting what he wants."

Clay asked, "What's his name, so we'll know who to be on the lookout for."

"All the name he gave was Smith. If he's part of that Smith family from around Cuero, he could be bad news. The Smith's and the Thompson's have been at each other for several years. I wouldn't be surprised if they don't end up killing each other before long. Both are hot-tempered and looking for trouble."

"Thanks for giving us the heads up. Where do we sign?"

"Right here. I can have the title ready for your signature by tomorrow. Will you be around that long?"

"We will be around as long as it takes."

Ellen asked, "Oh, by the way, are there any other properties available for homesteading in the vicinity? We have two friends who want places close to us."

"Let me check the book."

After looking at several pages, he said, "There is a lot of open land to the north and east of your place. There aren't any maps or plats on any of it, so they'll just mark off six hundred forty acres, and file on it. Then they'll need to show that they've made improvements and live on the place for five years. After that, they get clear title to the land."

"So, just pick a spot and put down roots. Right?" "That's it."

"What time tomorrow should we come by to sign the deed and pick up a copy?"

"Check with me around noon. I should have it by then."

Clay and Ellen went to the hotel dining room, had a lovely meal and went to their room. They were so excited to have gotten the place they wanted; they had a hard time getting to sleep.

Breakfast next morning was interrupted by a big loud mouth man storming into the dining room griping to the man with him, about someone beating him to that place. "I'll find them and put a stop to that. I've had my eye on that place for over two years, and just when I am ready to buy it some come lately thinks he can jump in ahead of me. He's got a rude awakening coming. Nobody does that to me."

Ellen was wide-eyed and pail in the face. She asked Clay in a whisper, "What are we going to do?"

"Well, I don't want to start trouble here. So, let's don't do anything. We'll sign the papers, get our copy of the deed and go home. We'll alert Willie and Luke as to what is going on. Maybe he will let off steam and forget about it. At least we can hope."

They finished breakfast and returned to their room. At noon, Clay and Ellen walked into the land office. The papers were ready, they signed and got a copy. Thanked the man and told him what happened at breakfast. "Yeah, that was him. He came here all ready to sign. When I told him it's already sold, he had a fit. Claimed he had first shot at it because he was in yesterday and said he wanted it. I told him you all had been in three days ago and said you wanted it and came back yesterday with the money, and signed all the papers. He wanted to know who the buyer was; I told him I couldn't give out that information."

"What did he do then?"

"Well, he said it didn't make any difference. He would find out who the scoundrel was and take care of him. Said he would be back to get a new title drawn up in his name."

Ellen was worried, "Clay, this sounds like trouble. Do we want to get mixed up in this?"

Clay said, "We aren't going to start anything, but if he comes around causing trouble, we can handle it. I'm not too worried."

"You may not be, but I am."

"Ok, let's get home as fast as we can so we can warn Willie and Luke."

They hurried to the livery stable, got saddled, and were on the road home in five minutes.

They kept the horses at an easy gallop for the first thirty minutes. Then they alternated between a gallop and a walk every thirty minutes. It took them two hours to reach home. Clay was riding Trouble; Ellen was riding Black Night. The two horses looked identical, except one was a mare, the other a gelding.

It was just past noon when they arrived. Luke and Willie were not there, so they quickly rode to their place. They were just eating lunch when Clay and Ellen came charging into the yard.

Before Clay could reach the front door, it opened with Luke standing there with his pistol pointed right at Clay's stomach.

"Hold your fire; I'm peaceful," Clay blurted out.

That's when Willie stepped around the corner of the house with his gun out. "What's up, Clay?"

"We may be in for trouble," Clay proceeded to tell them what had happened in Clinton.

Willie and Luke thought it would be a good idea to spend the night at Clay and Ellen's place. If there was going to be trouble, that's where it would happen.

Luke and Willie said they would be along as soon as they got saddled. When Ellen and Clay got home, Ellen made a pot of coffee while they waited for Luke and Willie. They all sat around the table drinking and talking until Ellen was falling asleep. She excused herself and went to bed. Luke and Willie said they would sleep in the bunkhouse. If they heard anything strange, they could cover it from two sides.

However, the night passed quietly. They were sitting around the breakfast table, finishing up with coffee, when they heard horses approaching in a rush.

They all grabbed their rifles; Ellen went to a front bedroom window, Luke and Willie went out the back door. Clay went to the front door to welcome their guest. He opened the door but remained inside the house. He was holding the door open with his right hand, and keeping the rifle behind the door, out of sight of the men outside.

Clay said, "Good morning, gents. Out riding early today. What can I do for you?"

The big loud mouth from the diner yesterday was sitting his horse in front of five other rough looking men.

He said, "For starters, you can pack up and get off this place."

Clay laughed, "Now why would we want to do that? We just moved in."

Loudmouth said, "You have until noon to be out of here, or we come back and move you off."

"By whose authority do you make these demands?"

"By my own authority. Just don't be here when we come back at noon."

"And if we are?"

"You heard me. Let's go boys."

They turned their horses and charged out of the yard in a cloud of dust.

When they were gone, Ellen came out of the bedroom with tears in her eyes, "What are we going to do?"

Clay answered, "We will set up a welcoming party for them. Let's walk outside and make some plans. We don't want them to feel slighted when they come back."

Both Clay and Willie had been in the war, so they knew something about defenses and attacks. Clay said, "They will probably come at us from the front in a group like they just did. They'll probably expect us to be in the house. Did any of them see either of you?"

They both said no. "We stayed out of sight, so they don't know how many are here."

"Ok, here is what I suggest. We have about five hours. Let's call it four, to be on the safe side. Let's walk up here to these trees."

They walked about fifty yards, went into the edge of the trees. Clay turned around and looked toward the house. "This looks like a good place. How about we dig a foxhole about here? This side of the house and the entire yard and barn can be covered from here. Now let's walk over to the other side."

They went about the same distance to the other side of the house. There was a pleasant little grove of trees that would prevent anyone from getting behind them and gave them some cover. Again, Clay suggested they dig a foxhole about here. "You will have the same advantage as from the other side. And, they won't even know you are here until you open fire. We will have them in a crossfire. I don't like this any more than anyone else. But if we don't put a stop to it now, we will be fighting them from now on. Do you agree?"

Both men said they did.

"Ok, I will be at the house with Ellen. She will be at the front bedroom window; I will be at the window in the living room. None of us shows ourselves. I will do the talking from behind those thick walls. If they start shooting, be sure to get that big loudmouth first. That will probably take the fight out of them if there are any left."

They returned to the barn and found two shovels. Luke and Willie started digging on both sides of the house. Clay went back inside to help Ellen get ready and tell her what was going on outside.

He laid out all the ammunition they had for the rifles, and pistols, dividing it evenly between all of them. Everyone had enough ammo to fight a war. Which they probably were.

Clay went back outside to check on the digging and lend a hand. He distributed the ammo, gave both men a full canteen of water, and relieved first one, and then the other on the shovels.

By the time the four hours were up, everyone was in position.

The men had all been in a position like this before during the war.

But, Ellen was a nervous wreck.

She said, "I talk big sometimes, but I sure hope I don't have to kill anyone else. That horse thief was bad enough."

Clay reassured her, "This is our home, we are not going to let anyone run us off. We are here to stay, raise our horses and kids, all twelve of them."

"Silly, we already have more than twelve."

"I was referring to kids."

"If that's what you are planning, you can start sleeping in the barn."

Clay said, "We still have some time; I'll take the men a pot of coffee." He divided the coffee into two canteens and took it to Willie and Luke.

As he was returning to the house, he heard them coming. They were charging down the hill toward the house, apparently trying to scare them. Clay hurried into the house and barred both front and back doors. Ellen had raised her window just enough to get the rifle barrel out. Clay did the same in the living room.

The group came charging up to the front porch, sliding their horses to a stop. Big mouth yelled out, "Alright, come on out of there. I told you to be gone. But since you didn't take my warning, we will help you move out."

Clay called out from behind the door, "Who are you that you think you can run us off our place?"

"My name is Jacob Smith; I run this part of Texas."

"Well, Mr. Jacob Smith, let me put it to you like this. You may used to run this part of Texas, but that was before we got here. So, you can mark this area of Texas off your map. You don't run this part anymore. Furthermore, the first man that touches a gun is the second man to die, right after you. You will be the first one with a bullet right between your eyes. Now, I am through talking. If you think you are big enough to back up your big mouth, come on and try."

Smith shouted, "Alright men, let 'em have it!"

They all went for their guns at the same time. Before they could get off a shot, four of them, including Smith, were falling out of their saddle. The two remaining, wheeled their horses, firing shots back over their shoulders as they stormed away.

Willie put some well-placed shots at the horse's heels to hurry them along.

After they had stormed out of sight, Clay cautiously went out to check on the men laying in the front yard. All of them were dead. Smith had a hole dead center between the eyes.

Willie and Luke came up. Luke asked, "What are we going to do with them?"

Willie suggested, "How about we catch up their horses, tie them on, and send them home?"

Clay said, "I like that idea. I'll attach a note to Mr. Smith, telling anyone who sees it, 'This is what happens when a bully attacks a peaceful family.'"

The horses were brought up, and the bodies tied on. The reins were looped over the horn of the saddles. The horses were given a slap on the rump and sent on their way.

For the next three days, the men stayed close to the house, working around the barn and bunkhouse, cleaning and getting everything back in top condition.

On the fourth day, Luke and Willie rode out to check on possible locations for their homestead. They were gone most of the day. When they returned just in time for supper, they were as excited as Clay and Ellen had been. They were telling about what they had seen and where they planned to homestead. They found four water holes that are fed by streams that run into the Guadalupe River. They didn't know if they stayed wet year-round, but since this is late October, and they are still running, one could assume they will supply water all year.

Clay asked, "Are they situated so you can cover all four in your two homesteads?"

Willie said, "We can do that, but they won't join your property, but they'll be close enough that there isn't room for another homestead in between. So, we could control all that area from here to the other side of our homesteads."

"That sounds great, guys. When do you plan to file it?"

Luke said, "We figured it would take us most of two days to get it marked off and staked. Probably be Monday before we can get to town to file. Oh, by the way, we saw a lot of cattle while we were looking around.

None of them have a brand, but they are like the ones we saw on your place, wild as deer. But I bet we could round up a pretty good size herd. Could probably drive it to Indianola, or one of those other towns along the coast, and get some pretty good money for them."

Clay said, "Well, that land has been sitting there all this time, and no one has claimed it, so two more days shouldn't make a difference. But, I like your idea of rounding up those cows. We could use that money to help fix up our places. We will need several more men to help with the roundup and the drive. Those cattle are wild. They've been running lose all their lives; they ain't gonna' take too kindly to being pushed around. When you go to town Monday, ask around, see if you can find three or four good men to help us."

Luke and Willie spent the next two days staking out their homesteads and went into Clinton on Monday to file. While they were there, they went to the local saloon and asked about anyone looking for work. The bartender looked around the room. Only a few men there at that time of the day. He pointed to two young men sitting together, drinking beer. He said, "You might talk to those two. They just came home from fighting in the war and haven't found a job yet."

Willie said, "Give us two more beers, and two more for them."

Luke and Willie walked over with the four beers and said, "You all mind if we join you?" He put the beers in front of the two. They smiled and said, "Heck no, you can join us all day as long as you're buying."

Willie said, "We are looking for a few good men to help us with a roundup and a drive down to the coast. You all interested?"

One of them said, "Let me check my schedule, see if I can work it in." He went through the motions of looking in an appointment book, said, "No, looks like I can fit it in. When do we start?"

Luke and Willie looked at each other and said, "We are ready to start right away. How about the day after tomorrow? By the way, I'm Willie Stanton. This is Luke Wilson."

The two introduced themselves as Leftie Knox and John Williams. Leftie was a tall, slim, redhead with a permanent smile and a jolly personality. He stood around six feet two and weighed about one-eighty-five. John Williams was about five-ten and weighed about the same, with sandy blond hair and blue eyes. Both said they had worked cattle before and were not afraid of the wild longhorns. Both had grown up around here, so were familiar with the area. Luke asked them if they knew the old Locke place, out north of Cuero about ten miles. Both said they did.

Clay asked them both, "Can you be there Wednesday morning? And if you know anyone else looking for work, bring them along. I don't know how long this is going to take; I guess that will be determined by what we find when we start rounding up."

Both men said they would be there.

Tuesday evening, John and Leftie came riding in with two other young men. They introduced them as Gerald and Matt Cordis. Both had grown up in the area and were accustomed to working with the wild longhorns. They had made two trips to Indianola with a herd.

Clay said, "That's just what we need. Someone with some experience."

They stowed their gear in the bunkhouse and came to the house for supper when Ellen yelled, "Come and get it!"

Next morning, they all saddled up and headed to the north side of their property intending to make a sweep south. The Cordis boys suggested going much farther north. "This is all open land. No one owns it; all the cattle have run wild here for years. When all the men went away to war, there was no one to do any branding, so you have large herds here for the taking."

There was a large open meadow on the land between Luke's place and Clay's, so they decided to use that as their holding ground. There was plenty of water and grass for several weeks. By then they would be on their way to the coast.

The first three days, they worked from sunup to sundown. They were bringing in from thirty to forty head each day, but it was brutal, hot, tiring work. They had to change horses at least twice each day.

The new hands were impressed with the horses Clay was supplying. Although most of the horses knew nothing about working cattle, they were learning fast. Even the young horses recognize that a cow with a six-foot spread of horns could be very dangerous and gave them plenty of room. When they encountered a big longhorn bull that showed fight, they rode around him and left him to his own business.

They would come back later and take care of him.

After one week of rounding up some of the wildest cattle in the state, they were satisfied that they had all they could handle on the drive with seven men.

The herd was hard to keep together in the meadow because they were accustomed to coming and going where they pleased, so the men stayed busy day and night. Two men remained on guard at the holding area. The cattle were nervous and on the verge of stampeding. That had the men nervous too because they had all seen or heard what could happen if a herd this size started to run.

They all agreed they had about all they could handle. They started for Indianola first thing the next morning with three-hundred and forty head.

Ellen said she was not staying here alone, and they would need a cook, and someone to watch after them to keep them out of trouble. Clay did not want to leave her here alone either. The men hitched the mules to the wagon, and all their camping gear was loaded, along with a generous supply of food. The sun was just peaking over the eastern horizon when they left the ranch.

Getting the herd moving in the right direction took everyone's help. By the time it was somewhat organized in a strung-out line, the horses were worn out. One at a time they went back to the remuda, which was being handled by Ellen, until they got things going, picked a fresh horse, and returned to the herd.

John Williams took over the horse herd. Ellen tied her horse to the rear of the wagon, climbed to the seat and followed the cloud of dust.

They let the cattle graze as they walked along. They did not push them, just enough to keep them moving. The men were spread out around the herd and had their hands full keeping them from scattering.

Gerald Cordis was riding point since he seemed to know the country better than the others, there were two men on each side and two riding drag. They were all kept busier than a one-legged man in a kicking contest.

The horses were worn out again in just a couple hours. At this rate, they were afraid they didn't have near enough horses to make this drive. But, they had what they had. If they had to stop early, they would just have to stop.

Along about mid-afternoon, they came to a stream with a good flow of water and decided to call it a day. The men and horses were worn out. They let the cattle spread out along the creek but kept a close watch on them and didn't let them stray too far.

Ellen set up her wagon, built a fire, and started cooking supper. The men came in one at a time to get coffee, and eat when supper was ready, then back to the herd. They knew they would have to be on guard all night.

By morning, the men were so tired they were dazed, but they knew they wouldn't get any rest until tonight. Then it wouldn't be much.

Ellen was up early and had breakfast ready before the sun was up. Again, the men took turns coming in to eat and get coffee. Clay helped Ellen get all her gear packed up.

When he returned to the herd and started gently pushing them to get them moving, an old cow with a wide spread of horns took the lead, and all the rest fell in line behind her.

They took a noon break, as much for the horses as the men. Two stayed with the herd, the others came in, got lunch and coffee, and fresh horses, two returned to relieve the two there so they could eat. Each man was allowed about an hour to rest, sleep, or whatever. Most of them went to sleep as soon as they laid down.

CHAPTER 19

They had just gotten the herd moving again when Gerald came galloping back to Clay and told him there was a group of horsemen up ahead coming their way.

Clay told Gerald to stop Ellen back there.

He then rode around the herd telling all the men to bring their rifles and come to the front, spread out along a line there about twenty feet apart. They created a seven-man front. If the men coming wanted to start something, they would be in for a real battle.

By now, the herd has become accustomed to following the old cow up front, and she is used to following the horse in front of her, so none of them seemed to notice there was no one behind them. Clay and his men kept riding so as not to break the rhythm of the herd. They did not want to give them any reason to get excited.

A few minutes later the two groups of riders met. They stopped about twenty feet apart.

Clay said, "Good day, gentlemen. Is there something I can do for you?"

A big, rough looking man stepped his horse forward a couple of steps and asked, "Where do you think you're going with these cattle?"

"We are driving them to Indianola to sell them. Why do you want to know?"

"What makes you think you have the right to sell someone else's cattle?"

"I don't have that right, but as you can see, none of these cattle have a brand on them, so they are not claimed by anyone, and they were on my property, so I am claiming them. Anyone who wants to argue with that better come loaded for bear because no one takes anything of mine from me. By the way, what is your name?"

"I am Westley Thompson. All these cattle are mine, I just haven't gotten around to branding them yet, and you are not taking them out of here."

Thompson was a big burly man with an attitude to match. He was probably three inches taller than Clay and would outweigh him by at least fifty pounds. He gave off the opinion he is used to walking all over other men because of his size.

Clay had his gun on his left hip for a cross draw; his right hand was on the saddle horn just inches from it. All the men spread out like Clay planned it, with their rifles across their saddles.

"Well, Mr. Thompson, seems like I ran into a friend of yours the other day. A Mr. Smith. He tried something like what you are trying. Didn't turn out to be his day."

"So, you are the one who killed Smith."

"Take that any way you want to. But I'll tell you, just like I told him, anything you take from me won't come cheap. Now, unless you have something else on your mind, I'd appreciate it if you all will move out of the way and let us get on with our business."

"I'm not through with you yet. Like I told you, you are not taking those cattle anywhere."

Clay turned his horse a little to the right, so he would have a clear shot if he had to draw his gun. Thompson saw that move and understood what it meant.

"Ok, Thompson, let's settle this right now, between you and me. No point in any of these other men getting involved."

Thompson sat there for a few moments, thinking that over. Here is a situation he has not run into before. Most people take his warnings and back away, afraid to get in a fight. This man apparently was not of that caliber. No one had ever stood up to him before. He couldn't let this happen and lose face in front of his men.

Thompson dismounted, removed his gun belt and hung it on his saddle horn. "Ok, wise guy, if you think you are as big as your talk, come on. Let's see just how bad you are."

Clay stepped down from his horse, removed his gun belt, hung it over the horn of this saddle.

He turned to his men and said, "If any of his men interfere, shoot them."

That's when he heard Ellen say, "Don't worry about them. The first one who makes a move gets it right between the eyes."

Clay looked around to see Ellen, standing there on the ground, with her rifle aimed across her saddle.

Clay just smiled. "Thompson looks like you don't have any better sense than your friend Smith."

Clay hung his hat on the horn of his saddle with his gun.

The two men walked toward each other and started circling, watching for an opening.

Thompson made the first move, coming in with a big roundhouse swing that Clay had no trouble avoiding. He ducked and gave Thompson a fist up to his wrist in his gut. As Thompson bent over, trying to get his breath, Clay hit him three more times in the face, then another in the gut. Thompson went down. But struggled back up and charged, trying to knock Clay off his feet. Just before he reached Clay, Clay's knee came up and busted Thompson's nose. Blood spurted all over his face, and down the front of his shirt.

Thompson staggered back, with a puzzled look on his face. He looked around like he was asking for help but saw all Clay's men and Ellen with rifles pointed at his men. At that point, he knew he had it to do all by himself.

He came in again with his fist in front of his face, weaving and bobbing like he knew what he was doing.

Clay timed Thompson's weaving and bobbing and let loose with a straight left to the nose. Clay had put everything he had into it. Thompson went down and stayed down.

Clay looked around at Thompson's men, told them, "Take your big bad man and get out of my sight. If I see any of you following, or even looking like you want to cause trouble, we will shoot you at first sight. When you threaten our lives and livelihood, I don't play no gentlemen's game. Thompson, can you hear me?" Clay took his canteen from his saddle and poured its contents in Thompson's face. He came up spitting and sputtering, looking around like he didn't know where he was. When his eyes focused and saw Clay standing over him, he tried to jump to his feet. Halfway up, he staggered backward and fell on his butt. He sat there for half a minute, getting his head straight. He looked at Clay again, said, "I'm going to kill you."

Clay walked over to Thompson's horse, took his gun belt, walked back to Thompson, tossed it on the ground in front of him. "There you are, Thompson. Put that on and stand up like a man. You want to kill me, here is your chance."

Clay got his gun belt and gun and strapped it on.

Thompson looked at the gun, then at Clay. A big smile came to his face. He slowly got to his feet, picked up the gun belt, being careful to keep his hand away from the gun, and strapped it on.

They were standing only about ten feet apart. Thompson started backing away to put more distance between them.

Clay said, "What's the matter, Thompson, are you leaving? I thought you wanted to kill me."

Clay walked toward Thompson, keeping the distance at about ten feet. Thompson didn't like that at all. He wanted to get as far away as possible, so he would be harder to hit. He knew if they drew at this distance there was a good chance both would get a bullet.

Clay was watching his eyes; the farther Thompson backed away, the more Clay walked forward keeping the distance the same. Thompson was sweating; Clay could see the fear in his eyes. Clay kept walking, "Come on, tough guy, I thought you wanted to kill me. You can't do it if you keep running away. You're not a tuff guy at all, are you? You've been pretending to be tough so long you have started believing it yourself. First, you showed you couldn't fight; now you are showing yellow, afraid to draw. Either draw or drop that gun and ride out of here. Either way, you are through in this county. Nobody is going to be afraid of you after this story gets around."

Thompson backed into his horse and couldn't go any farther. He knew he was trapped. He made a feeble attempt to draw his gun, but by then, Clay was too close. Just as Thompson's gun cleared its holster, Clay slapped it out of his hand. Then quick as a wink, Clay slapped him across the face with an open hand, then backhanded him with it coming back. Thompson staggered back and fell under his horse.

Clay looked up at Thompson's men who were sitting there with a disgusted look on their faces. One by one they turned their horses and rode away. None of them looked back. Thompson was still laying on his back.

Clay picked up Thompson's gun from where it had fallen; then pulled the rifle from the scabbard on Thompsons saddle, ejected the shells, and returned it to the scabbard, but took the pistol with him.

While all that was going on, the cattle had scattered some. By the time they got them all bunched up again it was time for the noon break. Clay told the men, "Keep your eyes open. I don't expect any trouble from his men, but there is no telling what Thompson may do. I wouldn't be surprised if he tried to back shoot some of us."

Ellen said, "Clay, I just have one question. Where did you learn to fight like that?"

"Well, in the outfit I was in there was a man who grew up in the town where the world heavyweight champion, John G. Heenan, lived. That man loved to work with kids. He taught every boy who wanted to learn to fight. One of those kids was in my outfit. He taught me and a couple of others, just like he was taught. I guess I picked it up pretty good."

After their noon break, they got the herd moving again with Gerald Cordis still riding point. The rest of the men were rotating positions, so no one was eating dust at the rear all the time.

The next day when they passed by Cuero, Ellen and Clay took the wagon into town to replenish their supplies while the men kept the herd moving.

Gerald told them it was roughly seventy to seventy-five miles to Indianola. They figured they could make it in about seven days.

On the third day, they passed by Victoria. Four more days, they were in Indianola crowding the herd of longhorns in the pens at the dock.

Clay looked up the cattle buyer who was buying and shipping to New Orleans. They made a deal for twenty dollars per head. The buyer paid with a draft on the bank in Victoria.

Ellen commented, "I have never seen so much money until I married you."

Clay smiled and remarked, "And that is only one of the benefits of being married to me."

Ellen winked and said, "Yeah, there is one other benefit that isn't bad either."

Clay checked all of them into the hotel for the night; then they went to a restaurant where they ate T-bone steaks and drank lots of coffee followed up with big helpings of peach cobbler.

When Ellen and Clay were back in their room and ready for bed, Ellen asked Clay, "Do you know what birds and animals do when it is nesting season?"

"Yeah, they start building a nest, and laying eggs."

"Well, we have already laid the eggs and built the nest. Now, all we have to do is wait for the egg to hatch."

Clay was speechless. "What are you saying, that we laid an egg? How was that?"

"No, we didn't, I did."

"I'm not following you."

"Clay, we are going to have a baby!"

"What, a baby, how did that happen?"

"Mr. Wade, if you don't know, I'm not going to try to explain it to you."

"But, but, but, when did this happen?"

"Sometime around six weeks ago. Probably on the boat ride from New Orleans. Sure had enough chances."

Clay was still in shock. "A baby." He grabbed Ellen and swung her around the room, "A baby. When?"

"I'm guessing around next April or May." "Wow, a baby."

"Yes, a baby."

"Hey, we have to get home," Clay said nervously. "We have got to buy a lot of baby things. We need a bed, a crib, a spoon. Oh my gosh, a baby."

Ellen laughed and said, "Calm down, Clay. All those things will come in good time. We have almost eight months before he gets here."

"He, it's going to be a boy?"

"I don't know that, but we can hope if that's what you want."

"A little girl would be nice if she is like her mother," Clay said. "Be right back." He ran from the room; Ellen heard him charge into the first room where the men were, "We are having a baby!"

Someone asked, "Now?"

"No silly. Not now."

Ellen heard the men congratulating him on becoming a father. She was still laughing at the way he was acting.

The next morning, Clay insisted Ellen ride in the wagon. He thought riding a horse would be too rough for the baby. She went along with him and rode in the wagon. Clay tied his horse on behind and rode with her.

CHAPTER 20

On the way through Victoria, they stopped at the bank and cashed the draft, so the money could be deposited in their account in Cuero when they got there.

It had taken seven days driving the cattle to get to Indianola; they expected to make it home in four. That meant three nights camping out on the trail. They were not in a big hurry, so they took their time and didn't push the animals.

When they arrived back home, they found everything just as they had left it. Ellen was tired, so she prepared a quick meal, ate and went to bed. The men sat around the table, drinking coffee, and planning their next roundup and cattle drive.

Clay said, "You know, we've heard there are thousands of cattle just running wild in the brush between here and Mexico. What do you all think about continuing to round up everything we can get our hands on and drive it to Indianola, as long as there is a market for them there?" Willie said, "I am all for it, but we need two or three more men, a regular chuck wagon, and a cook. Ellen won't be able to go along next time."

"Yeah," Clay said, "That brings up another problem. We can't leave Ellen here alone. We don't know if we are through with the Smiths and the Thompsons. I'll have to get someone to come and stay with her. Hey, how about Aunt Maddie? Willie, do you think she would come? She would be a big help to Ellen while we're all away working cattle."

"I'll send her a letter and invite her to come live with us," Willie said. "But, she won't be any help if there is trouble with Smith or Thompson, or someone else. We need a couple of men to take care of the places and all the horses we have here."

"Ok, you work on that. Now, do any of you know two to four more men we can get to work with us. Maybe an older man, or an older man and his wife. They could live in the other house where you all are staying. You will be building on your homestead, won't you?"

"Yes, we will," Willie said. "But all that's going to take a lot of time, building two houses, barns, fences, furniture."

"Yeah," Clay agreed, "I guess we should wait until next spring to do another roundup and drive."

"We made enough on this drive to pay for the material to build a house and barn," Said Luke. "I'm pretty good with a hammer, so get me the material, I can build a house."

"If Aunt Maddie agrees to come, we'll have to work out how we are going to get her here. But we have plenty of time," Clay added.

The meeting broke up; the men went to the bunkhouse, Clay went to bed with Ellen.

It took them a long time to get to sleep that night. They were lying there holding each other, talking about everything that had happened since he walked out of the hospital in Richmond just six months ago, the baby coming in the spring, the ranch to build, cattle to brand, the roundup next season and drive to market somewhere.

Suddenly, the window beside the bed shattered as gunfire rocked the night.

Clay yelled, "Get down, on the floor. Stay there!"

He rolled onto the floor, grabbing for his clothes, then his gun belt and gun. He had his boots in hand as he ran for the front door. Just as he reached it, a bullet came through leaving a large splintered hole.

He ducked to the side of the front window and peeked out. At first glance, he saw nothing. Then there was a flash from the hill in front and another from the north side. That told him there are at least two shooters. He heard shots from the bunkhouse. Willie and Luke are in on it too.

Probably whoever is attacking them doesn't know about Willie and Luke. Since they have their own places, they wouldn't be expected to be in the bunkhouse here.

Clay ran back to Ellen, who was still on the floor by the bed. "Are you ok? You didn't get hit, did you?"

"No, I'm ok."

"Thank you, Lord. You scared me, when I said stay there, I never expected you to do it."

"What are you going to do?"

"I'm getting my rifle and going out there after them. I can't stay pinned down in here. I can do more good out there. When I go out, you bar the doors and stay away from the windows. No matter what happens, you stay in here. We have to know where everyone is all the time, so we don't shoot each other. Got it?"

"Yes, but you be careful." She threw her arms around his neck and gave him a kiss and hug. "Go do what you have to do."

Clay went to the back door and surveyed the area visible from the kitchen. After seeing no gun flashes, he assumed all the shooting was coming from the front of the house. Willie or Luke was still shooting every time they saw a gun flash.

He opened the door a crack and called out, "Willie, Luke, I'm coming out, don't shoot me."

"Come on."

Clay ran to the bunkhouse and informed them of what he had planned. They told him where they saw the gun flashes. It looked like only two shooters, one in front, one on the north side.

When he left the bunkhouse, he stayed against the wall in the shadow. Keeping the bunkhouse between himself and where he thought the shooters were, he moved into the trees and around toward the front of the house. If he could get this one in front out of action, they would only have one to deal with. Clay hoped to get between the shooter and his horse. If he made a break for it, he would run right at Clay. At least, that was the plan.

Clay could see and hear the man firing a rifle about thirty yards in front of him as he continued to close in.

He heard a low whistle, like a signal. There was no more shooting, but Clay heard the men running. A minute or so later, horses could be heard leaving the area.

Taking a guess where they might be, Clay emptied his rifle as fast as he could in their direction. He heard a grunt and thud, like a body falling. Clay knew better than to go running up on a wounded man in the dark, so he moved slowly and quietly in that direction. He had only gone a few yards until he heard talking. It sounded like one man was trying to get another on his horse.

Clay tried to get to them before they got away, but he was too far away and couldn't move fast in the dark. By the time he got there, they were gone.

He knew he wouldn't have any trouble finding this spot tomorrow in the light of day, so, he returned to the house. Before he got within sight, he called out. "I'm coming in. Don't shoot. It's all over."

Ellen threw the door open and rushed out to grab him and give him one of her patented bear hugs.

"Are you ok?"

"Yeah, I'm fine."

Willie and Luke came up and asked him, "Did you see anyone?"

"No, but I shot one of them as they were riding away. I heard him fall off his horse. It sounded like the other one was trying to get him back on, but they rode away before I could get there."

Willie said, "Looks like we'll have some tracking to do in the morning."

"Well, I will," Clay said. "I would like for both of you to stay here. I don't want to leave the place, and Ellen unprotected."

"Ok, Luke or I will be up on the hill where we can see for a mile or more. If anything comes this way, we will be ready."

Clay suggested, "I think I would have three horses saddled if you see more coming than you think you can handle, get out of here. No one's life is worth anything we have here."

"We'll do that, but you be careful. This guy has shown he is not above bushwhacking you in the back."

Clay said, "I just had a better idea. It's too late to get any more sleep, so, I'm going to ride into Cuero and see if anyone has shown up at the doctor's office within the last few minutes. I might even catch up with them on the road. If they don't show up in Cuero, I'll ride over to Clinton and check the doctor there. I know if that guy was hit hard enough to knock him off his horse, he's going to need a doctor. Ellen, can you fix me a snack and coffee while I saddle Smokey?"

"Sure, it'll be ready in a few minutes."

Clay went to the barn and saddled his horse, led him to the back porch and tied him to the railing. When he went to the kitchen, Ellen had coffee, ham, and eggs waiting at the table.

She pulled out a chair and sat beside him as he ate. Clay could tell she was nervous. She kept wringing her hands and looking out the window.

Clay asked, "What are you worried about?"

"Clay, I am scared to death something is going to happen to you." Tears were running down her cheeks. "All this fighting and killing is not my idea of a happy life. I didn't bargain for this. I just want it to stop. I am ready to pack up and go somewhere else where we don't have to be on our guard twenty-four hours a day. It's just not worth it; I can't sleep, I can't eat for fear of a bullet coming through a window and hitting one of us."

"Can you give me one more day? I'm going to put a stop to it today. I know who's behind it, and I know where to find him. When I come back today, it'll all be over; then we can get on with our life. Just hold on one more day, ok?"

"I'll try, but it won't be easy with you out there and me not knowing where you are, if you are hurt, or if you are even still alive."

"Would you feel safer if you went into town and stayed at the hotel until I can wrap this up?"

"It's not me I'm worried about."

"Look, Honey, I went through four years of some of the worst fighting in the world and came away with a little scratch on my side. The Thompsons and the Smiths have attacked us here five or six times. I know we have been lucky so far, but a lot of that luck is because we know what to do in these situations. I am almost positive Westley Thompson is the one responsible for all our trouble. If I find he is, I plan to take him out of circulation permanently, no matter what it takes. I just need one more day. Ok?"

"I think I can hold out one more day. But, you promise me you are not going to get killed. Do It!"

"I promise I won't get killed."

Clay stood up took Ellen in his arms, held her for a long time, kissed her, and walked out to his horse. Willie and Luke were waiting for him. Both wished him good luck, shook his hand, and watched him ride away. Smokey was the happiest when Clay let him have his head and set his own pace. He set the pace at a fast gallop for the first two miles; then he settled down to a smooth, ground covering gallop until they were almost to Cuero. Clay pulled him down to a trot to let him cool off before they rode down the main street.

The sun was just peaking over the horizon when Clay stopped Smokey in front of the doctor's office. He didn't see any other horses tied nearby, but that didn't put him at ease. He was as tense as he had ever been.

The doctor opened the door at Clay's knock and informed him no one had been there with a gunshot wound. Clay thanked him, mounted Smokey and headed to Clinton.

Clay arrived in Clinton an hour later.

The doctor's wife opened the door when Clay knocked. She didn't invite him in, just looked at him and asked, "What can I do for you?"

She was holding the door open only about four inches, just enough for her to see and talk, but not enough for Clay to see inside.

He asked, "Is the doctor in?"

"Yes, but he's busy now, can you come back later?" Something told Clay everything was not right here.

Clay stepped back off the porch, said, "Thank you, Ma'am. I'll come back later."

She slowly closed the door. Clay walked back to his horse, mounted and went to the sheriff's office.

Sheriff Helm was just pouring himself a cup of coffee when Clay walked in.

Clay introduced himself, told the sheriff he had just bought the old Locke place out north of town.

"What can I do for you, Clay?"

"A couple of men attacked us again early this morning. None of our group was hurt, but I wounded one of the attackers. I think he's at the doctor's office right now. I just came from there, and the doc's wife was acting strangely. She didn't invite me in, said the doctor was busy, could I come back later. Didn't ask what I needed or anything. Very strange."

"Yeah, that doesn't sound like her at all. Did you see anyone else around? Any horses, or anything else that looked out of place?"

"No, I didn't want to look like I suspected anything, so I came straight here."

The sheriff said, "I think one of us needs to get where we can see the back door; the other can watch the front door."

"You know this town better than I do. I'll take the front door. What's across the street from the doctor's office?"

"There's a saddle shop a couple of doors down."

"Is there a back door?"

"Yeah, there's a vacant lot, you can tie your horse right at their back door."

"Then we wait to see who comes out?"

"That's the plan. Pretty elaborate, huh?" said the sheriff.

"Yeah, don't know how you come up with all these crazy plots."

CHAPTER 21

Clay led his horse down the street in the opposite direction of the doctor's office until he came to an alley that cut through to the next street. He mounted and rode to the vacant lot, saw the saddle shop, tied Smokey at the back door and went in.

The saddle maker looked up when Clay walked in, asked, "What can I do for you?"

"I'm Clay Wade, I don't mean to disturb you, but the sheriff and I are on a little mission. I just need to watch out your front window for a little while."

"Why, what's going on?"

"The doctor and his wife may be in a little trouble. We are going to let it play out and see what happens."

"You all are going to sit around and let them get hurt or killed?"

"No, it's not that serious. We think there are two men in there; one is getting treated for a gunshot wound, and don't want to be seen. We are waiting for them to leave so we can follow them. If it works out that way, no one gets hurt. That's the best that can happen. The worst thing is we go charging in there, and everyone gets shot, including the doctor and his wife."

"I see your point. There's hot coffee over there, help yourself." "Thanks, don't mind if I do."

Sheriff Helm crossed over to the block behind the doctor's office where he had a friend living. From the friend's back door, he could see the back door of the doctor's office. The two sat there visiting like nothing was happening. Thirty minutes later, the back door opened, and two men came out. One heavily bandaged about his shoulder and chest; the second was supporting him until he got him on a horse.

The sheriff watched but didn't think the wounded man was going to stay up there. He didn't recognize the wounded man, but he did know Westley Thompson as the one helping him.

When they rode out of sight, Sheriff Helm walked to the doctor's back door and went in without knocking.

Both Doctor McDonald and wife were surprised to see him. She asked, "How did you know?"

"Clay Wade told me. He said you were acting strange when he came to the door. Those men attacked his place again early this morning. Clay got a lucky shot as they were running away. He figured one of them was going to need a doctor, so he came here first. When he suspected foul play here, he came and got me. We have been watching for the last half hour or so."

Sheriff Helm stepped out the front door and signaled to Clay. Clay thanked the saddle maker for the coffee and walked across the street. When Clay walked in, the sheriff had just asked the doctor, "What went on here?"

"I was just getting out of bed when there was this banging on the back door. I told them to hold their horses; I'm coming. When I opened the door, this Thompson barged in dragging this other guy with blood all over him. I told him to put him on that table. A few minutes later, there was a knock on the front door. Thompson ordered us not to answer it. I told him, 'I am a doctor, I have to answer it.' He didn't like it but said open it but tell whoever it is to come back later. That's what my wife did."

Sheriff asked, "How bad is that man hurt?"

"He's hurt bad, but he will live if he doesn't get an infection and if the bleeding doesn't start up again. He's lost a lot of blood, but, if he gets the care he needs he can make it."

"Did either of them say anything about what happened, who shot him, or how it happened?" Sheriff Helm asked.

"The wounded man, said his name is Will Cothran, was cussing Thompson, said, "I told you that was a fool idea. Every time we've attacked that place we get shot to pieces."

"Thompson told him to shut up, or he would shut him up."

"When I got him patched up, I told him he needed to stay here two or three days and let me take care of him. Thompson said he was taking him with him now, and if anyone came around asking questions, we are to keep our mouth shut."

Sheriff Helm looked at Clay, "You have any questions?"

"No, I been standing right here, and I didn't hear the doctor, or his wife utter a word. The two most close-mouthed people I ever met. Can't get a word out of them."

"Yeah, I might have to lock her up until he talks. You folks have a nice day."

Clay and Sheriff Helm left the doctor and his wife and went to get their horses.

Clay said, "I'll meet you out back."

It didn't take but a minute to pick up the tracks they wanted. They were the freshest ones on the trail heading north out of Clinton. They could tell they were moving at a walk, so the sheriff and Clay increased the pace to a slow gallop.

A half mile out of town the trail left the road and went in a northeasterly direction across the open country. "This is the direction of the Thompson ranch," the sheriff pointed.

Clay asked, "How far is it?"

"About seven or eight miles."

"Is all the terrain open? Like this?"

"Yeah, rolling hills with groves of trees scattered here and there."

"So, we should be able to see them long before we catch them. Right, Sheriff?"

"Unless they take a notion of laying up in one of those groves."

"In which case, they could see us long before we could see them," added Clay.

"You are pretty smart for a boy from Tennessee."

"Heck, Sheriff, I feel like a native. I've been here going on two months; been shot at so many times, I'm getting to like the smell and taste of lead and gun smoke."

A few minutes later, "Sheriff, you notice anything about their trail?"

"Now that you mention it looks like they turned, so they go into that grove of trees up there."

The dew was still on the grass, so the trail showed up good.

"What do you think about us not making the turn and go on to the left of it? We could circle and pick up the trail on the other side if they came out. If we don't find the trail over there, we'll know they stopped and are still in there. Might save us from riding into an ambush."

"I like that part about not riding into an ambush."

They didn't turn when the tracks turned, just kept galloping in a straight line which would take them to the north of the grove of trees.

When they had gone approximately a mile and were out of sight of anyone in the grove where the trail led, they swung to the east. That put another hill between them and where they thought Thompson might be.

Clay and Sheriff Helm slowed their horses to a trot, so they wouldn't kick up a dust cloud that could be seen for a mile or more. When they got in the area where the trail should be, if Thompson didn't stop, they slowed to a walk. After riding farther than they thought they needed to, they still didn't find the trail.

"Sheriff, looks like we created a problem for ourselves."

"It sure does. We know they are back there in one of those groves, but we don't know which one, and I'm not anxious to ride in there and let him take a shot at me to find out."

"Ah, Sheriff, where is your adventurous spirit?"

"I left it at home today. But, if you want to ride in there, I'll wait here for you."

"I think we should get out of sight and wait for them to show up. How about on top of that hill in that grove. We can see them coming a long way off."

"Sounds like a workable plan."

"How far do you figure it is to the Thompson spread?"

"Probably another three miles, or thereabout. Couple more hills between here and there."

They reach the top of the next hill and found a secluded place behind some underbrush where they tied the horses. They each found a tree to lean back against where they could see the area behind them and wait.

"I sure wish we could have a fire and coffee."

"Sheriff, you have spoiled yourself sitting around the office, drinking coffee, getting lazy. Even your horse is glad to get out and work a little."
"You keep interfering with my daily routine - I'm going to find a reason to arrest you."

"Now, Sheriff, where would you be if I wasn't around?"

"In my office drinking coffee."

"Oh, yeah."

After almost an hour, they saw movement in the grove across the way. Two riders came into view, one supporting the other.

Clay said, "I'll get the horses ready."

It took about ten minutes for the riders to reach the grove where Sheriff Helm and Clay Wade waited. Their horses were hidden farther back in the underbrush. Clay and the Sheriff were hiding behind trees where Thompson would have to ride between them if he kept to his same course.

Just before Thompson entered the grove, either Clay's or Sheriff Helm's horse whinnied, Thompson's horse answered, Thompson dropped the lead rope on the other horse, put the spurs to his, cut to his left, and was gone. Clay made a break for his horse, when he raced back by Sheriff Helm, he shouted, "I want Thompson!"

CHAPTER 22

Clay was thankful he was riding Smokey. He didn't think there was another horse in the territory that could outrun him. If there was, Smokey could outlast him.

From the direction Thompson was headed, Clay figured he was going home, and he had to catch him before he got there and forted up.

He gave Smokey his head and let him run. He was enjoying it and gave it all he had. He settled into a smooth gate that Clay thought he could keep up as long as necessary. He knew Thompson's horse would run out of steam soon, so he didn't push Smokey more than needed.

When Clay came around the end of the grove that had been blocking his view, Clay figured he was maybe a half mile behind.

He could see Thompson whipping his horse with a quirt to get more speed. Clay leaned forward and talked to Smokey, stroking his neck. He felt another surge of power, and longer strides as Smokey got the message. Another quarter mile and Clay could see they were gaining.

Thompson looked back and saw Clay gaining and laid the whip to his horse again, but nothing happened. He was already doing all he could.

As Clay kept gaining, Thompson kept looking back and saw he was losing the race. Desperation kicked in.

With one mile before they reached the Thompson headquarters, there was a small creek at the bottom of the hill. When Thompson's horse attempted to jump it, he didn't have the strength necessary. When he landed on the far bank, his front legs collapsed, and he took a nosedive into the ground. Thompson flew in the air and landed on his head. Clay pulled Smokey to a stop with his revolver in his hand. Thompson wasn't moving, and his head and neck was twisted at an odd angle. Clay stepped down from Smokey and approached with caution but didn't expect to see any movement from the way Thompson was lying.

After checking for a pulse, and not finding any, Clay returned to his horse and rode to the Thompson headquarters, which he could see in the distance. When he rode slowly up to the front of the house, a young man came out onto the porch.

Clay introduced himself.

The young man introduced himself as Sam Thompson and said,

"Clay Wade, yes, I know who you are. This is a surprise. I never expected to see you here."

"I wouldn't be here now except that your dad and another man attacked my place again this morning."

"Clay, I've never been part of the problem. That was Dad's business.

I never took a hand in it."

"I regret I am the one who has to tell you, but your dad is dead. His horse threw him and broke his neck."

"Where did this happen?"

"At that little creek about a mile back. His horse tried to jump it and didn't make it.

"Thanks, Clay, I'll take it from here. I won't be causing you any trouble."

Clay thanked Sam, turned his horse and rode back to where he had last seen the sheriff. He wasn't there, so he assumed he had taken the wounded man back to town, and to the doctor, and then to jail. He followed the tracks until he came to the trail leading to the BAR W.

He needed to get home and let Ellen know everything was settled.

He could talk to the sheriff later.

When he rode into the yard at home, Ellen came running to meet him. He slid to the ground just in time to catch her as she jumped into his arms.

Luke came to take care of Smokey and led him away to the barn. Ellen and Clay went inside where she had coffee and cookies waiting.

"I want to hear what happened, Clay."

CHAPTER 23

The leaves are turning red and gold, the days are getting cooler, the nights colder. The whitetail bucks are parading around with their big racks of horns trying to attract the does. The geese can be seen and heard flying south every day indicating there is colder weather on the way. There is frost on the grass almost every morning.

It has been relatively quiet the last several weeks and things are shaping up around the BAR W ranch. So quiet in fact, that the men had let their guard down and were carrying on their daily work in a more relaxed atmosphere. Clay, Willie, and Luke have all registered brands at the county seat in Clinton. Luke Wilson registered a brand in his name as the LW. Willie Stanton registered his as the WS, Clay registered his as the BAR W.

The new year kicked in with a hard freeze dropping the temperature into the mid-teens. There was no snow, just ice. The ponds were frozen over for three days straight. The men worked at keeping the horses' water troughs clear of ice and the wood boxes by the stoves and fireplace full of wood. The Longhorns were left to fend for themselves, after all, the ice wasn't that thick, and they have been doing it all their lives. Wouldn't want to spoil them now.

Ellen was getting bigger every day. When she saw the doctor in Cuero he told her what she already suspected. The baby should get here around the middle of April. About three and a half months to go, and she was feeling fine, except she got tired quicker than she did before she got pregnant.

Luke Wilson and Willie Stanton have completed their new houses on their homesteads but are still waiting for furniture that has been ordered from San Antonio. Luke's barn was almost finished, but they haven't started on Willie's yet. They were still spending most nights at the Wade ranch, especially when it got as cold as it has been the last few days. One day each week was spent cutting firewood and stacking it close to the houses to be convenient when needed. But when the temperature was in the twenties and lower, everyone sat around the fireplace or the stove burning that firewood.

The cold spell lasted six days. Over the next three days it warmed up into the sixties again and it felt almost like summer. That is one of the advantages of living in south Texas, the winters are usually mild and short.

Luke and Willie were putting the finishing touches on Luke's barn when suddenly, out of nowhere, a bullet slammed into Luke as he was nailing down a shingle on the roof. He rolled off the roof and landed on the ground next to the wall of the barn.

Willie was inside the barn building stalls and feed bins. He heard the shot and saw Luke fall from the roof. He ran to him, saw he wasn't hurt too bad and dragged him inside the barn.

"Luke are you ok?"

"Sure, I do this all the time. Nothing new." Said Luke, grimacing in pain.

"Let me check that." Willie opened Luke's shirt to examine the wound. "Doesn't look too bad, just caught the top of the shoulder. Tore some muscle, but not life threating. Let me wrap that up until we can do a better job."

Clay and Ellen were riding toward Luke's place to help with the barn when they heard the shot. Although she was getting big with child, she still liked to ride Black Night with Clay when he was going out.

Clay told Ellen, "Stay here."

He put the spurs to his horse while he was pulling his Spencer from the scabbard. When he reached to top of the hill overlooking Luke's place, he pulled up behind a mesquite bush to look things over before he went rushing in and got himself shot. At first, he didn't see anything, but then there was another shot and he saw the puff of blue smoke at the top of the hill to the south. So, he knew where the shooter was, but he didn't know what he was shooting at.

To be on the safe side, he waited until he saw movement at the barn. Willie came to the corner of the barn with a rifle in his hands and peeked around. Another shot came from the hill. Willie ducked back behind the wall. That was all Clay needed to see to know what was going on.

He took note of where the shooter was and circled around to get behind him. He went back down the hill, turned to his left and galloped toward the shooter. When he figured he was directly behind him, but far enough back to not be heard, he tied his horse, took his rifle and began moving as silently as possible up the hill where he thought the shooter was. He had only gone a short distance when he came upon a horse that he didn't recognize tied to a tree. Assuming this was the shooter's horse, he removed the saddle and took it about a hundred feet away and hid it behind a large bush. Returning to the horse, he tied the reins to the tree in a hard knot. It was going to take a while to work that knot loose. This was all just in case the shooter should get by him and get back to his horse. He could still hear shooting coming from the top of the hill, so he continued in that direction, keeping as quiet as possible. After a few more minutes, he saw the shooter standing behind a large pecan tree, using it as a rest for his rifle. He was only paying attention to what he was shooting at and didn't hear Clay coming up behind him.

When Clay was twenty feet from him, the shooter raised his rifle for another shot. That's when Clay cocked the hammer back on his rifle and said, "Put the rifle down and turn around slowly. One wrong move and I put a bullet in your mangy hide."

The man stiffened like someone had poked him with a hot iron. He started to whirl around with the rifle still in his hand when Clay put a bullet in the tree right by his face. When the splinters and chips from the tree hit him in the face, the rifle was dropped like it was red hot. His hands went up and he was standing there with a horrible frightened look on his face.

As Clay was walking toward the shooter with his gun pointed at his gut, he asked him, "Who are you, and why are you shooting at those men down there?"

"That's none of your business, I'm not telling you anything."

Clay just smiled and said, "Don't matter to me. I won't have to make a marker for your grave if I don't know what to put on it. But I would think you would want your mother to know what happened to you and where you are buried. Don't you think so?"

The man looked like he was in his late teens or early twenties, maybe five feet ten inches with a slim build, long shaggy dirty blond hair down over his shirt collar.

Clay asked him, "Who sent you here to do this?"

"Nobody sends me anywhere."

"I am afraid you are about to learn a new lesson, fellow. I am going to tell you what to do, and if you don't do it when I tell you to, I am going to put you in so much pain you will wish you were still at home in your baby diapers. Now, start walking down the hill. Move."

The man just stood there until Clay slammed the butt of his rifle in the man's stomach. The shooter went down, holding his gut and groaning. He rolled around on the ground until Clay booted him in the ribs,

"Get up and start walking."

"I can't, you must have broken something."

"Well, If I didn't that time, I will next time. Want me to try again?"
"If you didn't have that rifle I would tear you apart with my bare hands."

Clay laughed out loud, "You couldn't tear me apart if you had all your friends to help you. Now, get up and start moving."

The shooter struggled to his feet, bent over and holding his stomach. Clay gave him a shove, "Get moving." When they came out into the open, Clay waived his hat, so Willie and Luke wouldn't shoot him. They saw them and stepped out from behind the barn.

As they got closer, Ellen came over the hill and walked her horse down to meet them at the barn.

Luke and Willie wanted to know, "What have you got there? Smells like a skunk."

"Yeah, acts like it too. He's a real stinker."

"Who is he?" asked Luke.

"Don't know. Won't give his name. So, I guess we will just bury him up there on the hill with the others. Maybe if someone misses him they will come asking about him and we can tell them where he's buried."

Ellen stepped up and asked Clay, "Why don't you do him like you did those others we had to kill. Tie him on his horse and send him home with a note?"

Luke said, "I like that idea, but who gets the pleasure of killing this piece of scum?"

Willie stepped up, "I think it's my turn. You did the last one."

The shooter had turned white, his knees were shaking so he could hardly stand. "Wait a minute, you can't kill me just like that. Just because I put a few bullets in your barn."

"And one in Luke. You were trying to kill him, Why?" Clay asked. "My brother said to run all of you off or kill you."

Clay asked, "And just who is your brother that goes around ordering people killed?"

"He's Dan Thompson, he took over when Dad was killed. What he says goes. When he hears about what you've done to me, he'll come over here and wipe all of you out."

All of them, Luke, Willie, Ellen, and Clay all started laughing.

That really infuriated young Thompson. He obviously was used to people quivering in fright at the mention of the Thompson name.

Willie told him, "Apparently you haven't heard about the meeting between your dad and Clay Wade here."

"You've met my dad?"

"Yes, I have," Clay said. "I am sure he never forgot that meeting either. You see, he and a few of his men tried to run us off a few weeks back."

"What happened?"

"Who wants to tell our young friend here what happened?"

Ellen said, "I'll tell him, but he won't like it. He seems to think his daddy was such an important man in these parts. Well, here is what happened. Your daddy challenged Clay here to a fist fight."

Young Thompson was smiling, knowing what the outcome of that fight would be.

Ellen continued, "Your big important daddy didn't get in one punch. Clay beat the stuffing out of him and sent him packing with his tail between his legs."

Thompson yelled, "NO, you couldn't!"

Clay asked, "When was the last time you saw your dad?"

"I saw him the day before he was killed, why?"

"I guess he had time to heal, it has been over a month since that happened. Had he been home all that time?"

"No, he was away on a business trip."

Ellen laughed, "Yeah, I'll bet he was. He crawled into a hole while his wounds healed."

Clay asked, "What is your name?"

"I am Charlie Thompson."

"How old are you Charlie?"

"I am nineteen, why?"

Clay said, "I don't know, I think I would feel bad about killing a kid. I guess I'll have to take you to Clinton and turn you over to the sheriff. Let them try you for attempted murder."

"That will never happen, Dan will have me out of there in five minutes."

"That may happen, but if any of us see you around here after today, you will be shot on sight. Do you understand that?"

"You sure talk big, standing there holding that rifle."

"You ask any of the men who were with your dad the day I whipped his behind. Get them to tell you if I can back up my talk. Willie, how about saddling Luke's horse, he can ride in with me and see the doctor while we are there. While you are doing that, I will get his and my horse from up on the hill. Luke, you keep a gun on him. If he tries to run, shoot him."

"It will be my pleasure, I hope he does."

It took Clay about twenty minutes to get both horses and return. Luke's horse was saddled, Thompson was tied to the horn of his saddle, and a lead rope was attached to the horn of Clay's saddle.

When they were ready to ride out, Ellen asked if she could ride along, saying she needed to pick up some things in town.

Clay said, "Sure, be glad to have you along."

The ten-mile ride to Clinton took about two and a half hours. When they arrived, Clay took Thompson to the sheriff's office while Ellen and Luke went to the doctor's office to get Luke patched up.

At the sheriff's office, Clay pushed Charlie in ahead of him with his hands still tied, met sheriff Jack Helm, "Morning Sheriff."

"Good morning, Clay, what have you got here?"

"Sheriff, this young man says he was told by his big brother Dan, to run us off or kill us. He tried to do that this morning."

"Yeah, I know this young man. He thinks he can run roughshod over everybody because his daddy has been doing it for years. I've told him and his daddy, Charlie is going to end up in prison, or dead, if he keeps this up, but they think they are bigger than the law."

"I'm filing charges of attempted murder against him. He wounded one of my neighbors in his shooting spree."

"Where is this neighbor now?"

"At the doctor's office getting the hole patched up. The only reason he is still alive is that this piece of trash can't shoot worth a darn."

"Ok, Mr. Wade, fill out this report telling what, where and when it happened, so the judge will know what he's being tried for. Come on Charlie, got a room all ready for you."

Just as Clay was completing the form, Luke and Ellen came in. Luke's shoulder was bandaged, and his arm was in a sling.

The sheriff asked, "Is this the victim?" "Yep, I'm Luke Wilson, Sheriff."

"Ok, Luke, I'm Sheriff Jack Helm, fill out this form telling the judge exactly what happened, where and when."

When all the forms were completed, Clay asked when the trial would be. He was told, "The Judge is making his rounds of all the county seats and is due here a week from Thursday. You and any witnesses will need to be here to testify."

"We will be here."

They left the sheriff's office and went to the café for lunch.

CHAPTER 24

Clay, Ellen, and Luke were having lunch when Ellen noticed Clay was not with them. He was there at the table, but his mind was somewhere else.

"Clay, where are you?"

"Oh, I was just thinking about all that has happened in the last six to eight months and wondering if the move here was such a good idea."

Ellen asked, "What do you mean, are you having doubts about coming to Texas?"

"I'm just thinking about all the trouble we have had so far and wondering if it will ever end. I'm worried about you being here in the middle of it. I don't want you to get hurt."

Ellen reached over and took hold of his hand. "When I married you, I accepted everything that came with you. The good and the bad. I don't think we have done so badly so far. We have a baby on the way, a beautiful home, lots of land with cattle on it, two good neighbors, what more could we ask for?"

"The opportunity to live our lives in peace and quiet, raise our children without fear of someone hurting them. Is that asking too much?"

Luke said, "Clay, don't worry so much. We can handle this like we did that trouble in Tennessee. We just stick together and watch each other's back. It's worked pretty well so far."

"Maybe you are right. I guess we don't have a choice now. We are committed. We have too much invested to back out now."

They finished eating, paid their bill, left and mounted their horses.

As they were riding out of town, they met five men riding into town.

Ellen recognized them first, "Oh, no. That one in front looks like a Thompson."

Clay, Luke, and Ellen instantly removed the thong from the hammer on their pistols. Clay and Ellen were wearing theirs on the left hip for a cross draw.

They continued riding toward Thompson with their right hands resting on their saddle horns just inches from their guns. They moved to the right side of the road and kept riding. When the two groups came together, Clay tipped his hat and kept riding.

Thompson looked like he wanted to start trouble but didn't know these people.

After passing Thompson and his men, Clay pulled his horse up and turned him around facing Thompson.

Clay called out, "Hey Thompson."

Thompson stopped his horse but didn't turn around.

"You probably haven't heard yet, but your brother, Charlie, is in jail, charged with attempted murder. Said he did it on your orders. Is that true?"

Thompson turned his horse to face Clay.

What he saw was Luke and Ellen sitting their horses with revolvers pointed at his men. Clay was sitting his horse just as he had been, with his right hand on the horn of his saddle.

Thompson just sat there with that killer look in his eyes.

After what seemed like a long time, but was only a few seconds, Thompson and his men continued toward town without saying one word.

That night at home, around the dining table, all four of them were eating and talking when Clay came up with a suggestion.

"How about this, since we can't make another gather and drive until spring, why don't we spend our time this winter branding all the young stuff we can round up. Get our brand on everything we can before someone else does."

Willie said, "That sounds like a great idea to me. If we don't someone else will. They could come in here and drive everything off and we won't have a leg to stand on."

"I agree," said Luke.

"Ok, the first thing we need to do is build a holding pen. There aren't enough of us to try to do this out in the open range. We can build it about in the middle of our three properties. If we can get those two brothers that helped us on the drive, what were their names?"

Ellen said, "Cordis, Gerald and Matt Cordis."

"Yeah, that's the ones. Luke, you and Willie found them in Cuero last time. Do you think you can find them again?"

Luke said, "Sure, they told us where they live. I think I can find them if they are still around. Want me to ride in and get them?"

"Do you feel like doing it? How does the shoulder feel?"

"If I don't move it, it doesn't hurt much. It may be a lot sorer tomorrow."

"That's what I'm afraid of." Clay said. "I think we need to wait a day or two to bring them out. We need to locate the trees and brush we can use to build the fences. Then when they get here we'll be ready to go to work. Maybe we need to get the other two men also, Leftie Knox and John Williams, since this is going to be a lot of hard work."

"So, what do you say, tomorrow we scout around and locate the timber? We can use the mules to drag it down to where we want it. When you all go to town, take the wagon and get more supplies.

"Also, scout around to see if you can find a cook."

After a little more discussion, they all agreed it was bedtime. Luke and Willie said goodnight and went to the bunkhouse, Clay and Ellen went to their bedroom.

As Ellen and Clay were lying in bed cuddling, Clay suddenly jumped and said, "What was that?"

Ellen broke out in laughter, "That was your son kicking you."

"You got to be kidding."

"No, put your hand right here."

Clay put his hand on Ellen's stomach. After a few seconds, he felt it again. His face lit up with a big smile. "That has got to be a boy, with a kick like that."

Ellen said, laughing, "You might be surprised how hard a girl can kick."

CHAPTER 25

All the next day, the three men scouted the area to find the best material for the fence. They knew to be able to hold the wild longhorns, it would have to be high enough and strong enough that they couldn't go over or through it. They located what they considered the best place, about a mile from where the holding pen was to be built. There was a large grove of young post oak and elm that would do nicely. It would be hard, but they could make it work.

The next morning at breakfast, Clay asked Luke, "How is the shoulder? Can you make it to Cuero and back without it hurting too much?"

"Sore as the devil, but if I don't get in a fight or wrestling match, I'll make it ok."

"I think it will be safer, and smarter if Willie goes with you. You can cover each other's back in case there's trouble. That ok with you, Willie?"
"Sure, I'll get my horse and tie him behind the wagon. Might come in handy if we run into trouble."

"Sounds like a good idea."

Ellen said, "Here, take this with you. It is something to eat along the way."

Clay helped hitch two of the mules to the wagon and saw them on their way.

When they were out of sight, Clay saddled Trouble and rode out to the top of a hill overlooking the trail to Cuero. He could see a long way, except in the groves of trees and tall bushes. An army could be hidden in there and he wouldn't be able to see them.

He searched the entire area, watching for any movement that may indicate trouble. Didn't see anything that looked suspicious. Then he turned back toward the house and checked out everything in that area.

Just as he was about to head back to the house, he saw something move in the tree line on top of the hill where they had stopped that first day to look the place over. He remained perfectly still, knowing if he could see what was there, they could see him if he moved. After a few minutes, he saw it again. Looked like a man on foot sneaking toward the house. He was carrying a rifle. His hat was pulled low over his face, so he couldn't be identified from this distance.

Clay figured he was in a good position to cover the house from here. He was only about a hundred yards away and could see all but the opposite side of the house. He decided to wait a little longer to see what this fellow was up to before he made his move.

If he had seen Willie and Luke ride away in the wagon, he would know there were only two people here. Apparently, he didn't see Clay ride away or didn't see him stop at the top of the hill, but it was obvious this guy was up to no good.

Clay kept watching. The man was headed in a direction that would take him to the other side of the house from Clay. When he went out of sight behind the house, Clay tied his horse to a tree, and quietly ran down to the house and slipped in the back door.

Ellen was in the kitchen and saw Clay coming. She met him at the door, "What's up?"

"A man sneaking up on the north side of the house. Get your gun and stay in the middle bedroom. I don't want to wonder where you are." Ellen ran to the gun rack and strapped on her gun belt, checked to make sure it was ready to fire, grabbed her rifle and went to the bedroom. Clay moved to the bedroom on the north side of the house where he could look out the window. Standing back across the room, he could see the tree line where they had dug the foxhole when Smith was attacking the house.

After a couple minutes, he saw movement in the trees. Ellen stuck her head in the door and said, "Clay, there is another one coming down in front."

"I'll check the back," Clay whispered. He moved around so he could see out the back window toward the barn. A moment later he saw a man sneaking up behind the barn and bunkhouse.

"Ok, we can't let them get any closer and get set up. I'm going to shoot the one on this side, you take the one out front as soon as you get a good shot. Shoot to kill. They've had enough warnings."

Ellen went back to her station in the front bedroom. It wasn't but a minute until Clay heard her shoot. "I got him. He won't bother anyone else."

Clay didn't have to wait but a couple seconds to get his shot. The man had just moved from behind a tree and started toward the house, probably hearing the shot on the other side of the house, was thinking whoever was in the house was looking the other way. As he cleared the tree, Clay put a bullet in his chest, knocking him down. He grabbed his chest and groaned, then he started screaming, "Help me! I'm shot, help me!" Clay looked out the back window to see where the third man was.

After a couple minutes he heard him calling to the other two, but, he wasn't getting any answer.

Another couple of minutes and the man was seen creeping back the way he came. Clay waited until he came from behind a bush and put a bullet in his upper thigh. The man crumpled to the ground, grabbed his leg and started cussing a blue streak.

Clay and Ellen waited in the house another fifteen minutes. When they didn't see or hear anyone else, Clay cautiously walked toward the wounded man, keeping his rifle pointed at him all the way.

When he was within thirty feet, he told the man to throw his gun off to the side. He fumbled around and finally found it and threw it back toward Clay.

"Clay asked him, "Do you have any more weapons on you?" "No."

"If I find out you have lied to me, it's going to go rough on you. Want to answer that question again?"

"Ok, there's one in my boot."

"Throw it out here."

When that gun was thrown away, Clay asked him again. "You have any more on you?"

"Just a knife in the other boot."

"Throw it out here. Any more?"

"No, that's all."

"You better be right."

Clay approached, squatted beside the man and asked, "Who are you?" "Ralph Lucas."

"Ok, Ralph Lucas, who are you working for? Who sent you here." "No one sent me. We heard you were worth a thousand dollars dead to someone."

"Really, now who would pay to have me killed?"

"I don't know. We were to see a guy in Clinton to collect our money when we showed him proof that you were dead."

"What were you supposed to show him as proof?"

"Look, I'm bleeding here. I need to get to a doctor or I'm going to bleed to death."

"You say that like I care. How were you going to prove I'm dead?" "Your body."

"Who is supposed to pay you? What is his name?"

"Maurice Garland."

"Where is this Garland located in Clinton?" "We were to ask for him at the saloon."

"Do you know what he looks like?"

"No, never met him. Are you going to stand here and let me bleed to death?"

"Ok, on your feet. We are going to go meet this Mr. Garland."

"I can't walk, you shot me in the leg."

"The legs not broke. Get up."

About that time Willie came riding into the yard on a winded, sweaty horse, and his rifle in hand, "What happened? We heard shooting and I got back as fast as I could!"

"You are just in time. This fellow and a couple of his friends were trying to collect a thousand-dollar bounty on my head."

"Well, now, that's interesting. Who put a bounty on you?" Ellen came walking up with her rifle at the ready.

"This is Mr. Ralph Lucas. Says he don't know. But a Mr. Maurice Garland is supposed to pay out the money. So, we were just about to go see this Mr. Garland. Where is Luke with the wagon?" asked Clay.

"He's coming. Should be here in a minute or two."

"Ok, let's tie him up. When Luke gets here we will throw him in the wagon and take him into town. Why don't you get a fresh horse and see if you can find three horses somewhere around here? Do you know where they are, Lucas?"

In a pain-racked shaky voice, Lucas said, "Mine is behind the barn in that grove of trees, the other two are out front, on top of the hill."

"Ok, I'll get 'em," Willie said.

Lucas struggled to his feet. Clay watched him limp toward the front of the barn. When he reached a bench in front of the bunkhouse he sat down. "I can't go any farther."

Clay took Lucas' scarf from around his neck and tied it tightly around his leg. The flow of blood gradually slowed until it stopped.

Luke came in with the wagon. The mules were winded and sweaty, so Clay told him to turn this team loose and use the other one. While that was being done, Willie came back with three horses, tied them to the back of the wagon. When the fresh mules were hooked up to the wagon, they drove around to where the other two victims were lying. Both were dead, so they were loaded into the wagon with Lucas. He didn't like that at all, but he wasn't given a choice.

When asked who his partners were, he said just a couple guys he met who agreed to take a hundred dollars each to help him collect the reward.

"So, you are the ringleader in the murder plot," Clay decided.

When everyone was ready to go again. Ellen said, "I'm not staying here alone. Will someone saddle my horse, please?"

Dark Night was saddled and brought out. Ellen mounted and put the rifle in the scabbard.

Luke was driving the wagon with the two bodies and Lucas. Clay, Ellen, and Willie riding behind, when they came into Clinton and went straight to the sheriff's office.

When Clay walked in the sheriff looked up and said, "Hello, Wade, did you bring me some more residents?"

"I sure did. Got him right outside."

"Hey, I was just kidding."

"I'm not. I have one for your hotel here, and two for the morgue." "What the hell happened?"

"I just happened to see one of them sneaking up on the house. While I was watching him, my wife saw another one coming from the other side, then a third one coming from the back. They had us surrounded and outnumbered. I couldn't let them get set and start picking us off. When we got the chance, we shot them first. Killed two of them, wounded the third. He tells me he was trying to collect a thousand-dollar bounty that someone has placed on my head. He was to show my body to a Mr. Garland, who he is supposed to meet at the saloon. Do you know this Garland?"

"I have heard of him. A shady character, from what I hear."

"I am going to bring him in and file charges of attempted murder against him too." Clay said sternly. "Is Charlie Thompson still staying here?"

"Yes, he is. His brother came storming in raising hell, wanting him released right this minute. I told him he would have to wait for the circuit judge to get here. I can't set bail on an attempted murder charge. He didn't like that a darn bit."

"The judge is still due here next Thursday?"

"I ain't heard anything different."

Clay left to get the prisoner and bring him in. He was put in the cell next to Thompson. They could sit there and compare notes.

Clay told the sheriff, "I'm goin' over to the saloon, ask for Mr. Garland, see what happens."

"Ok, but you be careful. I told you, I've heard he's a shady character."
"What does he do for a living?"

"I've heard several different things, a cattle buyer, horse trader, gives legal advice, don't know if he has a law license or not, that's just a rumor."

Clay returned to the wagon, where Luke, Willie, and Ellen were waiting. Clay suggested to Luke, "How about you go in the saloon and ask for Mr. Garland? If you are asked why you want to see him, tell him you were shot by me, and you want to file a lawsuit. That ought to be convincing since your arm is in a sling."

"Ok, here I go."

"Willie, how about you follow him in a couple of minutes later and keep an eye on things? I'll be a couple minutes behind you. I don't think anyone here knows me, but let's not take any chances."

Ellen asked, "What do you want me to do?"

"Oh, Willie, do you have the shopping list? Give it to Ellen, she can be doing the shopping while we handle this little problem."

"Little problem." Ellen said, "It's a big problem if you ask me."

Luke walked into the saloon, went to the far end of the bar and ordered a whiskey. When the bartender had served him, Luke asked if Mr. Garland was around.

The bartender looked Luke over from top to bottom, saw the arm in a sling, and asked, "What do you need him for?"

Luke answered, "I hear he is a lawyer, is that right?"

"He does some lawyer work. Why?"

Luke said, "I want to file a lawsuit against the man who shot me."
"Who was that?"

"Clay Wade, do you know him?"

"No, but I have heard about him. Supposed to be pretty salty."

"So, what about Garland, is he here?"

"That's him sitting at the corner table by the window."

Willie came in just in time to hear that last remark. He ordered a whiskey, never looked toward Garland, just stood facing the bar and sipped his whiskey. He could see what was happening behind him in the mirror behind the bar.

Clay came in and went to the bar, stood beside Willie and ordered a whiskey. Willie nodded his head toward the corner where Luke and Garland were sitting.

Clay nodded his head to Willie to follow me. They picked up their drinks and walked over to the table. Both pulled out chairs and sat down. Garland had a startled look on his face when he asked, "Can't you see I am talking with this gentleman? Wait your turn over there. I'll call you when I'm finished here."

Clay asked, "You are Maurice Garland?"

"Yes, I am. Who are you?"

"Well, Maurice Garland, I am Clay Wade."

Garlands face went snow white. He looked like he would faint.

Clay said, "I understand you are offering a thousand dollars for my dead body, is that correct?"

"No, where did you hear that ridiculous thing?"

"From three men who tried to collect. Two are dead and the other is in the jail talking his head off. Now, I am going to ask you some questions, if I don't get the right answers, I am going to take you out behind the barn and start stomping the life out of you until I get the right answers. Do you understand what I just told you?"

Garland was still in shock. He couldn't get a word out.

Willie got up and turned his chair, so he was facing the bar and the bartender.

Clay asked, "Garland, do you hear me?" Garland nodded his head.

"Ok, here is the first question. Who wants me killed enough to pay a thousand dollars to get it done?"

"I don't know what you are talking about."

Before Garland could blink an eye, Clay had slapped him open-handed and backhanded him across the face. Garland fell back in his chair, grabbed his face and whimpered.

Willie came out of his chair with his gun in hand pointed at the bartender, "I wouldn't do that. Just keep your hands on top of the bar and you might live to sleep in your own bed tonight."

The bartender put both hands on the bar with a sheepish look on his face.

"I'll ask you one more time. Who is paying to have me killed?"

"I can't tell you. He will kill me."

"Take your pick, him or me. I'm here now, ready to kill you now if I don't get the answer I want. You tell me who it is, and I'll protect you, so you can testify against him in court. Now, who is it?"

"Dan Thompson."

"I'm not surprised. Did he tell you why he wants me dead?"

"He said you were getting too big for your britches. You had to go."

"How were you going to let him know when I was dead?"

"He has a man come to check every day to see if I have heard anything."

"What time does he usually come?"

"Usually around four in the afternoon."

"Is it the same man every day?" "Usually."

"What does he look like. How would I recognize him?"

"He is a big man. Over six feet weighs close to three hundred pounds, rides a huge black horse."

"Ok, here is what you are going to do. When he comes in, you tell him you have my body, but you aren't showing it to anyone except Thompson, and you want your money. Got that? By the way, how much are you getting out of this deal? What is Thompson really paying to get me killed?"

"He's paying fifteen hundred. I was to keep five hundred."

"I ought to let him take you and skin you alive or do it myself. You are a sorry excuse for a man, you know that, Garland?"

"Look, Mr. Wade, Thompson gets and does what he wants around these parts. I don't want him killing me. It didn't sound so important."

"Paying to have someone killed, is not so important?"

"I told you, if I didn't do it he would kill me."

"Alright, when big man comes in, we will be right over there. You tell him what I told you. When Thompson comes in and asks where the body is, you can just point to me. I'll take it from there. Got it?"

"Yeah, but you promised to protect me. Remember?"

CHAPTER 26

Clay asked Willie and Luke if they would stay here and keep an eye on Garland, Make sure he doesn't get word to Thompson, ok. You can take turns going to lunch, just make sure one of you is here all the time. I will meet Ellen, go to lunch, and stay out of sight. I'll see the big man when he comes in and be ready to meet Thompson when he gets here." Willie and Luke said they would, Clay left and found Ellen in the mercantile buying enough supplies to feed an army. Most of it was already loaded on the wagon.

She wanted to know what was going on. Clay gave her a summary of what had happened, "I'll tell you more later. Let's go to lunch."

"Good, I'm starved."

They walked to the sheriff 's office and filled him in, then went to lunch.

They sat drinking coffee and talking. It was going on toward mid-afternoon when they saw the big black horse, carrying the big man, come down the street. He dismounted and tied his horse in front of the saloon and went in. A couple minutes later he came out, mounted and galloped back out of town. At that speed, he wasn't going very far, so Thompson must be close by.

Clay told Ellen to wait here, "I'm going to talk to Willie and Luke, see what went on."

He hurriedly walked to the saloon. When he walked in, Luke and Willie were sitting at a back table, one facing the door and Garland, the other facing the bartender. Garland seemed as nervous as a cat on a hot tin roof.

Clay asked, "What happened?"

Willie said, "Big man came in, Garland told him what you said, and he left."

Clay turned to Garland, "How long will it take Thompson to get here?"

"Probably at least an hour. Look, Wade, I don't want to be here when he gets here. He will kill me as soon as he sees you."

"Ok, come with me. We'll put you in a safe place."

"Where are we going?"

"To the jail, where all murderers go, sooner or later."

"But I'm not a murderer, I haven't killed anyone."

"You are an accomplice, same thing. Get up, move."

Clay frisked Garland and found a two-shot derringer in his vest pocket. When they walked in, the sheriff looked up at Clay, "Wade, I'm going to need a bigger jail if you hang around here much longer. Who is this, and what has he done?"

"This is Maurice Garland. He is working hand in hand with Thompson to get me killed. He is an accomplice to an attempted murder. He is the one who was to pay whoever killed me, then collect from Thompson."

"Is that right, Garland?"

"Look, I wasn't supposed to kill anyone. I was just the go-between.

All I was to do was handle the money, not kill anyone."

Sheriff Helm said, "That makes you an accomplice. Follow me." He removed a ring of keys from his desk and led Garland to the cells in back. He put him in the cell with Lucas, the bounty hunter.

Clay explained to Sheriff Helm that Thompson was due in town in about an hour to view his body and pay Garland. Of course, the body he was going to view would not be dead.

Sheriff Helm laughed, "I'll bet that is going to be a big surprise. I'd like to see that."

Clay said, "Why don't you. You can be in the back room watching and hear everything. It may come in handy when he is tried for trying to have me killed."

"Good idea. What time is he going to get here?"

"Not less than an hour. Unless the big man met him on his way to town. In that case, he could show up any time."

The sheriff said, "Let's go wait in the saloon. When we see him coming, I'll step into the back room. Better take that bartender with me, he and Thompson are close. Wouldn't want him tipping him off."

Sheriff Helm took a double barrel shotgun from the gun rack, dropped a handful of shells in his pocket and said, "Let's go."

On their way to the saloon, Clay stopped at the diner to let Ellen know what was happening, then went with the sheriff. They took tables in the back near the door to the storeroom.

Willie was sitting on the bench out front with his legs stretched out, leaning back with his hat covering his face, pretending to be sleeping. Luke was sitting at a corner table at a front window, directly across the saloon from where Garland had been sitting.

The four corners of the room had Clay in one, Luke in the other, the sheriff in the third, and the fourth one was vacant, where Garland usually sat.

When Thompson walked in the door with two of his men following him, the first thing he did was look for the bartender. He was in the backroom with the sheriff. Then he looked in the corner for Garland. He wasn't there either. The only people in the room were the two men sitting in opposite corners. As his eyes became adjusted to the dim light, he saw the man in the back corner stand up and ask, "Are you looking for me, Thompson?"

Dan Thompson looked like he would fall over in a faint. He started stuttering, "What are you doing here?"

"Why, am I supposed to be dead or something?" Clay asked as he walked across the floor. "That's what you expected, isn't it? It's time we came to an understanding, Thompson. I've been patient with you and your bunch too long. It's over. Time to answer for your sins. Why are you willing to pay someone to kill me? Why don't you do your own killing? Are you too yellow to even try? You even sent your kid brother to do your killing for you. It could have gotten him killed. When he couldn't get the job done, you put out the word that you will pay a thousand dollars to anyone who kills me. Why?"

Thompson looked over his shoulder to see if his men were still there. They were, but he didn't see that Willie was behind them with a gun in their back, and he had taken their guns.

"Go ahead, go for that gun. You have been acting like the big bad guy around here for so long you have come to believe you really are. Well, I think you are just a big bag of wind. All your dirty work is done by your hired thugs because you don't have the guts. Isn't that right, Thompson?"

"No, you're going to have a different opinion when I get through with you."

"Then why did you hire someone to kill me? Why didn't you do it yourself and save fifteen hundred dollars? That is what you agreed to pay, isn't it? Come on Thompson, admit it, you are just a big overgrown coward."

Willie had moved off to one side to get out of the line of fire, in case Thompson went for his gun.

Clay was now within four feet of Thompson. Thompson looked like he was ready to duck, expecting Clay to hit him at any second.

Clay taunted him some more, "Are you going to draw that gun or drop it on the floor. Whatever you're goin' to do, do it now."

Thompson licked his lips, tried to back up some more, but couldn't. "You have three seconds, Thompson, then I am going to walk all over you. Before Thompson could blink, Clay slapped him across the face, then backhanded him. When Thompson brought his hands up to protect his face, Clay landed one in his gut that doubled him over.

Clay stepped back, "What's the matter, Thompson? Too yellow to fight me?"

Clay turned to Thompson's men and said, "This is the man you follow. You do everything he tells you? Look at that, don't that just make you proud to work for a yellow coward like that? He won't even stand up and fight like a man."

That was the last straw. Thompson had finally had enough. He charged Clay like a bull. It was so unexpected that it caught Clay sleeping. They both went down, with Thompson on top, and being the larger man, he had the advantage. He tried to pin Clay's arms down with his knees. Clay was expecting that, so he raised his hands over his head, brought them together, palms open, as hard as he could over Thompson's ears. Thompson screamed, grabbed his head, fell to the side and rolled onto the floor. Apparently, both eardrums were busted. Clay got to his feet, walked to Thompson's head, grabbed a hand full of hair and lifted him up. "Well, you did have some guts after all."

The sheriff came from the back room, walked up to Thompson, lifted his gun from his holster, pointed toward the door, "Let's go. Got a nice cell waiting for you. You can share the one with your brother."

"You can't lock me up, I ain't done nothing."

"You put out a contract on Wade to get him killed. I am guessing that ought to be good for at least ten years."

"You will never be able to prove that. You don't even have any witnesses."

"Oh yes, we do. Got two in fact. Both singing their heads off."

"Helm, I will have your head for this!" yelled Thompson.

"Like you were going to have Wade's head? That's another charge, threatening an officer of the law. That ought to be good for another five years."

As they were going out the door, Willie asked, "What do we do with these men?" Referring to Thompson's men.

Sheriff Helm stopped, turned to them and told them in no uncertain terms, "You men will leave DeWitt county today. If I see you anywhere in the county again, I will run you in and charge you with everything I can think of. In fact, when I get to my office, I'm going through all my wanted posters to see if I have anything on any of you. If I do, you can continue spending time with your boss."

One of the men asked, "Which way is the closest county line?"

Sheriff Helm pointed west. They mounted up and left town at a fast gallop.

Thompson was marched to the jail and locked in the cell with Charlie.

Clay was instructed to fill out the report. "You should know how it's done by now."

When the reports were all filled out, Clay went to the diner to meet Ellen. She had done all the shopping and had it loaded in the wagon ready to go home.

Luke drove the wagon, Willie, Clay, and Ellen rode along behind. They weren't expecting trouble this soon, but they weren't taking any chances. The way things had been popping up, it could happen at any time.

Two and a half hours later, they were home unloading the wagon.

That's when they remembered the men they went into town to hire.

Clay said, "Looks like we will have to make another trip."

Ellen pointed out, "The trial is in three days. Can't it be done then?" Clay answered, "Yes, it can, but we lose at least three days if we wait.

If Luke and Willie are up to riding in tomorrow, we can probably get started the next day, which is Wednesday. They can be working while we are at the trial. It's going to take at least a week to build that fence, maybe longer."

Willie asked Luke, "Are you up to the ride?"

"Yeah, if I don't have to fight anyone I'm fine, just sore as the dickens. I can't do any lifting, but I can point and say, 'Do that, do this.'"

Ellen said, "That's good. Every job needs a boss."

Willie said, "We will leave early, be there by mid-morning; if we find them right away, and they can come out now, we should be back by mid-afternoon."

Clay said, "While you all are doing that, I'll be repairing that fence the horses pushed down."

Ellen had breakfast ready before the sun was up, and Willie and Luke were on their way to Cuero.

She was cleaning up the kitchen while Clay went to work on the horse pasture fence.

As they predicted, Willie and Luke were home by one that afternoon. The two Cordis brothers were with them. When they rode in the yard, Clay could tell something wasn't right. He put his tools down and went to meet them at the barn.

Willie told Clay, "We got a problem."

"Why, what happened?"

"Last night, as Sheriff Helm was ready to leave the jail to go home for his supper, four masked men came in, hit him over the head, opened the cells and let all the prisoners out. So, both Thompsons, Lucas and Garland are on the loose."

"How is the sheriff?"

"He has a sore head, but he's out with a posse looking for them," Willie said.

"I guess we better be prepared for trouble. Thompson's just liable to show up here any minute. You know he blames us for all his problems."

Luke said, "Yeah, and if we are way over there cutting trees and brush, we'll be leaving Ellen here alone. We can't do that."

"You are right, how about you all go ahead and get started, Luke, you and Willie know where we are going to be working, you can show Gerald and Matt what we want to be done. I will stay here with Ellen. If trouble shows up, I'll fire some shots, and you all come runnin'."

"Ok, but don't wait too long. I'll take us a little while to get here."

"I'll be in that grove of trees on top of the hill to the south of the house. I can see a long way down the road toward Cuero, and all the open country for miles around in all directions. That should give us enough notice."

The men gathered all the tools they thought they may need and loaded them in the wagon. Hitching one team of mules to it, they headed out to start cutting trees and brush.

Clay went into the house to let Ellen know what was going on. When he told her he was going to be on watch at the top of the hill, she felt more comfortable, but she still got her rifle and strapped her pistol around her waist, which was getting larger every day.

Clay took a canteen, and Ellen made him two large sandwiches from the deer steak. He was set for the day.

Along about mid-morning, he saw three riders coming up the Cuero road. He watched until he saw sun reflect off something on one of the men's chest, so he assumed it was either the sheriff or one of his deputies. When they were close enough that he was sure it wasn't a Thompson, he left his post and went down to the house to meet them.

When sheriff Jack Helm and his posse stopped at the front door, Clay invited them to step down and have a seat. "Good morning, men. You all out for a pleasure ride so early in the day?"

They all looked like they had had a rough night and day. The sheriff had a bandage around his head and looked a little pale. They must have been in the saddle since before daylight.

"No, Clay, we came to let you know that Thompson and the whole gang broke out of jail last night after dark. We couldn't do anything until after daylight this morning when we could pick up their track to see where they went."

"Yeah, I heard. Luke and Willie were in town early this morning and heard about it. We have been on guard ever since. Have you had any luck in tracking them down?"

Ellen came out the door, said hello to the sheriff and offered them a cool drink of water. They all accepted. She came back with a tray and a glass of water for each of the men, including Clay.

"Not much, the tracks led over into Gonzales county. I notified the sheriff over there, so they can be on the lookout for them."

"What do you want me to do if they show up here?"

"Do whatever you have to do to protect yourself."

Clay assured the sheriff, "Thompson has already shown he is not above shooting from ambush, hiring killers and put a price on my head. So, if he shows up around here, I am going to instruct all my people to shoot on sight."

"That sounds like the safest way. Just be careful. Don't let him sneak up on you."

"I'll do my best to see that he doesn't. Is there a reward on any of them?"

"No, not yet. I'll have to see if the county will do that. That might help get them back in custody or shot. Or, keep them totally out of the area."

Ellen Said, "Either way works for me."

Clay agreed, "Yeah, me too."

After the sheriff, his men and horses had a breather, they mounted and headed back toward Clinton.

Clay asked Ellen, "Do you want to ride over where the men are working, see how things are going?"

"Sure, that sounds like fun."

"Well, may not be fun, but it will get you out of the house for a little while."

Clay saddled Dark Night and Smokey, who hadn't been ridden in a while, and led them back to the house. Ellen came out in her riding clothes, with the gun strapped to her hip and rifle in her hand. She slid the rifle in the scabbard on the saddle and mounted. They rode out of the barnyard at a walk, in consideration for Ellen's condition.

Only took them about twenty minutes to reach the work site. The men had quite a pile of posts cut and stacked, along with piles and piles of brush that would be stacked on the pole fence, once it was finished. Just anything to keep the crazy longhorns from being able to see through it. Everyone seemed pleased with the progress they had made. But, they all agreed, it was still going to take at least a week to get the job done, maybe longer.

Ellen asked Luke, "How are you holding up, Luke? You look tired."

Luke said, "I am tired, but I really haven't done much to help, just dragging poles and brush out of their way so they can work."

"I'm sure that's something that needs to be done, so you are helping."

Clay told them about the sheriff 's visit, and what he told him about shooting Thompson on sight.

"So, keep your guns close and be prepared to use them if anyone shows up and starts causing you trouble."

CHAPTER 27

Clay and Ellen started back to the house. Before they had gone but a couple hundred yards, they saw a dust cloud. Looked like it was coming from the Cuero road and headed toward their house. Clay and Ellen changed their direction and headed for the hill to the south side of the house. Clay wanted to see who was stirring up all the dust from there. He wanted to get there before the other party reached the house.

Clay asked Ellen, "Are you up to a faster pace?"

"Sure, let's go."

They kicked the horses into a slow, comfortable gallop and circled around behind the hill. When they reached the grove of trees on top, they slowed to a walk until they reached a good spot where they could see the front of the house and down the road for half a mile or more.

The group of horsemen was nearing the turnoff to come to their house. Clay thought he recognized both Thompsons. There was a total of five men. Thompson still has four men willing to follow him. Or, maybe they were more family members.

"Ellen, how about you ride back and get the rest of the men. Have them come up on the other side of the house. You stay back out of firing range."

She turned her horse without a word and took off.

After she was gone, Clay took Smokey down the back side of the hill and tied him out of danger. He then went back to his lookout point and settled down behind a big tree and waited to see what they were going to do.

He didn't have long to wait. When they took the turn and reached the top of the hill overlooking the house, they stopped and were looking the place over.

Clay already had his sights on Dan Thompson. If he made any kind of threatening move, he was going to be a dead man.

He saw Thompson direct his men to spread out along the top of the hill to his left and right. One of the men was coming straight at Clay. He didn't want to open fire too soon. He would like for his men to get in position first. But he knew it was going to be several more minutes before they could get here, and his men didn't know where Thompson's men were going to be. He would have to trust them to know how to handle themselves.

He kept his eyes on all the men he could see moving around, trying to get into position to attack the house. The one coming directly to him wasn't being too careful about it. It was apparent he had never been in the war or any other fight, for that matter. Clay could take him out any time he wanted to. That one would have to be the first to go because when Clay opened fire, he would give away his position, then Clay would be a sitting duck for this man.

Clay kept looking back toward the direction his men would be coming from. He eventually saw their dust and knew they would be on the other side of the house in another minute or two.

He drew a bead on the one coming toward him, waited another half minute and pulled the trigger. He had aimed to hit him in the shoulder. He really didn't want to kill him, but if this didn't take him out of the fight, then he would have to.

He quickly turned back toward Thompson's position. He could see him trying to take cover behind a tree, so he put a bullet where he thought he would be. It must have been close because Thompson jumped out the other side of the tree. But, before Clay could work the lever and get another round in the chamber, Thompson was back behind the tree.

Clay could see one of the other men across the way on the other side of the house. He had a clear shot at him, so he took it. The man crumpled to the ground and never moved again.

About that time all his men came charging into the yard, firing at Thompson's men. He heard movement behind him. He whirled with his rifle ready to fire.

Before he pulled the trigger, Ellen screamed, "Don't shoot, it's me!"

"Oh, my god, Ellen, what are you doing here? I almost shot you! You are not supposed to be here. That's exactly why I told you to stay back, so I would know where you are. How do you think I could live with myself if I shot you?"

"I just wanted to help."

"I know that, but I need you alive more than I need your help right now."

"I'm sorry, Clay, it won't happen again, I promise."

"Ok, go back with the horses, and this time, please stay there."

"Ok, I will."

Clay watched until he was sure she was safe, then he returned to the business at hand. He knew two of the men were down. He went over to the first one he had shot to see if he was dead, or alive. As he approached the downed man, he kept his rifle pointed at him. He didn't see any movement, but he could see he was breathing. When he reached the man, he removed all his weapons and got them out of the way. Then he examined the wounds. The bullet had gone all the way through, and there was a lot of blood. The man was young. Maybe twenty at the most. Pulse was strong, but a little fast, but that would be normal for someone who was just shot.

Clay opened his shirt to look at the wound. There wasn't much he could do for it right now, so he tore off a piece of the man's shirt and stuffed it in the two holes, front and back. Maybe that would slow the bleeding until this fracas was over.

He picked up all the guns and carried them with him back to his place of concealment. He checked the guns, saw none of them were as good as his own, but he might need them if this battle lasted very long.

It took a couple minutes to get everyone located again. He saw Thompson was still hiding behind the same tree. He took a good bead on the tree and waited for Thompson to show himself.

Meanwhile, there was more shooting going on between his men and Thompson's other two men. Clay couldn't see the other men, but occasionally he would see a puff of smoke from one of their guns. He was finally able to locate their positions. He was watching all three, just waiting for one of them to give him a target.

He saw some movement from Thompson and was hoping he was getting ready to move to get a better position. Clay was ready when

Thompson came from behind his tree and sprinted toward the house. He let him get almost to the next tree before he shot him. Thompson grabbed his chest and collapsed to the ground, kicking and rolling around. After a minute or so, there was no more movement. Clay waited another minute, then called to Thompson's men.

"You men down there, Dan Thompson is dead, and two more of your men are dead. There's only two of you left. Throw down your weapons and come out with your hands up, or we will kill you too."

Clay just realized, one of the remaining men must be Charlie Thompson, the youngest son. Clay called, "Charlie, Dan is out of it. You have nothing to fight for anymore. Come on out, we will hold our fire if you come out with your hands empty. If you don't, you will be killed too."

They all waited for Charlie to make up his mind. Time was dragging on and it was getting late. The sun was going down across the Guadalupe River. It would be dark in another hour.

Clay called out again, "Charlie, you have three minutes, then we are going to come and get you. If we do that, we will kill you. Dan may still be alive. You may be able to save him if you get him to a doctor. Another of your men is still alive, but he's wounded bad. He needs a doctor too. What's it going to be, Charlie? You got two minutes."

"Alright, hold your fire, we are coming out!" Charlie yelled.

Clay watched as two men stood and dropped their guns and came walking out in the open. Willie and Luke moved in on them. Searched them for weapons, found none, tied their hands behind their back and herded them to the house. The Cordis brothers rounded up the five Thompson horses and brought them in.

Clay and Willie went to get the first one Clay had shot. He was still alive, so they laid him across a horse and brought him to the house and laid him on the front porch.

Ellen came with a pan of hot water and cleaned and bandaged the wound. He was still unconscious. The second one Clay shot was dead, as well as Dan Thompson.

When Charlie saw his brother was dead, he started yelling and screaming. "No, Dan, you can't be dead. Nobody can kill you. Dan, get up, Dan, you can't be dead."

Clay asked the men to bring the wagon down from the work site, so these men can be hauled into jail and the morgue.

Thirty minutes later, the wagon was loaded with the dead, the wounded, Charlie and the other man, who had never given a name.

Three hours later they rode into Clinton. It had been dark for a couple hours, but they still attracted a lot of attention coming down the street. A wagon loaded with dead and wounded and two tied up like a pig for the market. Clay and Willie were riding behind, leading five horses. Luke and Matt Cordis stayed at home with Ellen.

When they pulled up in front of the sheriff 's office, a crowd gathered out front. Sheriff Helm came out, "Well, Clay looks like you are still doing my job for me. Who you got here this time?"

"I brought one of your escapees back, one for the doctor and two for the morgue."

"Who you got for the morgue?"

"Dan Thompson, and one other man. Don't know his name. Charlie probably knows who he is."

"Unload the three for the jail here and drop the other two off at the morgue. I'll send someone for the doctor for the wounded one. Then you need to come in and fill out the forms that you seem to like so much."

"Ok, Sheriff, be right back."

Clay delivered the bodies to the undertaker, came back and filled out the report.

"Sheriff, what about the judge, is he still around, or do we have to wait for a month until he comes back around?"

"No, he's still here. We probably can have the trial tomorrow or the next day."

"How soon can we know? We have a long ride to get here."

"He probably has already turned in. I'll check with him first thing in the morning and send a rider out to let you know."

"Ok, Sheriff, we're going to head on home."

They had just left Clinton, headed toward Cuero when they felt the temperature getting cooler, and there was the smell of rain in the air. Willie said, "I sure hope this holds off until we get home." It didn't. A few more minutes and the temperature had dropped another ten degrees, and the wind was picking up. They all took their coats from the back of their saddle and put them on. A few minutes later, the rain came. It was a blowing, slanting rain, coming straight out of the north, hitting them in the face. The temperature dropped another ten degrees in about ten minutes.

Luke shouted, "This is what is known in Texas as a blue norther."

The mules kept chugging along, hardly paying any attention to the weather.

It was almost midnight when they pulled into the barnyard. Matt came out with a lantern, "You all go on in and get warm. I'll take care of the animals."

They all rushed the back door. Ellen was standing there with the coffee pot and five cups on the table. There was a roaring fire in the fireplace and the kitchen stove. Both putting out all the heat they could. The men gathered around as close as they could get without burning themselves, each holding a hot cup of coffee warming their hands.

It wasn't long before the coats started coming off. Then the men were getting sleepy and snuck off to bed in the bunkhouse. Luke had a fire going in the heater there also.

The next morning, the weather was even colder, and the rain was still coming down.

Clay made his way to the bunkhouse to meet with the men and tell them to sit by the fire today.

That afternoon a rider from Clinton came to tell them the trial would be held the next day, starting at ten, to give them time to get to Clinton. They thought Clay and Luke would be the only ones who would need to testify.

The next morning, they had an early breakfast and Luke and Clay mounted up and headed to Clinton. They arrived a little before ten and went to the café to get coffee and take advantage of the big wood heater in the center of the room.

At ten they were all in the saloon, which had been converted to a courtroom by moving all the tables against the walls and stacking them two high. The chairs were lined up in rows across the room. A table had been set up in front to act as the judge's bench.

The room was packed with standing room only. Most of the people in the area had suffered at the hands of the Thompsons at one time or another. They were here to see justice served to those deserving.

At precisely ten o'clock, the judge pulled his gavel from his robe pocket and banged on the table. "Court is now in session. Mr. Short, you are the prosecutor in this case?"

"Yes, I am, Your Honor."

"Who is your first victim?"

"The accused is Charlie Thompson. He is accused of firing shots from ambush at Mr. Luke Wilson, wounding him in the arm and endangering his life. He is charged with attempted murder. Mr. Wilson and Mr. Clay Wade are here to testify as a witness to these facts."

The judge called on the defense attorney, "Mr. Andrews, you are acting as the defendant's attorney in this case?"

"Yes, I am, Your Honor."

"Mr. Short, call your first witness."

"The prosecution calls Mr. Luke Wilson."

The trial proceeded rapidly from there. Luke told exactly what happened, even told about Charlie telling them his daddy and Dan had told him to do it.

The defense attorney objected to that statement as being hearsay. The judge overruled.

The defense attorney had no questions for Luke.

Then Clay was called, and he told how he and Ellen were riding to check on the work when they heard the shots. How Clay had managed to capture the shooter in the act, seeing him firing shots at Luke and Willie, and bring him in to be locked up.

The defense attorney had no questions for Clay.

The sheriff testified about the jailbreak and the prisoner's escape. Clay was recalled to testify about the shooting at the BAR W,

how Thompson and one other was killed and one wounded. Charlie Thompson was re-captured, and one other involved in the attack was brought in for trial.

The judge listened to all the testimony from the witnesses, then turned it over to the defense attorney.

He had no defense. He asked a few questions of each witness but none of them changed their stories.

When both sides rested, the judge sentenced Charlie to fifteen years in the state pen at Huntsville, Texas.

The other man that was brought in with Charlie Thompson was the next to be tried. Clay and Luke testified as to his part in the attack on the ranch. The judge sentenced him to five years in Huntsville. The man who was wounded by Clay in that fight was also sentenced to five years. The judge had other cases to hear, but Clay and Luke were finished.

They went to the café, had lunch and headed home.

The weather was still cold, hovering around forty degrees, but no rain. The wind was still blowing, which made it feel a lot colder than it really was. They bundled up as much as they could. It was a cold two-hour ride. They arrived back home around three in the afternoon. The sun was just trying to peak through the clouds but was having a tough time doing it.

Luke went to the bunkhouse, Clay went to his house. Both sat as close as they could to the fire trying to get warm.

Ellen brought Clay a cup of coffee and cuddled up on his lap. Clay said, "Hey, with you around, who needs a fire and coffee?"

Ellen rubbed her tummy, "Better take advantage of it. I won't be able to do this much longer."

CHAPTER 28

By the next day, the sun was out, and the temperature was back to being tolerable, so the work began again on cutting the material for the fence.

This time, Clay went with the workers and Luke stayed at the house with Ellen, working around the barn and repairing fences.

The first thing they did was cut a large stack of firewood and built a fire where they could get warm if they got too cold to work. But, they found swinging an ax and pulling a crosscut saw worked as well as a fire.

By the end of the day, they had a large stack of posts and a larger stack of brush, consisting of the smaller limbs from the trees they had cut to get the posts and poles.

This was the routine for the rest of the week. By Friday, they thought they may have enough, so they started pulling it all down to where the pen was to be built. Each of them had his own idea of how the fence should be built. After kicking them all around, one design was decided on and the work began. They had marked off about a two-acre plot. They worked until noon on Saturday, took the rest of the day off and all-day Sunday to rest up. All the men, except Clay, went into Cuero on Saturday night to have some fun.

Monday morning, it was easy to tell which ones had the most fun or the most to drink. A couple of them were slow getting started, but by noon everyone was back in the swing of things.

The fence was beginning to make the area look more like a corral. A large span was left open, so the cattle could be driven in. Two long strands of fence were run off at about a forty-five-degree angle from the opening. Once the cattle were driven between those two long arms, there was only one place they could go, that was straight ahead into the enclosure.

It was Friday by the time they called the fence complete. They took the weekend off and got ready to start their roundup and branding on Monday.

The men had heard there was a dance at the schoolhouse in Cuero on Saturday night, so they all got spruced up and headed to town. Clay asked Ellen if she would like to go. She thought about it a couple seconds, "Sure, why not. We deserve to have some fun occasionally."

"I thought we were already doing that."

"I don't mean that kind of fun, Silly."

Ellen put on the dress she wore when they got married, although the seams had to be let out several inches to allow her to get into it. Clay took a bath, put on his best and cleanest jeans and shirt, shined his boots, tied a scarf around his neck, and he was ready to go.

He hitched up the wagon and they were off. It took them just over two hours to reach Cuero. There was a crowd already gathered at the schoolhouse. Clay found a place to park the wagon, unhitched the mules and tied them to the wagon with an arm full of hay for each of them while they waited.

When Ellen and Clay walked in the door, everyone stopped and stared. Most of these people had not seen either of them before. The fact that Ellen was a beautiful lady, and was dressed like a new bride, had everything to do with it.

The band was already playing as they walked in the door. There was a fiddle, a guitar, and a bass fiddle. They made good music together.

The couple found a seat against the wall. Clay went to the punch bowl and got Ellen a glass of punch. When he returned to where he had left her, she was not there. He looked around, finally found her on the dance floor with Willie. They looked like they may have danced together before. After all, they did grow up in the area together, and they had dances there. Clay found himself feeling jealous that he didn't get the first dance. There were other young ladies there that looked unattached. Clay saw Luke and the two Cordis brothers doing their best to look smooth on the dance floor. They each had a young lady on their arm.

When that number ended, Ellen came back to Clay. He handed the two glasses of punch to Willie, "Here, your turn to hold the punch."

He and Ellen took the dance floor. He suddenly realized, they had never danced together. They make a good team though. It didn't take but a few dances and they were looking like old pros. Luke had to get a dance with Ellen, then it was Matt Cordis, then Gerald.

As it turned out they knew a lot more people there than they thought they did. There were the two other men who had helped them on the cattle drive to Indianola, Lefty Knox and John Williams. Of course, each of them had to have a dance with Ellen.

After the first thirty minutes, Ellen asked for a break. She finally got to sit and drink her punch. She was having a good time but needed the rest.

While Ellen had been dancing, Sheriff Helm came in. He went around the room shaking hands with all the people he knew, which was everyone in the room. He saw Clay and came over to shake his hand. "Well, Clay, I'm glad you brought your beautiful wife. She can meet some of the other ladies and get to know some of her neighbors."

"Would you mind introducing us?" Ellen asked. "We don't know anyone except the men who have been working with us."

"Sure, come on."

Clay took Ellen by the hand and followed Sheriff Helm around the room as he introduced them to everyone. Ellen was invited to all the town social events. She had to explain that she lived over two hours out of town and it would be impossible to make those events. Of course, they wanted to know where she lived. When she mentioned the Locke place, they all knew the Locke's and hated what had happened to them.

That's when Clay asked the sheriff what happened to them. The sheriff told him the bank of the Guadalupe River caved off with Mr. Locke and his horse. Both fell into the river. Locke hit his head on a rock and drowned. Clay asked the sheriff, "Do you think that is really what happened?"

"When I heard about it, I rode out there and looked around. I found a place where the bank had caved off, and there were horse tracks around.

But, no one could explain what Locke would have been doing there on the river bank. It was a mile or so down river from his place."

"Who found the body?"

"Now that's another strange part. It was one of Thompson's men. He said he was riding into town and heard a scream, rode over to the river to check, and found Locke floating in the water with blood all over his head."

"Did he have a good reason for being in the area at that time?"

"No, he didn't, and that ain't even close to Thompson's spread. But, with no eyewitness, there was nothing I could do."

"Maybe that explains why he was so upset when he didn't get the place. And, why he has been so determined to run us off. Even going so far as to put a bounty on my head. By the way," Clay asked, "Have you seen or heard anything from that fake lawyer, Garland?"

"No, not a word. I wouldn't be surprised if he turned up dead, to keep him from testifying against Thompson."

"Yeah, you probably have something there. Tell me about Thompson's family, any more sons who may cause trouble?"

"I've been meaning to warn you about that. He has three more sons. Charlie was the youngest. He tried to be as bad as the rest of them. If left alone, he would probably have made it. We can only hope him being sent to prison will cool the others off. But I wouldn't bet on it. You need to stay on your toes. They can be bad mean."

Clay saw his chance to get a dance with Ellen, excused himself from the sheriff, grabbed Ellen and hit the dance floor. He could tell by the look on her face, she was having the time of her life. She had to insist on taking a break, otherwise, she would be on the dance floor for every dance.

It was getting late, the party was winding down, and Ellen was dead on her feet. Thinking about the long ride home, in the cold, Clay decided to see if he could get a room at the hotel for the night. He asked the men to keep an eye on Ellen while he checked the hotel. He was lucky, they had one room left. He took it and returned to the dance. When he told Ellen, they would be staying the rest of the night at the hotel, she was thrilled. She had been dreading that long ride home in the dark and cold.

When they finally called it quits, Clay hooked the mules to the wagon and took them to the livery stable. No one was around this time of night, so he parked the wagon at the side of the barn, put the mules in the corral in back, threw them some hay and walked Ellen to the hotel. They were so tired, they both fell asleep as soon as their head hit the pillow.

They slept late the next morning, ate breakfast in the hotel dining room, attended church at the local Presbyterian church, had lunch at the Cuero café and headed home.

Monday morning, Clay told the men what he had learned at the dance about Thompson's other sons. The Cordis boys knew them but had never been friends with them. They discussed the plan to keep someone on guard at home. They would take turns, considering it a day off work. They built a covered watchtower on top of the hill in the grove of trees south of the house. From there, they could see all the approaches, hoping this would give them enough notice to prepare a defense. They took several extra rifles, that they had confiscated from Thompson's men, wrapped them in tarps to protect them from the weather, and stashed them in the lookout tower. The tower was camouflaged so it couldn't be seen from the road are any place beyond a hundred yards. Clay said he would buy a couple shotguns next time he was in town. They wouldn't be effective beyond about forty yards, but they would make a noise that could be heard over a mile away. When the men heard the shotguns, they were to come running. All the men were told to go fully armed and be prepared for anything.

"If any of you want to leave, now is the time. This could get dangerous."

Matt said, "Everyone needs a little excitement in their life occasionally."

Clay grinned and said, "You may get more than you bargained for. But I appreciate you sticking with us. Now, who wants to ride into Cuero and see if you can get Knox and Williams to come help us? Since we need to have one man on guard, it's leaving us a man short."

Luke said, "I can do that. I still can't do much with this shoulder, so I shouldn't be missed."

"That sounds good. Go to the house and have Ellen give you enough money to buy two twelve-gauge, double barrel shotguns, and lots of shell for them, double O buckshot."

"Ok, do we need anything else while I'm there?"

"Check with Ellen, if she needs too much, you will need to take the wagon."

"Ok, I'm on the way. I should be back by Friday."

"If you are not back by tonight, you are fired."

"You can't fire me, I'm a property owner."

"Oh, I forgot. While you are there, check with the blacksmith if the branding irons are ready."

Luke went to the house to get the money from Ellen, saddled his horse and left.

The rest of the men saddled their horses and went out to start rounding up Mavericks. Clay took the first watch in the tower. He had been there about an hour when Ellen came out to join him. Later, they laughed about it and said an army could have snuck up on them and they wouldn't have heard a thing.

Clay asks Ellen, "Is this going to be a regular thing for whoever is in the tower?"

She smacked him across the chest, and said, "If you keep up that kind of talk it just might be."

Clay took time to search the surrounding area but didn't see any movement. Ellen went back to the house to start lunch. The crew came in a few minutes later. Willie reported, "We have rounded up over forty head so far. They are in the enclosure, milling around looking for a way out. So far, the fence is holding them."

After lunch, and a brief rest period, the crew headed back to work. This time, Willie stayed in the watchtower and Clay went with the roundup crew.

Luke came in around mid-afternoon, with the two new shotguns and six branding irons tied to his saddle. He said Knox and Williams would be out tomorrow morning ready to go to work.

The crew came in at sundown. Ellen had a good meal ready. They sat around smoking and talking until bedtime. Willie said the cattle they are seeing and pushing into the pen are wild as deer. The horses have their work cut out for them to keep up with some of those rangy longhorns. On the other hand, the horses are learning how to herd cattle, and some of them are getting to be good cutting horses. They have about seventy head ready to be branded. It was decided, the branding will start tomorrow. They can't put any more in the pen and have room to do the branding.

Next morning, Luke went to the lookout tower, the rest of the men went to the branding pen. They got a good fire going, put the irons in the fire and waited until they were hot enough for the branding.

One man would rope an animal and drag it to the fire, where it was thrown on its right side and the brand slapped on its left hip.

Every third animal got the brand of either Clay, Willie or Luke. At the end of the day, each man had about twenty-five head with his brand on it.

When they were ready to open the gate, to let the cattle back out on the range, they did it very slowly. They didn't want them to stampede and run for miles. They were slowly driven to one of the ponds close by, so they could get a good drink. They had been in the pen for over thirty-six hours with no water. The men circled them until they quieted down, then gently rode away. They would eventually drift back to their familiar grazing area.

That was the routine for the next two weeks. The only thing that interfered with that routine was the weather. It was the middle of January. The winters in Southwest Texas aren't usually too severe, but it can get awfully chilly and wet at times. On those days, they laid around the bunkhouse and stayed warm while Clay and Ellen enjoyed the warmth in the house.

Late Friday evening, the Cordis brothers, Leftie Knox and John Williams said they would like to go home for the weekend. They would be back Monday morning ready for work.

When they were gone, it was just Clay and Ellen, Luke and Willie, the original four.

Clay asked Willie, "Did you hear back from Aunt Maddie, is she going to come out and join us?"

"Yeah, last time I was in town and picked up the mail, there was a letter from her. She said as soon as it warms up in the spring, she will come out. She is checking on transportation now. Seems there is a stagecoach runs from Knoxville to San Antonio. There are a bunch of stops and changing lines and so forth. But it can be done. Won't be easy. I figure if I know when she will arrive in San Antonio, I can take the wagon and ride over to bring her on down here."

"That should work. At that schedule, she could be here in time for the baby. Be cuttin' it close, but we can hope."

"I'll write her again and see if she has a schedule yet and tell her the plan. I'll have to make sure where she is going to land. Could be Victoria. The stage routes are so uncertain, they change almost every week."

On Monday they were all back at work. They had branded over two hundred head. There were a few grown cows with brands already on them. If she had a calf following her, they put the cows brand on the calf. They didn't know who owned the brand, but that was the law of the land. Several times things got lively there in the branding pen. Some of those old longhorns had a temper. With horns stretching out from one to six feet, they could be something else to deal with. If a horse, or man,

got gored with those horns, it was probably deadly.

Several times a cow had to be roped by two men and held back while her calf was branded. When that happened, she was led out the gate and released outside so she wouldn't hurt anyone.

To release her, she had to be thrown and her feet tied with pigging string. The ropes were removed from her head, the pigging string was left loose, so it would come off when she got up. The men made a mad dash for the fence or their horse before she got to her feet. It was dangerous work, but they enjoyed it and laughed about it later.

They were busy roping, dragging to the fire, slapping a brand on it when suddenly, they all stopped dead still. They heard two loud shots coming from the direction of the house.

Clay yelled, "Let's go boys!" They all had a saddled horse standing by. The ones doing the roping and dragging were already mounted. The other horses were tied outside the pen. They made a mad dash for the gate. Threw it open to let the ropers out, closed it, jumped on their horses. From there to the house it was a race. Clay signaled for them to split and go on each side of the house. As they got closer, they slowed to look the situation over before they went rushing in.

Luke was on guard at the house that day. He came out of the house onto the back porch. They came up to him in a cloud of dust. "What's up, Luke?"

"I saw a group of men coming up the Cuero road, but they turned off and headed cross country toward where you all were working. I didn't want you to get caught by surprise. They may be circling around to come at the house from the back."

"How many did you see?" Clay asked.

"Can't be sure, but there are at least four, and could be as many as six." "Let's assume there are six. Ok, Luke and Willie, you know the drill. Take two men with you, I will be in the house. Luke, you go back to the tower and keep a lookout. You can let the men below you know what is happening, they can get the word to the rest of us. Let's put the horses in the barn, so they won't know how many of us are here." "Got it."

They all took off, each to his assigned spot. Luke was in the tower with two men in the foxholes below him on the south side of the house. Willie and the other two men were in the foxhole on the north side of the house. Clay and Ellen were in the house.

The waiting dragged on for what seemed like hours. Probably wasn't over fifteen minutes when Luke told the men below him, "They are spread out and coming up behind the barn." Gerald Cordis made a run for the house to tell Clay, then ran to the north side to tell Willie. He then circled back around in front of the house, keeping the house and barn between himself and the approaching men.

Luke came down from the tower. He didn't want to get caught up there in a gunfight. The sides of the tower were only lined with brush that wouldn't even slow a bullet.

He whispered to Gerald and Matt, "I am going to circle around to the south and see if I can move in from the flank. If you see movement or hear shooting from over there, don't shoot me."

There was another wait. That was the worst part of a situation like this. But the first to move is usually the first to die, so everyone did their best to remain still and quiet.

Luke went straight down the hill to the south until he came to a small creek lined with trees and thick brush. He crossed over the creek and headed east, staying hidden behind the trees. When he thought he was probably behind them, he moved up to the top of the hill, removed his hat, laid down and crawled up until he could just see over the top.

He spotted two of them immediately. They were hiding behind the south corner of the barn, looking toward the house. He didn't see the others at first. Then he spotted movement off to the north, heading toward where Willie and his men were. There was nothing he could do to alert them. He would have to wait to see what their intentions were and depend on Willie to be on his toes.

One of the men at the corner of the barn moved off to his left, heading straight at Gerald and Matt.

Now it was obvious what they had planned. They were intending to have the house covered from three sides. Then it occurred to Luke that they may have men in front also. He couldn't see up close to the house, but he could see the hill in front. If anyone was up there he would be able to see them. The men on the sides would be able to see them also. It would be a long shot for him, over two-hundred yards. He had made shots that far before, so he wasn't too concerned.

They all waited some more.

When Luke guessed they were all in position, one of them called out, "Hello, the house!"

They waited for Clay to answer from the house. "Hello, come on in. The coffee is on and good and hot."

"Come out so we can talk."

"You are the visitor, you come on in. Who are you and what do you want?"

"I want to talk about buying some horses."

"Good, come on in. I have several to sell. How many do you want?" "Come on out so we can talk."

"Mister, if you want to talk to me, you are going to have to show your face and give your name. If you can't do that, you can mount up and ride out of here or we can bury you where you stand. Now, what's it going to be?"

"My name is Thompson, you killed my dad and my oldest brother and had my little brother sent to prison. We are going to wipe you off the face of the earth and bury you so deep, nobody will ever find you. Open fire, men!"

Luke had the talker spotted and had a bead on his head. When he gave the word to open fire, Luke put one in his left ear. He never moved again. By then, all the men were shooting. It only lasted about one minute. There were three men lying on the ground, either dead or wounded, two more were running back the way they came.

Luke put a couple shots near their heels to help them along.

When everything had been quiet for a few minutes, Luke moved out and headed down to the first man he had shot. He had no doubt he was dead, but he had to check.

All the other men came out and checked on the dead and or wounded.

There were no wounded.

The one that was headed toward Matt and Gerald's location was dead as well as the one on the right side where Willie, Knox, and Williams were stationed.

"That was a smart move, Luke. You had them from the get-go. Let's see if they have any identification on them," Willie said.

The one who said his name was Thompson had a wallet with his name engraved on it. The other two only had a name scribbled inside their hats.

Clay remarked, "That still leaves two more Thompsons out there somewhere. I am told by the sheriff, one of them is just as mean as their daddy was. The other one, Sam, is supposed to be not so bad. In fact, most people seem to think he is an ok kind of guy."

CHAPTER 29

Willie said, "We seem to keep having the same problem. What to do with the bodies."

"Better theirs than ours," said Matt. "Do we take them into town and turn them over to the sheriff, or throw them in the river?"

"I would like to just throw them in the river, but, I guess polluting the water like that's not such a good idea." Said Clay. "If we leave now, it will be dark when we get there. If we wait until tomorrow, the weather may be bad. I guess we better go now. Who wants to go with me?"

Gerald and Matt Cordis both volunteered.

"Ok, let's round up their horses and tie them on," Clay said.

The three men, with three bodies, rode into Clinton just after dark. Like before, a crowd started gathering as they rode down the street to the sheriff's office. Sheriff Helm heard the commotion and came to his door. He was standing there waiting when Clay and the men rode up with the bodies. Clay just stopped and sat there waiting for the sheriff to say something.

Finally, he shook his head and said to Clay, "Who you got there, Clay?"

"One of them is a Thompson, don't know the other two, but they and two others attacked our place this afternoon. The other two got away."

Sheriff Helm lifted each of the dead men's heads.

"Yeah, this is Westley, Jr., don't recognize the other two.

"Take 'em to the undertaker, you know the way by now. Clay, come in and fill out the report. You know the routine."

When Clay was finished with the report, Sheriff Helm read it, then read it again. "They don't seem to be getting any smarter, do they? Looks like they would learn that attacking you is not a good idea."

"Maybe you can pass that message along to the remaining sons. Because if they attack us we will do our best to kill them. I don't want to keep killing people. I thought that was over when the war ended. I seem to be killing just as many now just trying to stay alive and protect my family."

"I will have a talk with them. But, I doubt it will do any good." Clay asked, "Is there a Mrs. Thompson?"

"No, she left them years ago. I heard all the men were rough on that woman. She finally got tired of it and left."

"No daughters?"

"No, Just the old man and five boys. Now just two boys left."

"Are you going to send someone out to let them know about these two?" Clay asked.

"Not tonight, but, yes. I'll probably ride out there myself in the morning."

"Do you think it would do any good for me to talk to them?"

"I doubt it. But it can't hurt to try. Why don't you stay around town tonight? I'll bring them here when they come in, you can talk to them here. That way, there won't be any shooting."

Matt and Gerald Cordis had returned from the undertaker and suggested to Clay that they all spend the night at their house. He said they have plenty of room. Clay thought that was a good idea. Beats staying at the hotel.

They went to the Cordis home where Clay met Mr. and Mrs. Cordis. They had a modest home two blocks off the main street. There were the two boys and two girls. Both girls were married and didn't live here anymore, so, there was an extra bedroom that Clay took advantage of.

Next morning, after breakfast, they saddled their horses and led them to the café, tied up out front and went in. They ordered coffee and waited for the Thompsons to ride in.

An hour later, they saw the sheriff ride in.

Clay said to the Cordis boys, "How about you watch my back from here, I'll wait in the sheriff's office."

About another hour, a wagon came down the street followed by four rough looking men.

The wagon and men stopped at the sheriff's office. Two men went in, the others waited outside at the wagon.

Gerald and Matt had moved to a table by the front window where they could see the street and keep an eye on the Thompson's. They had their rifles laying across the table.

The sheriff and Clay saw them coming down the street. Clay stepped into the back room where the jail cells were. When they came in, Sheriff Helm said, "Have a seat. I assume you're here to pick up your brother's body. What about the other two. Are you picking them up too?"

"No, you can do what you want to with them. They ain't family." That came from the largest and oldest of the two.

"Didn't they work for you?"

"Yeah, but that don't make us responsible for them."

"There's someone here who wants talk to you. He just wants to talk, so there better not be any trouble. You got that?"

"Who is it, and what does he want?" asked the large one.

Sheriff Helm turned toward the jail cells and called out, "Come on in".

When Clay entered, the sheriff said, "This is Clay Wade. He wants to talk to you. Clay, I believe you know Sam, this is Robert."

"We got nothing to say to that murdering so and so," this coming from Robert.

Clay said, "Just to keep the record straight, I have not murdered anyone. I have not attacked your home and tried to kill you. All I have done is defend myself, my family and my property. Three of your family and your hired men have attacked us on three different occasions. On two of those occasions, one of your family was killed. The other time, your brother attacked us, wounded one of my men, and found himself in jail charged with attempted murder. That is three out of three. We don't shoot to wound people. We shoot to kill. If you attack us, you will be killed. Is that what you want? Look, there are only two of you left. And it's all your family's fault. They attacked us, on our home place. What is it you all want anyway?"

The same older Thompson jumped to his feet, pointing his finger at Clay shouting, "You come in here and start throwing your weight around, taking over land that you have no right to, killing the rightful owners, and you are blaming us for it!"

"Yes, I'm blaming you. See, the difference here, Thompson, is I bought that land all legal, with my own hard-earned money. On the other hand, you and your family are trying to get it illegally, killing the previous owner, now trying to run me off, so you can take it without paying for it. Do you see the difference?"

"That land was ours long before you got here!" shouted Robert.

"No, it wasn't. Your dad was just claiming it. He never did anything to own it. Then when I bought it, he started raising cane, threating to have me killed, tried to do it himself, but couldn't pull it off. He tried to stop me from driving cattle to market. That's when I beat the stuffing out of him and sent him packing with his tail between his legs. If you two knotheads have not learned anything from all this, then you deserve whatever happens to you. We will not be run off, we will defend our rights, if you attack us again, you will be killed. I guarantee it."

Clay's tone softened slightly, "You boys could have a good life here. You obviously have a big place with lots of cattle and horses. If you'll settle down, and stop trying to be something you are not, work at what you already have, stop trying to take things that don't belong to you, you could make a comfortable living and have a nice long life. If you keep up the way you are going, you have no life. Now, I am through talking. You know where I stand. What you do with it is up to you. I'm leaving now. I suggest you remain seated until I am out of town. I wouldn't want to have to kill you until you've had a chance to think about what I've told you."

With that said, Clay walked out the door, crossed the street to his horse, mounted, and rode out of town.

A mile out of town, he stopped and waited for Matt and Gerald. When they rode up they were smiling. Clay asked them, "What's so funny?"

"You should have seen them when they came out of the sheriff's office. That Robert was fit to be tied. The sheriff was standing outside his door with a shotgun just watching. He told them to get their brother and go on home."

Clay told Gerald and Matt what he had told the Thompsons. "I just hope they get some brains in their head and take my advice. I don't like living on pins and needles all the time."

When they reached home they put the horses in the barn, rubbed them down and gave them a scoop of oats and hay, then rushed into the house and bunkhouse to help keep the fire warm.

Ellen was waiting with a cup of coffee for Clay when he came in.

"How did it go in town? I was worried about you when you didn't come home last night."

"I wanted to talk to the Thompson boys, to see if I could put a stop to all this killing."

"Did it work?"

"Only time will tell. They seem to think they own everything in sight. Acted like their daddy owned this place. I set them straight on that count. Don't know if they believed me, or if they even want to."

By sundown the wind was blowing something fierce, a light, freezing rain was coming down. The next morning, everything was covered with snow.

Clay remarked, "Now, this is more like back home, except there it was a dryer snow. The humidity here cuts right through you. Makes it feel a lot colder than it really is."

"Yes, but this is still good snuggling weather."

"Yes, it is. Come here, let's snuggle."

She sat on his lap, as they sat in front of the fireplace enjoying their coffee, the quiet, and each other.

The weather was too bad outside to get any work done, so they all stayed inside out of the cold.

It wasn't cold enough for the snow to last long. By mid-morning, the sun was out, and the snow was all gone, except in the shade of the buildings and trees.

They still did not trust the Thompsons, so there was always someone in the tower. They took two-hour shifts, so no one got too cold sitting up there. It was enclosed on all sides, with shooting ports on four sides, so the wind was not a problem, but the cold still got to you.

The next day, the wind had shifted to come out of the south and had warmed up to a nice cool, sunny, pleasant day. After a good breakfast, the horses were saddled and ready to roundup more cattle for branding. Gerald drew the tower duty for the day. The rest of them went a good ten miles to the north before they started their sweep back south, driving everything they saw that didn't have a brand on it. A few with brands got mixed in, but they could cut them out later. It was brutal work, especially on the horses. They changed horses at least twice a day, sometimes three. Depending if they were close to home. In some places, the brush was so thick a horse and rider couldn't get through it. That was the favorite hiding place for the wild ones. They seem to know a horse couldn't get to them, so they would stand still and hope they weren't seen. When they were spotted, and a horse and rider came in after them, sometimes, they would run. Sometimes, they would fight. If they showed too much fight they were left alone. There were plenty more, so one cow or bull wasn't worth all the trouble. The big range bulls were the worst. They would fight like a grizzly when they got mad. If they went with the cows and didn't cause trouble, they were driven in with the rest of them. If they showed fight, they were left alone. The work continued day after day when the weather allowed. They were still in the middle of winter in south Texas. There were good days and there were bad days. So far, the good outnumbered the bad.

They took Saturday and Sunday off.

There was another dance in Cuero on Saturday night. Clay asked Ellen if she would like to go. "If the weather is good, not too cold, not raining and no Thompsons gunning for us - I would love to go."

"We will make arrangements to stay at the hotel as soon as we get there. Do you think you can ride or should we take the wagon?"

"I'm not that far along yet. Let's ride."

"Ok, we will leave right after lunch, give us time to get there and check in at the hotel, have a nice meal and get changed for the dance. How does that sound?"

"Terrific."

All the men were going to ride in, so they all went together. They arrived in a group around four in the afternoon. Clay and Ellen got a room at the hotel. All the men, except Willie and Luke, went home to get ready for the dance. Willie and Luke would go as they were. They were wearing their best, so changing wouldn't improve anything.

At five-thirty, Clay and Ellen were in the hotel dining room having supper when the two Thompson boys walked in.

They saw Clay. The older one gave him a dirty look, the younger one tipped his hat and went to a table across the room.

Ellen saw the look, "Who is that?"

"That is our friendly neighbors, the Thompsons." "Oh, no. Is there going to be trouble?"

"I wouldn't bet against it."

There were several couples in the room that Clay and Ellen had met at the last dance. They couldn't remember their names, but the faces were familiar. The same was true of the other couples. They waived and said hi.

Two minutes later, Willie and Luke came in. They looked around the room, noticed where the Wade's and the Thompsons were sitting, chose a table across the room where they were facing the Thompsons. They never acknowledged Clay and Ellen, acted like they didn't know them. But, when Clay looked over that way, he noticed both had removed the tiedown thong from their pistols. He was wishing he had worn his now. But he didn't want to alarm Ellen by looking like he was expecting trouble.

She saw the look on his face and saw him reach down where the gun would be.

She reached down and picked up her handbag that had her comb, brush, makeup and such. She tapped Clay on the leg and showed him the opened bag with the 32-caliber handgun he had bought her before leaving Tennessee.

"He smiled and whispered, "Keep that close."

"Oh, I intend to."

They finished their meal, had another cup of coffee, paid the tab and walked to the schoolhouse for the dance.

The Band was just getting warmed up when they walked in. Several people came over to say, "Hi". The men wanted to talk about range conditions. The women wanted to talk about cooking and clothes. One of the men, a Mr. Simpson, who owned one of the larger ranches in the area, struck up a conversation with Clay, "I've been hearing about the trouble you've been having. I understand you are about to run out of Thompsons."

"I hope they will get tired of it and leave us alone. I just saw the last two at the hotel a few minutes ago. Do they ever come to the dances?"

"One of them comes, has a good time, causes no trouble, loves to dance, most of the young ladies like to dance with him. They say he is a perfect gentleman."

Clay nodded, "I met Sam when his dad died. He sounded like a nice guy. Said he was not involved in the trouble I've been having. I hope that's true."

"Sam is the second youngest. He's the one I was talking about."

The band was going strong, the dance floor was filling up when Ellen grabbed his hand and pulled him onto the dance floor. "I didn't come here to stand around and talk."

They danced the first two with each other, then Luke took over, then Willie, then John Williams, then Lefty Knox, and then the two Cordis brothers.

While she was dancing with them, one of the wives came to Clay, "Looks like your beautiful wife has been stolen, and my husband is busy talking cows. How about you and I take advantage of that?"

"And to whom do I owe this pleasure?"

"I am Lucy Barton. We have the BB ranch west of town."

"I hope your husband is not the jealous type."

"When he gets to talking cows and horses, he doesn't know I'm around."

"Do you all have some nice horses?"

"Yes, we do. "You should come over and look at them. There are some real beauties."

"I just may do that, I need to get another stallion or two. Which one is your husband?"

"That's him talking to the man you were just talking to. He is Bob Barton."

"Thanks, I'll talk to him as soon as I get the chance."

They finished their dance and Clay walked her back to her husband where she introduced them.

"Bob, this is Clay Wade, he is looking to buy a couple stallions. I thought you may want to talk to him about it."

"Hi, Clay. I'm always willing to talk to anyone wanting to buy horses.

What are you looking for?"

Clay answered, "I have this nice herd of horses, but they're all related.

All from the same stallion or his sons and daughters. I need to bring in some new blood."

"Are you looking for any particular color or breed?"

"Not really, while I was away in the army they were left to breed freely, so, I have some that are inbred. But, although I haven't seen any ill effects from it yet, I can't let it continue. I would like to see what you have. Maybe we can work out a trade, some of my young fillies for your stallions. How does that sound?"

"Sounds like a workable solution to me. When can you come by to look at them?"

Clay said, "Are you and your wife staying in town tonight?"

"Yes, we are staying at the hotel."

"Good, my wife and I are staying there too. If you don't mind, maybe we can meet for breakfast and ride over together."

Ellen came over and Clay introduced them.

Lucy and Bob were about the same age as Clay and Ellen, so they hit it off from the start.

After the introduction, Bob asks Clay if he would mind if he had a dance with Ellen.

Clay said, "Not if I can dance with your wife."

They danced the next round and came back to Bob and Lucy's table where they were invited to join them. The rest of the night Ellen and Clay shared the table with Bob and Lucy.

Bob got Clay's attention and pointed out the young man who had just come into the room. Clay recognized him as the younger of the two Thompson boys. Bob said his name was Sam.

Sam went to the punch bowl and got a cup, then turned around surveying the room. When he spotted Clay, he paused a moment, nodded at Clay, then continued to look around the room.

Clay asked Bob, "Is this the one that's supposed to be the nice one?"
"Yeah, I've never seen him cause any trouble."

Ellen was looking at Clay with worry on her face when Willie came over and asked Ellen to dance.

Ellen hesitated a moment, then handed her purse to Clay, "Hold this for me."

CHAPTER 30

Clay knew why she had done that. Her gun was in the purse. Clay sat it beside his right hand with the opening toward him and continued talking with Bob.

As the night wore on, the crowd was thinning out. The foursome was talking about going to the hotel dining room for coffee before turning in when Sam Thompson walked up to the table.

Everything went quiet as a mouse around them because everyone in the room knew of the trouble between the Wades and the Thompsons.

Before anything could happen, Clay stood, held out his hand to Thompson, "Hello Sam. Good to see you again. How are things going for you?"

Sam shook his hand, "About as well as can be expected, I guess. I need to talk with you, in private, if we can."

Clay had already noticed Sam was not armed. That made things even in that regard.

Clay pointed to an empty table in the corner, "How about over there?"

They walked to the table. Clay took a chair with his back to the wall.

Sam noticed it and smiled but didn't say anything. When they were seated, Sam started the conversation.

"Look, Wade, like I told you before, I don't want any more trouble between us, but I can't speak for Robert. He has that same streak that my dad and Wes had, and it got them killed. I'm doing my best to convince him to do like you said, but he is hard-headed as a longhorn bull. So far, I ain't made much headway."

"Well, Sam, I appreciate what you are doing. I can promise you, if there is any more trouble, it won't be started by me. But I can also promise you if he comes after us; we will do everything we can to protect ourselves and our property. You've lost four family members, all because they attacked us and our home. We didn't have any other choice. I hope you can see that and not hold it against us."

"Yeah, I knew what they were doing. That's why I didn't go along with them. I knew it wasn't right."

Suddenly, Clay heard the room go quiet again. He and Sam looked up and saw Robert Thompson coming in the door.

Sam got to his feet and went to meet him. Sam was trying to get Robert to go back out the door, but he was having none of it. He was determined to get to the table where Clay was sitting.

Clay saw immediately that Robert was armed, the thong was off the hammer of his gun, and he had been drinking. He knew he was in trouble if he stayed where he was. He stood and walked toward Robert and Sam, wanting to get within reach if he went for his gun.

Before he reached them, Willie and Luke came up behind him. Willie politely lifted Roberts gun from its holster and stepped back out of reach.

Robert whirled around and grabbed for his gun, "What do you think you're doing? Don't you know who you are messing with?"

Willie said, "Yeah, I'm messing with a loudmouth drunk who is about to get killed."

Just as Clay reached Robert, Sheriff Helm stepped in the door with his customary double barrel, sawed-off twelve-gauge shotgun. He saw what was going on. Saw Willie had already removed Robert's gun. He put his hand on Robert's shoulder and said, "Come along with me, Robert."

"Get your hand off me. I'm not going anywhere with you. Get out of my way, I'm going to kill that murdering skunk."

"No, you are not, you are coming with me. You will spend the night in my jail. Now come on." Robert took a swing at the sheriff, he ducked it and cracked him on the side of the head with the butt of his shotgun.

"A couple of you men bring him over to my hotel."

Willie and Luke stepped up, handed Robert's gun to Sheriff Helm, picked Robert up by his feet and shoulders and carried him to the jail and deposited him on the bed. Sheriff Helm locked the door, thanked Willie and Luke and walked back to the dance with them.

When they entered, Clay looked at Willie and Luke, they gave him the thumbs up and went to their table across the room.

Clay was still sitting at the table with Sam Thompson. Sam was apologizing for the actions of his brother when Sheriff Helm came over.

"Sam, Clay, is everything ok here?"

"Yeah, Sheriff, Sam and I have an understanding. There won't be any trouble between us, but neither of us can be responsible for what Robert does. I'm afraid he is going to get someone killed, and I'm going to do my level best to make sure it's not me or mine."

"I can't fault you for that. Sam, do you think you could keep me informed of what Robert is cooking up, or warn Clay, so he can be on the lookout? Maybe I can stop it before he gets himself killed."

"I doubt it, Sheriff, he doesn't tell me what he's planning because he knows I don't approve of it. He just calls some of the men together and rides out. I don't know what he is doing or where he is going."

"Well, it was worth a try. I'll keep him locked up until tomorrow morning when everyone has left town. Maybe he will have cooled off by then."

Clay thanked Sam and returned to the table with Ellen and the Barton's.

Shortly afterward, they all left and went to the hotel dining room for coffee before turning in.

Next morning, the four of them met for breakfast. When they were finished, Clay and Ellen went to the livery for their horses. The Barton's had a buckboard pulled by a pair of matching sorrels. Clay and Ellen were riding Trouble and Dark Night, the matching black appaloosas.

When Bob saw Clay and Ellen's horses, he asked, "Is this some of your own breeding?"

"Yep, sure is."

"I'm impressed already."

Clay asked, "How far out to your place, Bob?"

"It will take us about an hour to get there."

They set a nice, easy pace and arrived there like Bob said, in one hour. Lucy invited Ellen in to join her unless she wanted to see the horses.

Ellen said she would like to see the horses.

They waited while Bob saddled horses for himself and Lucy. Clay was like Bob when he saw Bob's horses. He was impressed with the quality of what he was seeing.

The horses were in a pasture not far from the house. Clay could see before they ever got close that these were some nice horses. There were blacks, sorrels, grays, duns, and buckskins, with a palomino or two thrown in.

Clay asked Bob, "How many breeding stallions do you have?"

Bob said I have four. I'm like you, I need to get rid of them and get some new blood, or at least get a couple more to breed to the fillies that I'm keeping."

"Let's look at your studs."

"They are over here on the other side of the barn."

They rode over to the stud pasture. There was a high solid fence between the four pastures to keep the studs from seeing each other and getting into a fight through the fence.

"Do you want to part with any of these?" Clay wondered.

"I will let any two of them go. I'll either sell them to you or maybe trade even for two of yours. I'll have to see yours first though."

"When can you come to see them?"

"Are you busy tomorrow?"

"I'm never too busy to talk horse."

"Lucy, do you want to ride over with me tomorrow?" Lucy asked Ellen, "Is that ok with you, Ellen?"

"Sure, we've never had a welcome visitor before. They always come with guns blazing. This will be good for a change."

They all had a good laugh about that.

Clay and Ellen were invited in to have lunch before they started home.

Clay asked Bob if he knew where they lived. "You bought the Locke place, didn't you?"

"Yes."

"Then I know where you are. I knew Allen Locke. He was a good man."

"Is there a shorter way from here, without going back through Cuero? "Yes, there is. I'll show you where the cut off is when you are ready to leave. But, you'll take that cut off, follow it until you come to the Guadalupe River, follow it north until you come to a crossing, shortly after crossing you will hit the Cuero road just south of your place. Should take about an hour, maybe a little more."

"Back to your horses, Bob, I really like that buckskin and the dun. I understand if you cross a sorrel or a bay, with a dun or buckskin, you will get either a buckskin or a palomino. Have you heard that?"

"Yes, in fact, that buckskins momma and daddy are a sorrel and a dun."

"You said you would part with two, are you willing to let me have those two?"

"If that's the two you want, sure. Do you want to take them with you when you go?"

"That depends on the price you are asking."

"I figure good quality studs like that should be worth at least a hundred fifty each. What do you think?"

"I think that's a fair price. Ellen are you in agreement with this?" "Sounds good to me. I'm anxious to see the offspring from our sorrel mares and those two stallions. They should be some beauties."

"Good, but why don't you bring one when you come, and I'll take one now. That way we shouldn't have any trouble out of them while on the trail."

"That's a good idea."

An hour later, Clay and Ellen left for home, leading the buckskin stallion behind Trouble. They were told the buckskins name was Buck, naturally.

When they rode into the barnyard leading the new stallion, it was late Sunday afternoon. All the men were back from the dance, not looking any too worse for wear. The first one out, Lefty Knox, said, "Where did you find that bag of bones, Boss?"

"We found him staggering along the road, figured he wouldn't last much longer, so we drug him along. Maybe we can fatten him up and do something with him."

"I don't know Boss, you got to have something to start with. I think this may be a hopeless case."

All the other men were laughing and enjoying the joke. Ellen didn't know whether to take him seriously or not, but she soon realized they were just giving Clay a hard time about his new stallion.

Leftie took the lead rope and led Buck around so they all could get a look at him. "What do you think boys, should we just put him out of his misery?"

Willie finally said, "Man, that is one fine looking horse. Where did you get him?"

"Bought him from Bob Barton. He and his wife Lucy are coming over tomorrow to look at our horses. He may want a couple of those two-year-old studs out there, and maybe some of the fillies to breed to the studs that he has. Oh, he is bringing another stallion tomorrow when they come. He is a dun, built about like this one."

"Looks like we are going to have to build some more pens," Luke said. "These boys can't be running around loose."

"Yeah," Clay said, "That will make four stallions on the place. Blackie, Stormy, Buck, and Dunnit. That's what the other one is called. We got a real horse operation going here. We're going to have to start selecting which mares we breed to who and write it down in a book. That will be a good job for Ellen. We just have to give her the information, so she will know what to put in the book."

Willie said, "I don't think we can just go by names anymore. We have too many. We need to come up with a numbering system and brand it on their shoulder or hip. That way we will have a permanent record."

"Where did you learn all this, Willie?" Luke wanted to know.

"Oh, I read a book once."

"Why don't you work on a numbering system, and we'll see if we can get it going. I'll run it by Ellen and see if she has any ideas."

They put Buck in a stall in the barn, gave him oats and hay. Clay went into the stall with him to get a measure of his temperament - to see if he is going to be easy to work with. Buck stood there like this happened to him every day, and maybe it did. Clay didn't ask Bob about that, but he will tomorrow. Buck stood there and let him brush him all over, lift his feet, clean his hooves, comb his mane and tail.

When Clay went in for supper everyone else was already around the table ready to eat.

Ellen told him, "I thought maybe you had decided to sleep in the barn with your new horse."

"You'll have to get a lot meaner before I'll do that."

When all the joking was put aside, the men told Clay they thought Buck was a good addition to their horse breeding program. Clay told the men, "There are several of those big bay and sorrel mares that I want to breed to these two new boys. They are over two years old now, so they are old enough. They will be over three before the foals arrive. I'm hoping to get some palominos and buckskins out of them. I also want to see what we get when we breed Buck to Splotch. I bet we get a buckskin with a blanket. Anyone want to bet against it?"

Knox said, "Not me. I've seen what she produces. That'll be something to see."

The next day about mid-morning, the Bartons arrived leading Dunnit. The men and Ellen were as impressed with him as they were with Buck.

The Bartons were introduced all around. Ellen invited Lucy in for coffee. "You men can come in anytime you want to stop talking horse," she hollered back. When they were inside, Lucy wanted to know all about the baby, when it is due and so forth. Ellen was happy to have someone other than Clay to talk with about the baby. He loved talking about it, but, there is just so much you can talk about with the same person.

Lucy was curious about the gun strapped around Ellen's protruding midsection. Ellen explained, "We have had so much trouble with the Thompsons that we all go armed. We never know when one of them, or a bunch of them may show up and start shooting."

Lucy got nervous when she heard that, but Ellen explained, "They only show up when they think all the men are out on the range. That's why we keep a man in the watchtower on the hill, so we won't be surprised."

"Have they ever done that?"

"Oh, yes, just last week."

"What happened?"

"There were four of them. They came sneaking up from across the range behind the barn. Luke was in the tower and saw them coming way down the road and signaled the men. They all got here in a hurry and were waiting for them. Two of the Thompson men, including one Thompson, was killed. The other two ran."

"Ellen, how can you sit there and talk about it like it's an everyday occurrence? Aren't you afraid?"

"When Clay is around, I don't worry too much. I've seen him in action too many times. I know what he's capable of."

"How and when did you and Clay meet? Have you known each other long?"

"Practically all our lives, but, then Clay went away to war when I was fourteen. He was gone for four years. He didn't recognize me when he got back. You should have seen his face when he figured out who I was. He said, 'This can't be that little skinny freckled face brat that followed us around all the time.'"

"I didn't know you when you weren't expecting, but I bet you were a knockout. You still are."

"Thanks, Lucy, I'm getting so big, sometimes I don't feel very attractive."

It turns out, Bob grew up on his same place and inherited it from his family. They already had a going operation before Bob took over.

Ellen explained how they came to be here and why they moved from Tennessee.

After a while, Bob and Clay came in. Bob had seen all the horses and liked what he saw. He wanted two of the big bay two-year-old stallions, and two of the Appaloosa fillies. One of them was black with a white blanket and the other was a smoky gray with a white blanket. He and Clay were thrilled about the possibilities of their offspring.

The Bartons left at mid-afternoon headed back home. They all agreed to visit more often and stay in touch.

CHAPTER 31

Since there were no cattle in the holding pen to be branded, the men took time to build three new stud pens, one each for Blackie, Buck, and Dunnit.

They cut trees from the same area where they cut timber for the branding pen, drug it all down to the barn area. The pens were built with a twenty-foot wide space between the pens to keep the stallions from fighting over and through the fence. They put one of the older pregnant mares in the pens with them to keep them company.

They didn't think it necessary to have anyone in the tower since they were all working this close to home. That turned out to be a bad mistake. Three days into building the stud pens; while Leftie and John were cutting timber for post a mile from home, the men at home heard shots coming from that area.

They quickly saddled their horses and Clay, Willie and Luke made a mad dash to see what was happening.

The two Cordis brothers stayed at home to protect Ellen and the property there.

They stopped on top of the closest hill overlooking the grove where the cutting was being done. They didn't see anything immediately.

They eventually saw a puff of smoke coming from farther around to the east, on the same hill they were on. Looked like the same setup as when Charlie Thompson was shooting at the barn and wounded Luke.

Clay told Willie and Luke that and suggested they do the same thing he had done - circle round behind the shooter and take him from behind if they could.

They agreed and went back down the hill and galloped east until they thought they should be directly south of the shooter. It only sounded like one doing the shooting, but they could be mistaken. Just as they were tying their horses and getting ready to advance on foot, they heard a barrage of about fifteen shots, about as fast as a rifle could be fired, and then a horse leaving as fast as he could run.

They didn't know if they had given themselves away somehow, but it looked like the shooter had gotten away.

They still advanced carefully in case there was more than one.

They heard no more shots as they closed in on the location of the shooter. They found a double hand full of empty cartridge shells. Looked like from a forty-four caliber.

Willie and Luke went to check on Lefty and John while Clay searched the area looking for where the horse had been tied. When he found it, he studied the track for a long time. He thought he would recognize them if he saw them again. He found some hair from a horse tail on a bush. He removed it and put it in his pocket to study later.

When he got to the other men, Leftie had John's shirt open inspecting the wound. It was high on the right side, below the collarbone but above the lungs. He was in considerable pain, but it didn't look life-threatening unless it got infected. He had lost some blood. Leftie had put a pad over the holes front and back, made from John's shirt. Then he tore the shirt into long strips and had them wrapped around John's chest to hold the pads in place. John was conscious and aware of his surroundings.

Clay asked him, "How do you feel?"

"I can sure tell I'm alive." As he grimaced in pain.

"Do you think you can sit a horse to get you home?"

"Let me sit up and see how I feel."

They helped him sit, leaning back against a wagon wheel.

Leftie reminded him, "We have the wagon here, you can ride in it if you would rather do that."

John thought the wagon would be rougher than a horse, so they helped him get mounted and then helped Leftie get the mules hitched to the wagon. They all headed home. Willie and Luke rode beside John in case he started falling they could catch him.

They made it in about twenty minutes and John was still sitting his saddle. They got him off and in his bed in the bunkhouse.

Clay called Ellen and told her John had been shot. She grabbed her medical kit and came to see how bad it was. She cleaned it with hot water and told the other men to hold him. They didn't know why, but each of them got an arm or a leg. She removed a bottle of whiskey from her bag, gave John a big slug, and before he could react she poured a generous shot of whiskey into the wound. It took all the four men could do to hold him down.

When he could breathe again, he asked, "What did you do that for?"

"That's to kill any infection. I learned it from my dad. An old mountain man told him about it. He says he has never seen it fail."

Ellen fixed them all a good meal about sundown. John was sleeping and the rest of them sat around on the porch drinking coffee and planning their next move.

Clay told them he was going up there tomorrow and see how far he could track that shooter.

Willie said he would go with him. "I don't think it's a good idea to go alone. If you find him, and he gets a lucky shot in, you could be in real trouble."

Then Ellen said, "I think John needs to go into town and see the doctor. Those holes need to be sewn up. I am sure he can do a better job of doctoring it than I did."

They thought about that a moment. Then Clay suggested, "How about this. Leftie can drive John into town, Gerald and Matt can hang around here, keep a close watch on the place. Willie and I will track the shooter. How about that?"

Ellen wanted to know, "What are you going to do when you find him?"

"I guess that depends on what he does. We will give him a chance to explain himself. We don't have enough evidence to prove he is the one who did it, but I'll know those horse tracks if I see them again."

Ellen didn't like his plan, "I don't like you going after that man. There is too much chance of you getting hurt."

"We can't carry on our work around here and let him have free shots at us any time he wants. We are lucky no one has been killed yet. This is the fourth time someone has tried to kill some of us. We need to put a stop to it now, we can't go on living like this. Leftie, when you go into town tomorrow, let Sheriff Helm know what is going on out here, ok?"

"Ellen, do you need anything from town?" Knox wanted to know. "You could pick up the mail if there is any for any of us. I'll give you a letter to mail and a shopping list before you leave tomorrow."

They all had an early breakfast. Everyone helped hitch the mules to the wagon and got John loaded and comfortable.

The weather was cool enough to need a heavy coat, but the sun was shining and a light breeze blowing. They gave Lefty and John each a blanket to wrap in, knowing it was going to be a long cold ride there and back.

Before they left, Clay cautioned them to be careful, "You don't know who you may meet on the road or in town. That Robert Thompson is just crazy enough to try anything." They had their handguns and rifles, so they were as prepared as they could be.

Willie and Clay saddled their horses. Clay was riding Trouble, Willie was riding a large bay mare he had taken a liking to. He called her Martha, for no good reason.

They checked their guns. Made sure they were all loaded to the maximum. Even the revolvers had six rounds in the cylinders instead of the usual five.

They went to where the shooter had been and found the trail he left as he was leaving. It wasn't hard to follow. The horse was being pushed hard and had kicked up a lot of dirt. They were not in a hurry since the trail was almost a day old. There had been no rain the night before, so the tracks were plain as day.

The trail was leading them in a southeasterly direction. Clay knew Thompson's place was in this direction.

It was about noon when the trail turned more to the south. "Looks like he may be going to Clinton or Cuero." Said Willie.

"Yeah, if he does go into town we will have a hard time tracking, but maybe we can find some tracks that match. Not likely he will still be there though."

The tracks led them to the road between Clinton and Cuero. They could tell the rider had gone toward Clinton. There were too many tracks on the road to distinguish their shooters from any of the others, so they rode on into Clinton and went to see Sheriff Helm. He was in his office with his feet on his desk when Clay and Willie walked in. "No, not again. Who did you bring me this time?"

Clay told him, "This is your lucky day, Sheriff. We don't have any guests or bodies for you, yet."

"What do you mean, yet?"

Clay told him what had happened at the ranch yesterday. "We trailed him into town, but of course, we lost him with all the traffic here."

"Do you have any idea who it might be?"

"Oh yes, I have a good idea, but I can't prove it. Did you see Robert Thompson in town about mid to late afternoon yesterday?"

"I can't vouch for what time he got here, but he was in the saloon last night. I thought I was going to have to lock him up again. He was causing quite a ruckus, but it didn't get out of hand and no one was hurt."

Clay asks the sheriff, "Did you see what kind of horse he was riding?" "He usually rides a big bay. Why, what have you got?"

Clay showed him the tail hair he had gotten from where the shooters horse was tied.

After looking at it he remarked, "That could have come from a bay or a black. That does narrow it down some."

"Do you know if he put his horse in the livery stable, or left him tied at the hitch rail?"

"He was left at the hitch rail in front of the saloon. I saw him when he came staggering out and left town. He could hardly stay on the horse."

"I should have followed his trail yesterday. I might have caught up with him."

"How is John, was he hurt bad?"

"He will live. Bullet went through 'bout here and came out his back. He should be at the doctor's office now if they haven't already left. I didn't see the wagon when we rode in."

"They probably went to the doctor in Cuero. It would be closer."

"You're right. We will go back that way. Do you think we might learn something if we went to the saloon and talked to anyone who was there last night? When he got drunk he might have spouted off about what he had done."

"Guess it can't do no harm. Come on."

The sheriff picked up his sawed-off shotgun. Clay and Willie removed the thong from their pistols and headed for the saloon.

There were only five or six men sitting around. Some sipping drinks, some playing cards, some just sitting and talking.

They went to the far end of the bar where they could see everyone in the place. The bartender came to take their order. When he came back with the three whiskeys, Sheriff Helm asked him, "When Robert Thompson was in here last night, did he say anything about where he had been that day or what he had done?"

"I didn't hear him say anything. Of course, I was busy most of the night. He sat at that table over there by the front wall with a couple other rough looking men. They were all drinking, but they didn't get loud about anything he had done."

"Do you know who the other men were?"

"One was Malcolm Freeman. The other was Butch Goodson."

"Do you know anything about them? Where they work, where they live?"

"No, they have only been in a couple times, just in the last two weeks. What's this all about, Sheriff?"

"Just trying to tie up some loose ends. Nothing to worry about. Thanks for the information."

They finished their drinks. Clay left six bits on the bar and they left. They thanked the sheriff for his help, mounted up and went to Cuero. They saw the wagon sitting in front of the mercantile. They tied up to the hitchrail in front and went in. Lefty and John were waiting while the store owner filled Ellen's order. When he had it all stacked on the counter and tallied up, Clay paid him and helped Willie and Lefty carry it to the wagon.

John's right arm was in a sling and he had a big bandage on his shoulder under his shirt. Clay asked him what the doctor said.

"He said, 'What happened, did you get shot?' Leftie told him I was cleaning my knife and it went off. That doctor didn't let it get to him though. He just said, 'I've seen some knife wounds, but never one like that. Must be one heck of a knife.' No, he said it looked clean, whoever bandaged it did a good job. He didn't expect any problems, but if it started getting red and feverish, come back. I told him I would just have Ellen pour more whiskey on it. Know what he said?"

"No, what."

"He said, 'Sounds like a waste of good whiskey.'"

Leftie wanted to know if they caught their man. Clay and Willie told him where they had been and what they had learned. Leftie told him they had not seen or heard anything either.

They headed home with Leftie and John riding the wagon, Willie and

Clay following on horseback. The trip from Cuero to home always took two and a half hours with the wagon, but, just under two hours horseback.

When they arrived back home and got the supplies unloaded and put away, Ellen told them supper would be ready in one hour. That's when they all realized - none of them had had anything to eat since breakfast. Ellen made a big pot of coffee and they sat around drinking and talking until the meal was on the table.

At breakfast the next morning, Clay told them he was going to take one of the plain horses, so he wouldn't be recognized by his horse, his camping gear, a few days supplies of food, and follow Robert Thompson everywhere he went until he made a mistake. When he did, Clay was going to end all the shooting and killing. Ellen didn't like the sound of that at all, and she let Clay know it in a hurry.

Clay said, "I know how you feel, Honey, but we can't let this go on. Someone is going to get killed if we don't stop it now. We have really been lucky so far, but that can't last forever. I think this is the only way to handle it and keep the rest of you out of danger. I should be safe enough because he will never know I am watching him. I did a lot of this kind of thing for four years."

"Clay, take someone with you. It will be a lot safer and I will feel much better knowing you are not out there alone."

Clay responded, "But one can stay hidden much better than two."
"But if you get hurt you won't have anyone to help you. Two of you will be twice as safe."

"Ok, I give up. Matt, you know this country better than any of the rest of us. Do you want to go with me? It will get you out of building fence for a few days."

"Sure, I'll go. I don't mind building a fence, but I don't like Thompson shooting at me either."

Clay asked him, "Do you have a bedroll with you?"

Willie spoke up, "You can use mine, l won't be needing it."

"All right, we'll spend today getting everything ready and pull out of here around two this afternoon. That should put us at the Thompson spread in time to find a good lookout point and set up camp. That ok with you, Matt?"

"Sure, can't wait to get started."

The rest of the men returned to building corrals for the new stallions, while Matt and Clay assembled their camping gear, food, weapons, and ammunition. Clay made the remark that he wishes he had some binoculars. Matt said, "No problem, I have some in my saddlebags."

"I knew I chose you for some reason. Looks like we are going to need a pack mule to carry all this stuff."

While they were busy getting everything ready, Ellen was a nervous wreck, walking from room to room, wringing her hands, and doing her best to hide the tears.

Clay saw what was going on and tried to ignore it, without much success. Finally, he stopped what he was doing to try and comfort her, but it didn't work. Ellen said it felt like he was going away, and she would never see him again.

He assured her that was not the case. "I can do this without getting hurt, just trust me, please. Matt knows the country and has binoculars, so we can stay way back. Thompson will never know we are anywhere around until he starts something. That's when we step in and put a stop to all this nasty mess. Then we can carry on the way we planned and won't have to be looking over our shoulder all the time."

"I know, Clay, it sounds so simple, but it never is. There is always a danger, and one of these days you're going to get hurt, or worse."

"That's exactly why we have to put a stop to this now before someone does get hurt. Now, I need to get going. Just put your faith in me and let me do my job, ok? Look at it this way. With Matt and me watching him all the time, he can't sneak over here and hurt any of you because we will be right behind him. If I sit here and wait for him to come to us, we are sitting ducks. This way I can stop him before he even gets here. Now doesn't that make sense?"

"When you say it like that it does."

"Ok, I'm going now. Wish me luck."

"Ok, good luck." Ellen gave him a long kiss and a hug. Clay went to his horse. Matt was waiting with the pack mule and Clay's bay mare, so they rode away toward the south-east. But, before they got completely out of sight of the house, Clay suggested to Matt, "I think it will be a good idea to circle around the place to make sure Thompson or someone else isn't lurking out there just waiting for us to leave."

Matt asked, "You want to split up and go in opposite directions to cover the area quicker?"

"Sounds good, let's go. I'll ride out to the road to see if there are any fresh tracks since yesterday when we came in. I'll meet you out there."

Clay and Matt rode out looking everywhere a person might be, not expecting to find anyone, but still being very careful to not let any kind of sign slip by unseen.

When they met later, neither of them had seen anything to indicate anyone had been around lately.

It took them almost three hours to come within sight of the Thompson home place. When they topped out on the last hill to the northwest of the place, they made sure they came out in a grove of live oaks with lots of underbrush to conceal them from view. Matt said, "There is a good place over to the northeast of the house where we can stay hidden and have a good view of the whole place. The house and barns back up to that hill, so we will be pretty close."

"Ok, lead off, you know where we are going."

Matt led off, going back down the hill away from the house, then turned back to the east, staying out of sight of anyone who may be looking from the house. When they reached the spot Matt was looking for, it seemed to be ideal for what they wanted. They were only about a quarter mile from the home place, with a perfect view of the back of the house, the barns, the horse corral, and an outhouse. They moved back down the hill and found a thick patch of woods and brush. They pushed their way in, found a small opening just large enough to put up the two-man tent. Thirty yards on down the hill was a small stream where the horses were staked out close to the water. There wasn't much grass, just a little along the creek bank that would be gone in a day or so. Fortunately, they had thought to bring along some oats, because they knew they were going to have to remain hidden during the day unless they were out following Thompson.

It was just past sundown, but not quite dark by the time they had their camp set up. The campfire was concealed well enough that they didn't think there was a chance of anyone seeing it for more than a hundred yards. They got the coffee going, heated some beans, and ate them with bread and coffee. As soon as the coffee was ready they pulled the sticks back from the fire and let it die out. They sat around talking in low voices until they got drowsy and turned in.

CHAPTER 32

Before daybreak the next morning, Matt was getting a fire started while Clay brought the horses into camp and gave them a scoop of oats, saddled them, and tied them nearby.

Both were shivering from the cold before the fire was going good. Clay took Matt's binoculars and a heavy blanket up to the top of the hill overlooking Thompsons place. He laid out on his stomach behind some underbrush, wrapped himself in the blanket where he had a good view of what was happening below, and waited for things to come alive. At first, it was too dark to see anything except the lights coming on in the house. After a short time, he heard the familiar noises coming from the bunkhouse and barn as the men prepared for the day's work. With the sun gradually lighting up the area, Clay was able to see the people moving about, but couldn't recognize anyone yet.

Matt came up beside Clay, handed him a fresh cup of coffee, and stretched out beside him. "See anything?"

Clay handed the binoculars to Matt, took a sip of the hot coffee, and waited.

"That looks like Sam that just came out of the house headed to the barn."

He handed the binoculars back to Clay, "Yep, that's Sam. I'll bet we don't see Robert until almost noon. I don't think he is much help around here, from what Sam told me."

There were two men sitting on a bench outside the bunkhouse who looked like they were waiting for someone or something. They had three horses saddled and tied to the fence. One of them was a large bay that fit the description of the horse that Sheriff Helm said Dan used to ride. Clay was wondering if Robert had taken over Dan's horse, or did they have more than one horse on the place that fits that description.

When the sun was full up in the east, Sam and the rest of the men mounted up and rode out to the north. The two men by the bunkhouse were still sitting there when Robert came out. One of them handed Robert the reins to his horse. They all mounted up, Robert led them out headed east.

"Well, I wonder what he has planned. I can't see him out building a fence or branding cows and such. Can you?"

Matt said, "No, I have known him all my life, and I have never heard of him doing anything but causing trouble, for someone."

"Let's follow him and see what he's up to." Clay said, "This might get interesting."

"Think the mule and camp gear will be all right if left here?"

"It's hidden pretty well. Someone would just have to stumble upon it. If that happens they are probably doing the same thing we are doing - spying on Robert Thompson."

"Let's take our heavy coats and rain gear, just in case we need it."

After taking a long look to make sure which way Thompson and his two men were headed, Clay and Matt decided on a route that would keep them hidden until they reached the top of the next hill. Once there, they stopped long enough to locate their party, decided on the route, and moved out again. This continued until almost noon when Clay and Matt saw Thompson's group approaching what looked like a small farm. There were plowed fields, fenced pastures with several cows in them, a large shed with hay stacked in it. This is still January, so there were no crops in the fields, but they looked to be ready for planting when the time was right.

Clay suggested, "How about we move up to that patch of trees over there. That will put us close enough to get a good view of what they intend to do." With that said he spurred his horse into a slow gallop with Matt following close behind. As they moved up behind the grove of trees, they slowed the horses to a fast walk to keep down the noise and dust. It looked as if this patch of trees and underbrush had been left here intentionally to help break the north wind. They rode their horses into the thick cover, dismounted and tied them out of sight from the house.

Taking their rifles, they hurried to the edge of the trees and hunkered down behind some bushes where they could see and hear what was said. They were only about a hundred feet away and Robert Thompson was shouting loud enough to wake the dead.

A man and woman were standing on the front porch with three children who looked to be maybe ten to twelve years old. Thompson and his men were sitting their horses fifteen feet away in the yard.

"McDermott, I have told you for the last time, this is it. You are squatting on my land, and you are leaving now. You have ten minutes to load what you want and get off the pace. If you are still here, we will burn this flea trap down with you in it." Thompson pulled a watch from his vest pocket, "Time has started. You have ten minutes."

"I homesteaded this place, proved up on, and have clear title to it. You can't run us off. You don't have any right to do that."

"You have eight minutes. You are wasting time, McDermott."

Clay Whispered to Matt, "Cover me, I am going to come up behind Thompson and read to him from the good book."

"I'm glad I'm here to see this," Matt said.

Clay moved off to his right to get more behind Thompson before he started closing in on them. When he emerged from the trees, he was about one hundred feet back and closing. He quietly walked in until he was twenty feet away and stopped. McDermott and his wife saw him coming and probably assumed he was with Thompson until Clay motioned for them to remain quiet. Thompson and his two men had their pistols in their hands just waiting to use them on five defenseless people. Clay motioned for the McDermotts to go inside the house. It took a minute or so for them to understand what he was trying to tell them, but they finally got it. Mrs. McDermott grabbed the children and went inside calling for her husband to come with her. The door slammed with a bang.

Thompson told one of his men, "Cover the back, make sure they don't come out with a gun."

Clay levered a cartridge into his rifle barrel, and said, "Don't anybody move a muscle. You are covered from two sides by four guns. Now, drop those pistols. One false move and you're dead. You have two seconds. DROP 'EM, NOW!"

Three guns hit the ground at the same time.

"Step down off your horses and turn toward me."

When that was done, Clay ordered them to take four steps toward him. When he turned and saw Clay standing there, Robert Thompson almost had a heart attack. His eyes bugged out, his face turned beet red, then white. "Wade, what are you doing buttin' in my business again. Looks like I'm going to have to kill you yet."

"Sorry to spoil it for you, but this is not going to be the day. Now, tell me what you are doing here harassing these people."

"They have been told before to get off my land. I am here to make sure they leave."

"Mr. McDermott," Clay called, "Can you come out here, please?"

The door opened, and Mr. McDermott stepped out onto the porch holding a double barrel 12-gauge shotgun.

"Mr. McDermott, I am Clay Wade. I have a place over on the Guadalupe River, and I have been having trouble with the Thompsons ever since I moved here. But, now I see I'm not the only one. I heard you say you have homesteaded and proved up on this place. Do you have the papers to prove it? Not that I'm questioning your word, but I want to prove it to Robert Thompson. Then if you continue to have trouble with him, you will have me as a witness when he turns up dead."

"I'll get the paper. Only take a minute."

While he was getting the paper, Thompson lit into Clay, accusing him of butting in where he has no business, making threats, promising to kill him and his entire family.

McDermott returned with the deed showing the date it was homesteaded, and the date it was finalized.

"So, Mr. McDermott, you have been here almost six years, is that right?"

"This coming June will be six years."

"When did you first start having trouble with the Thompsons?"
"Right after his daddy died. This one and that other one, I think his name was Dan, started throwing their weight around - demanding we get out. This time they caught me outside without my shotgun or he would already be dead."

While this conversation was going on, Thompson was standing there looking from one to the other, giving them looks that said, 'I'm coming back and kill both of you.'

Clay thanked Mr. McDermott, "Sorry we had to meet under these circumstances, maybe next time we can visit some."

"OK, Thompson, I want you and both your men to sit down and pull your boots off."

"You must be crazy, Wade, if you think I'm goin' to pull my boots off for you."

"Here's how this is goin' to work. You can take your boots off, or I will take them off for you. I guarantee you don't want me doing it. You two, sit down, get those boots off, you have one minute."

"Or what?"

"Like I told Thompson, you can do it, or I'll do it for you, but you won't like the way I do it. Now, what's it going to be? You have a half of a minute left."

The four of them stood there looking at each other until the minute was up. Clay took three steps toward Thompson, swung the rifle, catching Thompson on the point of his chin. Thompson's feet flew up as he hit the ground on his back. He never moved. Clay reached down and pulled his boots off and threw them toward the porch. When he turned to the other two, both were sitting on the ground pulling their boots off.

"Mr. McDermott, could you bring some water? I do believe your guest has fallen asleep."

"I sure can, be right back."

McDermott returned with a bucket of water and splashed most of it in Thompson's face. He came up spitting and sputtering, wiping water from his face and eyes. When he realized what had happened, he lunged to his feet ready to fight. That's when he realized his boots were gone.

Clay stood a few feet away, waiting to see what Thompson was going to do. He couldn't seem to make up his mind. He wanted to fight, and kill, but there was something about this Clay Wade that made him hesitate. He never had that feeling before and didn't understand what was wrong. Always before, the Thompsons went where they wanted to go, did what they wanted to do, to whomever they chose, and no one gave them any trouble back. But, since Wade came into the county, things had not been easy for the Thompsons.

"Thompson, have you had enough for today?"

"I'm going to kill you, Wade, if that is the last thing I do."

"You got that wrong, Thompson. If you try to kill me or any of my friends or family, that will be the last thing you will ever do. Now, you three start walking."

"I'm not going anywhere without my boots."

"You think not, do you?"

Clay walked around them, pointed his rifle at the ground at their feet, and started firing as fast as he could pull the trigger and lever in another round. By the time he had fired seven rounds, the three of them were twenty-five feet away and moving as fast as they could pick 'em up and put 'em down.

Just to get in on the fun, Mr. McDermott let loose both barrels of his 12-gauge.

Mrs. McDermott came out with the three kids, gave Clay a big hug and introduced the kids, "Mr. Wade, you saved the day for us, and probably a lot more. I don't know how to thank you."

"You can start by calling me Clay. This mister stuff makes me feel old. By the way, you need to meet my sidekick."

Clay motioned for Matt to come and meet the family. Introductions were made all around and Clay and Matt were invited in to have lunch. That sounded good since they only had coffee for breakfast.

Before they went in for lunch, Matt and Clay caught up theirs and Thompson's horses and tied them to the hitching rack by the barn.

Mrs. McDermott put out a feast of vegetables from their garden along with pork chops from the smokehouse and fruit from the orchard.

"Clay asked, "What do you do with all the vegetables and fruit that you raise here?"

Mrs. McDermott told them, "We put up everything we can, smoke the meats, store the dry beans and such until we need them. We usually have a lot more than we can use, so we take it into Clinton and Cuero, and sell it to the store there."

After another hour of talking and sharing several more cups of coffee, Clay and Matt said goodbye, mounted up, and leading Thompson's horses headed back the way they had come. They were not in any hurry, knowing they would catch up with three very sore-footed and mad men before they had gone very far.

Matt asked Clay, "How far do you guess it is back to Thompson's place?"

"I'm guessing about ten to twelve miles. Their feet should be plenty sore by now. It's going to be dark before they get home."

"That's kind of what I was thinking."

"How about if we swing wide around them and get to our campsite before dark. We can watch for them from there."

Clay and Matt continued following in Thompson's tracks until they spotted them almost a mile ahead. Then they turned off to the right to put a hill between them and continued to their former campsite. When they reached there, everything was as they had left it. The pack mule was grazing contentedly by the stream, but he had eaten the grass down to the roots. Matt pulled the stake and moved it to a new patch of grass.

Clay took the binoculars to the top of the hill overlooking Thompson's spread, but there was still no sign of the sore-footed men yet.

Clay said, "As soon as it gets dark I'm going to take their horses back a mile or two and turn them loose. They will go home from there, and if I stay in this stream as far as I can, there won't be any tracks leading them back to us."

"Sounds like a good idea, want me to come along?"

"No, I think I can handle it. Shouldn't be any problem, unless I get lost in the dark."

"If you do, just fire a couple shots and I'll come and get you. As soon as it gets dark, so the smoke won't show, I'll get a fire going and have something to eat when you get back."

Clay waited a few more minutes before starting out. By the time he got to where he intended to turn the horses loose, it was dark enough to do what he wanted to do. He tied the reins to the saddle horn, slapped them on the rump, and sent them on their way. When he arrived back at camp, it was good and dark. He didn't see the campfire until he was within a hundred feet of it, it was so well-hidden in the thicket.

Matt had the coffee ready and was heating beans and frying bacon. Clay asked him, "Have you seen anything down below?"

"Not a thing. Haven't heard anything either."

After eating, Clay took the binoculars to the top of the hill to see if he could see anything, but it was too dark. The only lights were coming from the house and bunkhouse.

Clay was on the lookout at the top of the hill when the sky started to get bright in the east. Matt was making coffee and frying up more bacon. They kept the fire very small and used dry wood, so there was little danger of it being spotted from below.

As usual, just as it started turning light in the east, people started moving around, lights came on in the house and bunkhouse, talking and laughter could be heard.

Matt brought Clay a plate with bacon, beans and a cup of steaming coffee. The hot coffee really hit the spot, with the temperature in the low forties. Very little wind was blowing, so it wasn't too bad. It usually warmed up nicely during the day, or it has so far.

They ate their breakfast sitting behind a screen of brush watching what was going on below. Sam came out just about sunup. All the men had their horses saddled and ready to go.

CHAPTER 33

Sam was seen giving instructions to two different groups of men. They mounted and rode away, one going to the south, the other to the east. No sign of Robert and the two men with him yesterday, but the horses the three had been riding were lounging in the corral with several other horses.

Just before noon, a lone man came hobbling into view from the east. It looked like one of Robert's men, and he was having a hard time of it. Just barely able to pick his feet up and put them down again. Clay and Matt couldn't decide if he was that far behind, or if he had been sent on ahead to get horses and come back for the other two.

It took another hour for him to reach the bunkhouse. He went inside and didn't come out for an hour. When he did he had on boots, but he still wasn't walking very well. After saddling three horses, he headed back the way he had come. From that, Clay and Matt assumed the three had spent the night out, with no camping gear or food, not even coffee.

Clay commented, "I would sure hate to have to deal with Robert today. I'll bet he is madder than a wildcat with his tail caught in a bear trap."

"I wonder why someone didn't ride out to find them when their horses showed up without them." Matt wondered.

"They probably had no idea which way they went when they left here yesterday. Everyone was already gone when Robert and his crew rode out. On top of that, they probably don't care what happened to them. From what Sam told me, "Robert doesn't contribute much to the ranching operation."

All morning, Clay and Matt sat around in the shade drinking coffee and waiting for Robert to show up. Finally, right at noontime, they came riding in. Robert turned his horse over to one of the other men and went to the bunkhouse. When the other two had taken care of the horses, they joined him. None of them were seen again until late the next morning when they came limping out to saddle their horses.

"Looks like we better saddle up and pack up all our gear," Clay said. "Robert is going to lead us somewhere today and we may not be coming back here."

With that said they got busy breaking camp. The mule was brought in and loaded with all the camping gear. Clay was keeping an eye on Robert and crew while they were getting ready to move. By the time Clay and Matt were ready to hit the trail Robert and his two men were almost a mile away, heading west. "Well," Clay said, "They are heading in our direction, but they could be going to Clinton or Cuero. I guess we'll find out soon enough. Let's swing farther to the north just in case they turn that way we will be in a better position to get ahead of them before they reach our place."

Taking the lead rope on the mule, they cut down behind a hill and increased their speed. When they reached the top of the next hill and located Robert and crew they were almost to the fork in the trail that would take them either to town or to the BAR W. Clay pulled out the binoculars and was watching when Robert took the trail toward Clinton."

He said, "Well, since we're this close, may as well go in and see how Robert spends his day in town. Maybe we can make him mad enough to draw against me and we can put all this foolishness to rest."

When Clay and Matt rode into Clinton they saw Robert's horse tied in front of the saloon. They dismounted and tied their horses and mule next to them, removed the tie down thong from the hammer of their revolvers and strolled in and up to the bar. Robert and his men were sitting at a table in the back corner. Clay and Matt ordered a beer and turned their backs to the bar and surveyed the room. Clay looked straight at Robert Thompson, raised his glass, tipped his hat and smiled. Two other tables were occupied by two men each. Robert had been staring at Clay since they came in the door.

An hour later, Clay and Matt had finished three beers, and Robert probably had consumed at least six in that time. Clay decided it was time for them to leave. They left money on the table and proceeded toward the door. They were almost to the door when Robert Thompson spoke up, "Hey, thief, whose land are you stealing today, some helpless widow?" Clay and Matt didn't look back, just continued out the door and mounted their horses. Leading the pack mule, they turned up the street headed toward home when Matt pointed across the street, "Clay, is that your wagon and team at the grocery store?"

"I do believe it is." They angled their horses toward the wagon when Ellen came out the door with her arms full of bags and the store owner following behind. Ellen had just put her bags in the wagon when she saw Clay, waved and smiled.

Suddenly a look of horror came over her face. She screamed a blood-curdling scream at the same instant Clay felt a tremendous blow in his back. He felt himself flying out of the saddle but there was nothing he could do to stop it. The ground came up and hit him in the face. His last sensation was the smell of dust and pain through his body.

What seemed like forever, he was back on the battlefield wondering if he was going to live. He heard the cannons, rifles, screams just like before when he was wounded. He kept fading in and out and that same pain and voices, voices and pain, never one without the other. Then he was aware of someone sitting beside him holding his hand. He didn't want to move, afraid that image would go away. Finally, he turned his head, so he could see who was there. Ellen was sitting in the chair beside his bed with her head laid back, eyes closed, sound asleep. He watched her for a long time, just enjoying the view. When he squeezed her hand, she sat straight up and stared at him like she had never seen him before. "Doctor, he's awake." Then she leaned over and kissed him on the lips. Tears were running down her cheeks. She was crying and laughing at the same time.

"I think I've died and gone to heaven," Clay whispered.

"Oh, no, you don't get away from me that easy."

"What happened?"

Just at that moment, Willie walked in, "I'll tell you what happened! Robert Thompson and his two sidekicks came out of the saloon and shot you in the back. Ellen drew her revolver and before anyone else could react, she had shot all three so quick - I'm not sure if they died from the gunshot or surprise. But they were all dead before they hit the ground. The town hasn't stopped talking about it yet and it's been almost a week!"

"I've been here a week?"

"This is the sixth day," Ellen said holding up her fingers.

"How do you feel about having to shoot those men?"

"I haven't had too much time to think about it, what with you being shot and not knowing if you were going to live or not. But now that you are out of the woods, we need to get you out of here. We have a ranch to build and eleven more kids to raise."

"Eleven, but you said......."

THE END

Made in the USA
Columbia, SC
21 August 2019